BEAUTY AND THE
BROODING BOSS

BY
BARBARA WALLACE

AND

FRIENDS TO
FOREVER

BY
NIKKI LOGAN

MILLS &
BOON

Dear Reader,

There's this fantastic old movie called *The Enchanted Cottage*. In it, two wounded people hide from the world in a country cottage. While there, they discover their scars mysteriously disappear. At first they credit the cottage for weaving a magic spell, but in the end come to realise the real magic is the love they find with each other.

I couldn't help thinking of this movie when writing *Beauty and the Brooding Boss*. Like the characters in the movie, Alex Markoff has withdrawn to a country cottage to hide from a world that has let him down. In her own way Kelsey Albertelli is hiding too—she's protecting herself from life's bumps and bruises. When these two loners suddenly find themselves spending the summer together in the romantic countryside, their self-protective walls are chipped away. But the question is, will their relationship survive the outside world? Will their love be strong enough to weave a magic spell for them?

This book has a special spot in my heart because it's based in the Berkshire Mountains, where I grew up. I took a few liberties in creating the locations. Many of the settings, like Alex's woods, the Leafy Bean and the Music Centre, are loosely based on real locations. It was a lot of fun finding romance in my hometown.

I hope you enjoy Alex's and Kelsey's journey to happily-ever-after as much as I enjoyed writing it. Your comments are always welcome at my Web site, www.barbarawallace.com

Best wishes and happy reading,

Barbara

BEAUTY AND THE BROODING BOSS

BY
BARBARA WALLACE

All the characters in this book have no existence outside the imagination of
the author, and have no relation whatsoever to anyone bearing the same name
or names. They are not even distantly inspired by any individual known or
unknown to the author, and all the incidents are pure invention.

First published in Great Britain 2011
Harlequin Mills & Boon Limited,
Eton House, 18-24 Paradise Road, Richmond, Surrey TW9 1SR

BEAUTY AND THE BROODING BOSS © Barbara Wallace 2011

ISBN: 978 0 263 88859 1

23-0211

Harlequin Mills & Boon policy is to use papers that are natural, renewable
and recyclable and products and made from wood grown in sustainable forests.
The logging and manufacturing processes conform to the legal environmental
regulations of the country of origin.

Printed and bound in Spain
by Litografia Rosés S.A., Barcelona

Barbara Wallace has been a lifelong romantic and daydreamer, so it's not surprising she decided to become a writer at age eight. However, it wasn't until a co-worker handed her a romance novel that she knew where her stories belonged. For years she limited her dreams to nights, weekends and commuter train trips, while working as a communications specialist, PR freelancer and full-time mum. At the urging of her family she finally chucked the day job, pursued writing full-time and couldn't be happier.

Barbara lives in Massachusetts with her husband, their teenage son, and two very spoiled self-centred cats (as if there could be any other kind). Readers can visit her at www.barbarawallace.com and find her on Facebook. She'd love to hear from you.

For Peter — I couldn't do this without you.

And for the Moody Muses — the best support
group a gal could ask for.

CHAPTER ONE

ALEX Markoff WASN'T *really ugly*.

Nor was he scarred, horribly disfigured, or any of the other things Kelsey imagined a recluse to be. In fact, the man standing before her couldn't be described as anything less than stunning. He was tall, at least a half a foot taller than her, with a lanky athletic build that took up most of the door frame. Faded jeans hung low on narrow hips while a black golf shirt molded to expansive shoulders. With his right arm engulfed from biceps to fingers in a plaster cast, she wondered how he managed to put on such a well-fitting garment.

Storm-cloud-colored eyes bore down on her from above finely-honed cheekbones.

Nope, not ugly. But definitely unhappy to see her on his doorstep.

Other doorsteps and other unwelcome expressions threatened on the edge of her memory and she shook them away. This wasn't the same. Not at all.

Still, she couldn't stop that all-too-familiar uncertainty from creeping into her voice as she offered up a polite smile. "Hi. I'm Kelsey Albertelli."

When he didn't respond, she added, "Your new assistant."

Silence.

"From New York. Mr. Lefkowitz hired me to—"

"I know who you are."

His voice matched his physical stature. Kelsey nearly stepped back from its impact. *Or was it the barely veiled hostility?*

Driving up the Taconic Parkway with the windows rolled down had blown her topknot loose, and strands of brown hair were falling into her line of sight. She tucked a few of them behind her ear. "Good. For a moment, I thought maybe Mr. Lefkowitz's office forgot to close the loop."

"No, he closed it. Several times."

Kelsey nodded as an awkward silence settled between them. More strands of hair fell in her face. She tucked them back and waited to see what Markoff would say next.

The answer was nothing. He simply turned around and retreated into the house leaving her standing alone on the threshold.

Can't say you weren't warned. "Doubt you'll get much of a warm welcome," his editor had said. Clearly an understatement. "Just remember, he doesn't have a choice. You work for me, not him."

"Don't worry," she'd assured him. "I'm sure I'll be fine. Nothing I can't handle." *For the right price.* Thanks to Grandma Rosie, she was all about the paycheck these days. She'd have to work three or four jobs to earn what Mr. Lefkowitz offered. Besides, it wasn't as if she hadn't shown up unwanted on a doorstep before.

Coincidentally, that was thanks to Grandma Rosie too.

Since Markoff left the door open, she assumed he intended her to follow. By the time she realized and crossed the threshold, he was several paces ahead, and she had to rush to catch up.

"You're certainly tucked away up here," she said, reaching his shoulder. "You don't get too many sets of directions saying 'turn right at the big pine tree' in New York City. I think I turned right three times at three different trees."

"It's the one at the fork," he replied.

"I know that *now*." She emphasized the word. "Still, in most places when they give you a landmark, it's a building or a sign or something. Not a pine tree. I missed your driveway the first time driving by too. You can barely see your mailbox behind the bushes. But then, I imagine that's the point...."

Her sentence faded off. She was rambling. She hated rambling. Nervous chatter to fill up silence. Drove her insane. She'd had enough of it as a kid to last a lifetime. Got to the point, in fact, where she wanted to scream at the social workers to shut up. Yet here she was doing the same exact thing. Anxiously trying to break the ice with a man whose resentment at her presence poured off him in waves.

Still, she refused to feel intimidated. "Mr. Lefkowitz said you write all your drafts longhand. I assume that's what I'll be typing—your longhand draft, that is." Her gaze flickered to his plaster-encased arm. "I hope breaking your arm hasn't affected your progress."

No sooner did the words leave her mouth than he stopped short, turning his gray eyes on her. Kelsey found herself rooted to the spot by their intensity. "Did Stuart tell you to ask that?"

"I—I—" Kelsey honestly didn't know how to reply.

"You tell Stuart Lefkowitz he'll get his manuscript when he gets it. Bad enough he's foisted a damn typist on me—I don't need a babysitter too."

"I wasn't—that is, I'm not—" Scrambling to catch up once again, Kelsey found herself wishing she'd asked a few more questions during her job interview. *That's what you get for being motivated by money.*

When she first learned she'd be typing manuscript pages for Alex Markoff—the Alex Markoff—she thought the assignment sounded exotic. She'd been in high school when *Chase the Moon* debuted, but she remembered the book sitting on teachers' desks, and she remembered reading excerpts from it in literature class. Alex Markoff was The Author of the Decade. The one writer everyone clamored to read.

She stole another look at her new boss. Maybe she should have looked at a book jacket before arriving. His looks might not have caught her so off guard. It wasn't that he was stereotypically handsome—in profile some might consider the nose a tad long or his jaw too angular—but the strong features suited him. Hard to believe she imagined him disfigured. Then again, how else was she supposed to picture a man who went from bestselling author to hermit?

She really should have asked more questions during the interview.

Looking to her surroundings for answers, she could only see that Nuttingwood was as dark and masculine as its owner. It reminded her of an English cottage from some old black-and-white movie, all stone and ivy. The front room was similar in appearance, small with antique furniture and hunter green furnishings.

Turning the corner, however, Kelsey suddenly found herself thrust into a large space dominated by windows and French doors. Outside lay a sprawling garden awash with color so vivid it made both the dark wood interior and the green Berkshire mountains pale in comparison. Through the glass she could see birds darting back and forth amid the flowers, many of which she didn't recognize.

"Wow," she said under her breath. It was like standing in the New York Botanical Garden.

Footsteps pulled her from her reverie. Markoff had headed across the open space to a door on the opposite side. Following, Kelsey found herself in a room similar to the one she left, though smaller and with fewer windows. It was no less spectacular, however, thanks to a pair of French doors that opened onto a terraced rose garden. Adirondack chairs encouraged visitors outside, while inside a pair of plaid overstuffed rockers battled back with a comfortable invitation of their own. Clutter—mostly magazines, books and papers—littered the end tables and bookcases. A few crumpled balls of paper lay on the floor. For some strange reason, they seemed more like decorations than mess, complements to the room's lived-in atmosphere.

"Great office." In her mind, she could imagine him scribbling away by the window.

Markoff simply pointed to a large wooden desk tucked in the corner. "You can work here."

"No computer?" The desk was barren of electronics.

"You can use your own and save to a flash drive."

"Okay." Good thing she had brought a laptop. Wonder what else she'd need. "Do you get Internet up here on the mountain?"

"Why?" That laserlike intensity had returned to his eyes, and they now bore into her suspiciously, as if she'd asked him for the National Defense codes. "Why would you need Internet access?"

"So I can keep in contact with New York. Mr. Lefkowitz will want updates."

He made a noise in the back of his throat, a sort of quiet, guttural growl. Kelsey immediately recalled his babysitter comment. Just her luck to step into some sort of bad blood between editor and writer. "If you don't, I can find a place in town—"

"There's Internet."

"Great." She'd worry about access another time when he was in a better mood. *If he had a better mood.*

A stack of yellow notepads lay on the desk so

she turned her attention to them. "This is what I'm typing, I presume."

"Type exactly what's written," he replied. "Don't change a thing. Not a single word. If you can't read something, leave it blank. I'll fill in the word later."

Kelsey picked up the top notebook. Lines of gray masculine scrawl filled the page. Great. He wrote in pencil. And changed his mind a lot too. With all the arrows and slashes, the paper looked more like a sports play than a story. Looked like there would be a lot of blanks.

"Anything else?" she asked. One thing she learned as a temp was to learn an employer's quirks and rules upfront. Knowledge made adjusting to that much easier, and she figured Markoff's typing guidelines were merely the tip of the iceberg.

She was right. "I don't like loud noise," he continued. "No music, no loud voices. If you need to call your boyfriend or whoever—"

"I won't be calling anyone." Her quick answer must have caught him by surprise, because his stormy eyes blinked. "No boyfriend, no family." Why she felt the need to supply the information, she didn't know.

A shadow flickered across his face, momentarily quieting the turbulence in his eyes. The change threw her off balance. Without the glare, his face went from intense to downright arresting. It was most unsettling. Tucking her hair behind her ear, she looked away to the ground.

"Well, if you do need to make a call," she heard him say, "please go outside. Or better yet, wait until after work hours."

"Speaking of which, what hours did you have in mind? I mean, do you have a preference? So I don't disturb you?"

"Doesn't matter."

Because he didn't care or because she would disturb him no matter what? "Then if it's all right with you, I'm a morning person. I like to get an early start on the day."

"Fine."

Silence engulfed them once more, awkward and uneasy. Kelsey adjusted her appearance: her satchel, the hem of her T-shirt, anything rather than let Markoff's obvious displeasure get under her skin.

"Well then," she said, forcing a cheery note, "since we've covered where I'm working, what I'm working on and when, all that's left to settle is where you'd like me to sleep." Again, she found herself prodding his non-response. "Mr. Lefkowitz said you agreed to let me stay here." Amazingly.

"Upstairs," he replied. "The bedrooms are up-stairs."

"Is there a particular room…?"

"I don't care."

"As long as I don't steal yours, right?"

Her attempt at levity fell flat. More than flat, based on how his expression darkened.

"I appreciate you being so accommodating. The Berkshires are a popular spot apparently, because summer rooms are at a premium." She was babbling again. "Mr. Lefkowitz had his office call every hotel first."

"I'm sure he did."

Was that skepticism in his voice? What on earth? Did he think she chose to stay up here in the middle of nowhere? She took a deep breath and smoothed back her hair. "Look, Mr. Markoff, I know this arrangement wasn't your idea." She kept her voice as level and calm as possible. "And I'll be the first to admit the arrangements are less than ideal…."

"Or necessary."

"Be that as it may, I'm here for the summer. I promise I'll do my best to stay out of your way as much as possible."

"Good."

The blunt answer stung more than Kelsey expected. She tightened her smile, hiding the reaction. "It might help if we set some ground rules right now. For example, as far as meals go…"

"The kitchen's in the back. You're on your own for food."

Now why didn't that surprise her? "And the bathrooms?"

"The main one's upstairs, across from the guest rooms. You'll find towels and a tub. There's limited hot water."

"Guess that means I should catch the first shower."

He wasn't amused. Again, the reaction hurt. She chalked it up to a new location and old ghosts. *It's only for a summer,* she told herself. Any situation could be endured as long as it was short-term and she kept her personal distance.

"Don't worry," she amended. "I'm not one for lingering under the spray." Or anywhere she wasn't wanted, for that matter. Since he nodded in response, she assumed he approved the answer.

Meanwhile, she could tell Markoff was eager to end their meeting. So he could stomp off and rue her presence, no doubt. "My laptop is in the car. Why don't I go get it and start working. I'll print out the finished pages and leave them for your review."

As she spoke, she moved toward the door. Unfortunately, Markoff moved toward the desk at the same time and they inadvertently ended up in each other's personal space. The scent of wood and cloves drifted toward Kelsey. A warm earthy aroma that made her want to close her eyes and inhale deeply. Instead, she looked up to meet eyes that were stormier than ever.

Awareness, strong and instinctive, spread through her. "Sorry, I didn't realize you were…" For some reason her brain wiring had suddenly gone haywire, and she was having trouble putting words together. "I mean, I was heading…"

She slipped past him, into the vacant doorway. "Why don't I go get my laptop?"

Alex didn't respond. Good thing, since it took till she reached her car and some deep breaths of fresh air before the weird flustered sensation left her brain.

"Get a grip on yourself," she muttered to herself, unlocking the door. "You're going to be here all summer." Surely she wasn't going to spend the next three months rattled by her boss, was she?

When she returned a few minutes later she heard a voice coming from the office.

"For crying out loud, we're talking a couple extra months. Three tops. You can't wait an extra ninety days?"

Who couldn't wait? Markoff's voice was razor-sharp, cutting through not just the air, but her as well. "And I suppose I broke my arm on purpose too," she heard him say. "That why you sent the babysitter? To make sure I didn't hurl myself down another hill?"

Babysitter. He meant her. That meant he was talking to Stuart Lefkowitz. Trying to get rid of her perhaps?

Crossing the main space toward the doorway, she stopped shy of the entrance and peered through the crack. Markoff had his back to her. She could see his shoulder muscles rippling with tension beneath his shirt. When he turned, she saw a similar tautness playing across his profile.

"Did it ever occur to you," he said, "that I can't write with someone breathing down my neck twenty-four seven?"

Alex's jaw twitched while he listened to the voice on the other end. Suddenly, his eyes grew disbelieving. "What did you say? Yes, I know what 'breach of contract' means. You wouldn't..."

There was silence, followed by a slow controlled intake of breath. Incredulity had changed to outright fury. "Fine. You'll get your damn book."

Kelsey jumped as he slammed the cell phone on his desk. Breach of contract? They were threatening legal action? No wonder Mr. Lefkowitz had been so adamant about her staying. And no wonder Markoff resented her. He was right. She *was* a babysitter.

On the other side of the door, Alex let out a

frustrated groan, and she heard footsteps. Fearing discovery, she instinctively drew back, scrambling mentally for an explanation should she be confronted for eavesdropping. A second later, the banging of a door told her she was safe; that he'd left through the garden. Sure enough, looking outside, she could see him stomping off toward the woods.

With the angry conversation she heard fresh in her mind, she finally let out the sigh she'd been holding since her arrival.

This was going to be a long summer.

That night Kelsey unpacked, settling into the room that would be her home for the next three months. Since Alex never mentioned which bedroom would be hers, she selected one that looked like a guest room. Like the front of the house, the room she picked was dark and woodsy, draped in hunter green and brown. The only thing missing was a deer head hanging on the wall.

The aroma of cedar wafted from the closet, adding to the rustic appeal. As she unpacked her clothes, she tried to count the number of times she'd gone through this routine. And it was a routine. First came the bureau, taking up as little drawer space as possible—a throwback to sharing a room with multiple people—then the closet. The entire process seldom took more than fifteen minutes. She'd learned early to travel light and not get too settled, so all her worldly possessions fit into two large suitcases. This summer it was the most she'd ever packed, she noted. Then again, the two years she just spent subletting was the longest she'd ever spent in one place. Guess in sticking around, she'd acquired a few more things.

Closet done, she reached for her satchel, the final part of her ritual. Immediately, her fingers found her most prized possession. The ceramic mug was cool to the touch despite sitting in her bag all day long. Hard to believe that once upon a time, brightly painted flowers had circled its surface. They were nothing more than faded speckles of paint now. There was a crack along the top of the handle from too many washings. Smiling, Kelsey cradled the mug in her palm. She could picture the same mug, colors still bright, resting on a countertop, a female hand pouring coffee into it. If she tried really hard, she could picture her mother bringing the cup to her lips, though as time passed, that memory got harder and harder to conjure up.

All of a sudden she felt overwhelmingly small and alone, as if the simple act of remembering transported her back in time. For a moment, she wasn't a grown woman controlling her own destiny, but a little girl back in the system, gripping the last

talisman she had from her old life. Living with her
mother hadn't been great, but at least she'd been
wanted. At least that's how she chose to remember
those years.

She leaned against the headboard, knees drawn
close, the mug pressed to her breast. This was part
of the routine too, this momentary lapse into loneliness. She'd get over it soon enough. She always
did. Soon as she familiarized herself with the surroundings. Although this time the feelings were
stronger than usual. Hardly surprising given Alex's
animosity.

She gave herself five more minutes of self-pity,
then put the emotion back on the shelf and walked
to the window. Her bedroom overlooked a less
landscaped part of the garden, closer to the trees,
increasing the feeling of isolation. Outside, through
the tree line, she noticed the sky still bore traces
of daylight even though it felt far later. "Country
living," she mused, raising the sash. The greeting quiet was unsettling. Nothing but the rustle of
leaves and a few intermittent high-pitched trills.
How on earth would she sleep without the under-
current of traffic? Or streetlights? Didn't Markoff
believe in outdoor lighting?

Of course not, she answered with a roll of her
eyes. Lights would ruin the whole "darkness"
theme he had going.

To her right, a branch snapped. She leaned over the sill, half expecting—or maybe fully expecting—to see a wild animal dashing out from the trees. What she saw instead surprised her more. It was the silhouette of a man.

Markoff.

He was walking the perimeter of the property, just inside the tree line. Head down, he picked his way carefully, as if counting his steps. Kelsey watched him approach with a catch in her throat. He looked so alone. Not at all like the hostile man who had greeted her this afternoon. This man reminded her of a specter. That was the only word she could think to describe him. There but not there.

He came closer, and Kelsey drew back, not wanting to get caught watching. No sooner did she pull into the shadows than she noticed he'd stopped. His face slanted upward to her window. Kelsey stifled a gasp. What light remained hit his eyes just right, turning them to shining silver. Even from two stories up, she could see the emotion churning behind them, bright and unguarded. She couldn't name what emotion she saw, but whatever it was, it struck a familiar chord, pulling her in and making her insides twist. It felt like he was looking straight at her. Or rather, *inside* her. Which was silly, since he couldn't see her from where she stood.

Eventually he moved on, leaving the night air charged with his presence. Quietly, Kelsey lowered the shade. A few moments later, she heard footsteps on the stairs, followed by a bedroom door clicking shut.

His room was next to hers. She hadn't realized. Through the wall, she heard the scraping of a chair and she swore what sounded like a long, desolate sigh followed by another and another, each sounding more frustrated than the next. Suddenly there was the rattling rush of glass and paper punctuated by a groan. The door opened and footsteps, heavy, angry footsteps, sounded in the hall. Kelsey knew the front door would slam before she heard it.

Okay, so maybe she was wrong about the nighttime quiet. But she was right about it being a long summer. Maybe she should have stayed in New York and worked those three jobs after all.

And be tied to Grandma Rosie's debt for even longer.

Letting out a long breath, she collapsed backwards on the bed. "Thanks a lot, Grandma," she muttered. Looked like Markoff wasn't the only one who didn't have a choice.

CHAPTER TWO

"ALL I can say is thank God for coffee. Especially—" Kelsey took a long sip "—fresh-ground Italian roast. I swear this stuff might be the only thing keeping me upright today."

Her companion, a large orange tabby, said nothing. Kelsey had found the furry critter dozing on the terrace when she arrived at dawn, and he'd been keeping her company ever since. She suspected the animal was a stray. Unless Alex had a hidden soft spot, she didn't see him as the pet-owning type.

Then again, those eyes she saw last night definitely hid something....

Forget it. He didn't deserve sympathetic thoughts. Not after the way he kept her up last night with his continual pacing and sighing.

"I thought writing was a sitting profession, not one that required moving across the floor all night long." She took another drink and waited for the caffeine to kick in. She was going to need to be alert if she was going to spend the day deciphering his handwriting. "I'll tell you one thing, Puddin'-cat, I don't care how brilliant a writer he is, the man definitely needs to improve his social skills. He acts like my being here is some kind of plague. How much you want to bet he's annoyed that I helped myself to the coffee this morning?"

The cat pulled a paw over its eyes in response.

"Exactly," Kelsey replied. "Though seems to me, if you're going to leave a fresh pot brewing at the crack of dawn, you shouldn't be surprised when people help themselves." The smell alone had been nirvana after a sleepless night. "Fair's fair, right?"

"Who are you talking to?"

Kelsey nearly jumped out of her skin. Standing at the edge of the terrace was a very dark and both-ered Alex Markoff.

Immediately, her insides somersaulted. How was it he could look so intimidatingly perfect at this hour? He wore a navy blue T-shirt the same shade as his sling, the hem of which skimmed the waistband of his jeans. Jeans, she noted, that looked made to hug his hips. He'd been up and about from the looks of it. His skin glistened with perspiration, the moisture darkening the collar of his shirt. Dark curls peeked out from the back of his neck with the unruliness that only came from damp hair. Though it shouldn't, seeing them made her wonder what he might look like stepping from the shower.

"Good morning," she said once she caught her breath.

He stared at her with unreadable eyes. "You didn't answer my question. Who are you talking to?"

"Just the—" She pointed to the sunny spot on a terrace that was now deserted. "Myself."

"Do you always do that?"

"When there's no one else to talk with. What's that they say, 'You're your own best company'?"

"So I've always believed."

As she tucked her hair behind her ear, Kelsey swore he checked for an earpiece. Really, did he think she was lying? "Looks like I'm not the only morning person after all. I helped myself to the coffee, by the way."

"I heard."

Along with how much else? Quickly, she raised her mug, hoping he wouldn't notice her skin flushing. "Have you been up long?" she asked over the rim. "I would think after such a long night, you'd be sleeping in."

"Why do you think I had a long night?"

Why did he seem to scrutinize everything she

said as though she had a hidden meaning? Along with staring at her with those probing gray eyes?

"I heard you," she explained, resisting the urge to duck her head like a nervous teenager. "Kind of hard not to, actually. Old house, thin rooms. You sigh loudly."

"Oh."

Oh, indeed.

"I take it writing didn't go well last night?"

"Why do you want to know?"

"I don't know, to make conversation?" She shrugged. "Do I have to have a reason?"

"There's always a reason."

"Well, in this case, my reason was to be friendly. After all, we're going to spend the summer working together, we might as well be civil to one another, right?"

He gave her a long look. Gauging her sincerity? While she waited, the part of her not insulted used the standoff to study his face, catching the details she'd been too overwhelmed to notice before. Things like the tanned complexion, the faint scar on the bridge of his nose, the curve of his Cupid's bow.

And, of course, the emotion behind his eyes. Yet again it struck her that there was something sad and painful behind their turbulence. A kind of longing, perhaps.

Or loneliness.

What was his story? She really should have done some research before taking this job.

Her curiosity would have to go unexamined as the sound of crunching gravel on the other side of the house interrupted the standoff. Soon as he heard the noise, Alex's expression changed. Again. His shoulders straightened and a soft curse escaped his lips.

"What?" Kelsey was having trouble keeping up with his collection of abrupt moods. Naturally he didn't answer. Like yesterday, he simply turned and walked off leaving her to follow. She turned the corner in time to see a burly tree-trunk of a man step out of a green pickup with the words *Leafy Bean, Farley Grangerfield Prop.* painted on the side. The man looked from Alex to her with interest, but said nothing. Not surprising given the dark warning plastered all over Alex's face.

Continuing in silence, both men reached over the side of the truck bed and each grabbed two canvas bags laden with groceries. Alex, she noted, carried both with his good arm. As the stranger passed, he shot her another look. "Last two bags won't unload themselves."

Taking the hint, Kelsey hustled to the truck to see they'd, fortunately, left her what looked like the two lightest bags. She brought them into the kitchen where she found the two men wordlessly unpacking groceries and arranging them on the kitchen table. The door swung shut behind her, causing them to both look up.

"Where should I put these?" she asked.

"Counter," Alex replied. "That's not necessary," he added when she started unpacking.

"I don't mind." What else was she going to do, stand there and watch them? "You'll have to tell me where the stuff goes though. At least the first time. I'm pretty good at remembering where things go. Plus this way I'll see where there's space for my groceries."

Dammit, she was babbling again. It was quickly becoming a bad habit. But the quiet… It filled the room so completely. And those looks she kept feeling the grocer give her. Curious and full of implied innuendo. She had to say something just to hear something besides her own thoughts. Although the subsequent look Alex shot her made her wish she'd reconsidered.

"Bigger order'll cost you extra," commented the grocer shortly.

"Kelsey will be buying her groceries separately."

"Right," she said. After all, she was on her own for meals. Why would they do something as simple as combine grocery orders? "I'm Kelsey Albertelli,

by the way. Mr. Markoff's new assistant. I'm here
to help while his arm's broken. Are you Farley?"

The lack of denial suggested he was. "Need
three days' notice for delivery. You want your food
sooner, you have to pick up your order yourself.
Special orders take longer. And if I don't have the
brand, I'll substitute. No complaining."

Was everyone in Berkshire County this brusque?
At least Farley's silence felt different. Gruff though
he was, he lacked the anger and wary defensiveness
that surrounded her new boss. "Got order forms in
the truck," he said when the last grocery item had
been put away. They were the first words anyone
had said in a few minutes. "You want some, follow
me."

She did, feeling Alex's stare on her all the way
to the drive. "Normal delivery's every ten days,"
the old man was telling her. "First four bags are
free, after that you pay."

"I'll bear that in mind." Kelsey took the stack
of tri-colored forms he handed her. "You been delivering to Nuttingwood long?" she asked.

"Long enough"

"And that's been…?"

"Three, four, five years. I don't keep a calen-
dar."

She would have liked to have been surprised by
the vague answer, but deep down she suspected

that's all she'd get. Still, it was worth a shot. "Thanks again for the forms," she said, waving them in the air. "I'll see you soon."

Farley muttered something about having nothing better to do than drive around all day and shut the door. Kelsey stifled a smile. The answer was so grumpy and so over the top, she actually found it funny.

She waited until the truck disappeared round the tree-covered bend, then returned to the house. Where, she discovered, Alex hadn't moved. He stood flush against the kitchen sink, his eyes glued to the space beyond the window.

"Interesting character," she said, shutting the door. "Is that grumpy old man act for real?" *As opposed to yours, which I can't for the life of me understand?*

"I wouldn't know."

"Ever been to his store? The, uh," she looked at the forms in her hand, "Leafy Bean?"

"Once or twice."

"It as colorful as him?"

"The pastries are decent."

Coming from him, that was nothing short of a glowing recommendation. She made her way to the kitchen table where a few grocery items, mostly fresh produce, remained. Maybe she was imagining things, but Alex seemed pretty annoyed she'd

crossed paths with Farley. Then again, surely he
didn't expect, because he was apparently an antisocial hermit, that she avoid human contact too?
Did he think she'd spend all summer alone with
no one but him and a stray cat for company?

A strange, warm shiver ran down her spine at
the notion.

Alex had switched his attention from outside the
window to her. Eyes dark and murky, the scrutiny
ignited another set of shivers. Aw, hell. Why not
come right out and ask the question? "You don't
like him knowing I'm here, do you?"

"I don't like people knowing my business."

"I hardly think you having a temporary assistant
will be big news in town. If they even find out.
Farley doesn't seem like the kind of guy who talks
about anything let alone gossip."

"Everybody talks eventually, Miss Albertelli. I
don't have to help them out." He pushed himself
away from the counter. "And neither do you."

Everyone talks eventually.

She didn't know it at the time, but Alex's parting
remark was the last she heard from him for two
days. He disappeared Lord knows where shortly
after, leaving her to wander Nuttingwood alone.

"I see you more often," she said to Puddin' the
cat when he made his daily appearance on the terrace. "He's like a ghost, only showing up at night."

She knew he showed up then because she could hear him pacing the floor. Pacing and pacing.

"Maybe if he wrote something upbeat he'd be able to sleep." What pages she'd deciphered so far were darker than the man himself. Bitter too. Brilliant but bitter. About as far removed from *Chase the Moon* as you could get. "Like they were written by two different people," she told Puddin'. Maybe in a way they were.

With each passing hour she kicked herself a little harder for her lack of due diligence before taking this job. Instead of asking questions, she had let herself get distracted by the size of her impending paycheck. Sure the money was a priority, but why didn't she think to get a little more information about her boss? She'd really like to know what his story was. Why he seemed so angry at the world.

"I know, I know," she said to Puddin', "keep your head low and mind your business." That was the rule. "But if I knew why, then maybe I'd know if this disappearing act was going to play all summer."

It still wasn't too late to find out. Wasn't that what the Internet was for? Without giving it another thought, she rose from her seat, moving so fast Puddin' jumped too. Farley said he'd been delivering groceries between three and five years. *Chase the Moon* came out about six years ago.

Surely in six years there would have been some kind of news article written about Alex Markoff, right?

A dozen keystrokes later, she had her answer. The Actress and the Author: It's Love! screamed the tabloid headline.

Alex Markoff, in love with a movie star? Seemed incongruous if you asked her. But there was proof. A photo of Alex and a familiar blonde cozying up to each other over a cup of coffee. An odd kind of irritation settled over her as she read about their courtship. Apparently the starlet, Alyssa Davenport, met Alex at a book signing. A whirlwind romance followed and much to everyone's surprise the couple married and settled in Los Angeles where one of Alex's short stories was being made into a film. Alex's fame and her looks made them a favorite for the camera. A click of the mouse found dozens of photos. At fund-raisers. At movie premieres. On a producer's yacht. Of Alyssa's platinum-blond hair and perfectly formed features. In every photo Mrs. Markoff appeared lovingly perched on her husband's arm, her smile a glowing complement to Alex's somber, almost reluctant expression. Even living a fairy tale, he didn't smile.

Another click and the story changed. "What Went Wrong?" asked the headline superimposed over Alyssa's face. Other stories promised to reveal "Markoff's Dark Secrets."

Everyone talks eventually. And talk they did. Friends, acquaintances, even employees offered lurid "insider" details of the marriage, the breakup and the couple's intimate life.

"Did everyone who knew him give an interview?" she asked aloud.

"Short answer, yes."

Kelsey's stomach dropped. Slowly, she raised her eyes from the screen, coming face to face with Alex. Fury darkened his features. "What the hell are you doing?"

She tried to answer but the words stuck in her throat. Instead she ended up opening and closing her mouth like a fish gasping for air.

Meanwhile, Alex turned the laptop around and glared at the screen. Kelsey could feel the rage boiling up inside him. Which made his tightly controlled voice doubly scary.

"I'll ask again. What do you think you're doing?"

"I—I—" Tucking the hair behind her ear, she took a deep breath and steadied herself. A difficult task, what with the death stare Alex was throwing her way. "I'm sorry. I thought maybe if I knew more about you I could—"

"Could what, Miss Albertelli?"

The glare got worse, forcing her to look away. All of a sudden, her answer didn't sound so adequate. "Understand you better," she replied softly.

Apparently Alex didn't find the answer adequate either. His jaw muscle twitched as he looked from her to the screen and back. "You want to understand me better?" he asked finally, his voice even more maddeningly controlled than before. "Then understand this. My private life is that—*private*. You do not have the right to root around in my past, no matter what your reasons are."

I wouldn't have had to if you weren't such a mystery, Kelsey muttered inside her head. Still, she knew Alex was right. She dropped her gaze to her hands, feeling like a kid caught breaking house rules. It was a feeling she detested, although never so much as this particular moment, since she had no one to blame for her predicament but herself. "It won't happen again."

"Damn right it won't. Because you're leaving. Today."

Leaving? As in fired?

Stupid, stupid, stupid. Why didn't she listen to her own rules and mind her own business? No, she had to go poking around in Markoff's past and get herself fired. Fired as in out on the street with no reference. Who knows how long it would take her to find a new position? Images of collection notices flashed before her eyes. She was so screwed.

"Mr. Markoff, wait!"

Having issued his order, Alex had turned and marched out. Kelsey scrambled after him, catching him by the shoulder. "You need to reconsider."

He whirled around, lightning flashing in his stormy eyes. "I don't *need* to reconsider anything. I'm not the one who invaded my privacy."

"Please. I need this job." Lord, but she hated the pleading note in her voice. Another insult courtesy of Grandma Rosie.

"You should have thought of that before you went on Google."

"But—"

"Today, Miss Albertelli. Go pack your things."

Idiot. What was she going to do now? Maybe she could get Stuart Lefkowitz to intervene....

She didn't relish playing this gambit, but desperate times called for desperate measures, and if she had any hope of paying off Grandma Rosie's debt in a reasonable amount of time, she didn't have a choice. Alex was almost to the garden door. If he left, who knew how long he'd be gone.

"What about Mr. Lefkowitz? He's not going to be happy with another delay."

That stopped him. "Stuart's happiness isn't my

concern." He still sounded haughty, but a hint of wariness had crept in.

"I'm sure that's true," she replied, "but…"

His lips became a tight line. "But what?"

Now or never. Slowly, deliberately, she crossed the room, making sure her eyes stayed locked with his. It wasn't easy, what with the fluttering in her stomach that accompanied each step. "But you and I both know he doesn't want more delays."

He tried to disguise the hitch in his breath, but she heard it nonetheless. The cards were on the table. He knew that she knew about the breach of contract. For several seconds, the only sound in the entire house was the ticking of the hallway clock. Kelsey waited, holding both her ground and her breath.

Finally, he let out what sounded like a strangled groan. She recognized the noise as defeat. "Why won't the world just leave me alone," he muttered, jamming his fingers through his hair. "Is that so much to ask?"

The pain in his growl did little to ease her conscience as Kelsey watched him stomp away. Although he didn't say so, she knew she'd won the challenge. He wouldn't throw her out. This time anyway. She waited until she heard the front door slam before sinking to the sofa in relief. Relief accompanied by a hefty dose of guilt. Cursing, she smacked a nearby cushion.

So much for her getting on Alex Markoff's good side.

CHAPTER THREE

THAT night, Kelsey went out to eat. After the day's debacle, she wanted to put as much distance between her and Alex as possible. She ended up in town at the local inn. The two-hundred-year-old building featured a pub in the basement, so she tried drowning her guilt with a cheeseburger and Irish music. No such luck though. Her conscience still felt lousy. She could kick herself for being so nosy. Alex was right; his past was none of her business. After all, how would she feel if someone poked around in her life?

And yet, thanks to those shocking Web sites, here she was obsessing more than ever. There was something about the man she simply couldn't let go of. Something in the way he expressed his anger. In the way he begged the world to leave him alone. There was despair in those gray eyes of his that told her there was far more to Alex Markoff than some angry, mournful hermit.

What was he like before his divorce, she wondered. Carefree? Happy? She tried to picture him laughing and came up short.

How sad. Even she found occasion to laugh once in a while.

It was well past midnight when she returned to Nuttingwood. She might have arrived back earlier, but no sooner did she leave the restaurant than the sky erupted in a monstrous thunderstorm. Thanks to the torrential rain, the wind and the lack of streetlights, she couldn't see more than five feet in front of her on the drive home. As a result, she missed the fork with the pine tree and had to retrace her path.

Happily, Nuttingwood was dark when she pulled into the drive. Alex was, no doubt, avoiding her as well. She dashed to the front door, bumping her hip against the marble entranceway table the second she crossed the threshold. Cursing for not leaving a light on, she felt along the wall until she found the switch and flipped it upward.

Nothing happened.

She flipped the switch again. And again.

"You're wasting your time."

Lightning flashed, briefly illuminating the room and she caught sight of a dark silhouette at the great room window. "You're wasting your time,"

Alex repeated. "Lights went out thirty minutes ago."

Kelsey drew closer. Now that her eyes had adjusted, she could see Alex was doing more than simply standing at the window. He was kneading the muscles on the back on his neck. He wore a pair of loose-fitting sweatpants with no shirt. His hair was messed too. He must have been lying down when the storm hit. Seeing him so exposed felt queerly intimate, almost voyeuristic. For the first time since she moved in, Kelsey realized she shared a house in the woods with a flesh-and-blood man. A very handsome, very desirable man. The sudden awareness made part of her grow shaky while other parts became painfully awake.

"This happen often?" she asked. "Power outages, I mean." Nice to know how frequently they'd find themselves together in the dark. Because of a storm, that is.

"If the wind blows hard enough."

"And how often is that?" she asked, reaching his shoulder. He didn't turn around upon her approach, seemingly intent on studying the shadows in the garden. Lightning flashed, and she caught his reflection. His expression was much farther away than this room.

"Often enough. There's an emergency generator in the basement."

"You haven't turned it on yet?"

"I like the darkness."

Why am I not surprised?

"Did you say something?"

"Nothing important." She didn't realize she'd spoken aloud. Covering, she changed topics. "Lightning's putting on quite a show."

"Suppose."

"When I was little one of the other fost—other kids told me thunder and lightning were caused by alien attacks. Scared me so much I would hide under the covers." She could still remember cowering under the blanket, clutching her mother's cup to her chest like a talisman. "The stupid things kids fall for, huh?"

"Not only kids."

"What?" His voice was so soft, she missed part of his sentence, making it her turn to ask, "Did you say something?"

"Nothing important."

Intuition said otherwise, but she didn't press. He wouldn't admit the truth if she did. So instead, she stole what had to be the hundredth look at his profile. In the dark, she could only see the outline of his features. His expression was impossible to read. Even so, his magnetism was stronger than ever. Maybe because they were alone, or because the dark made everything that much more intimate, but she felt surrounded by him. There seemed no escaping his scent or the heat emanating from his body. She could even feel the rise and fall of his chest, his breathing strained as it filled his lungs. His desolation was palpable, so much so she hurt for him. She found herself wanting to reach out and soothe his pain.

"I'm sorry about this afternoon," she said softly. "I had no right to snoop behind your back."

"No, you didn't."

The corner of her mouth twitched upward with guilty amusement. "You don't believe in cutting people slack, do you?"

"If I cut slack to everyone who betrayed my privacy, I'd need a much larger supply of scissors."

She thought of the gossip articles and Web sites, and she understood. No one deserved to have their life splashed on the front page. "I'm sorry too, about your marriage."

"It was a long time ago."

"Still, you—"

"I don't want to talk about Alyssa, Miss Albertelli. Our marriage failed. End of story."

The myriad of emotions in his voice—anger, frustration, hurt—said otherwise, but seeing as how she was already treading on thin ice, Kelsey didn't push. "Did you say the generator was in the basement?"

"At the foot of the stairs." He sounded grateful for the change of subject.

"Mind if I turn it on? You can keep the lights out in this room, but I'd like to find my way upstairs without incident." Not to mention, shedding light might diminish the intimacy of their situation. Maybe, if she could see his usual stormy expression, she wouldn't feel his pull so intensely.

"Knock yourself out."

Finding her way to the kitchen in the dark was easier said than done. Nuttingwood was one of those houses that had been added onto over the years, leading to an abundance of twists and turns and unexpected corners. During the day, the eclectic layout gave the house character, but at night, in the pitch black, the layout became a pedestrian nightmare. Kelsey was certain she'd fall and break an arm too. Worse, she'd break some piece of furniture or irreplaceable family heirloom.

Eventually she reached the double-swing door leading to the kitchen, just in time to hear footsteps approach from behind.

"You'll need a flashlight," Alex said, giving the door a push. Kelsey followed in silence, trying not to think about how his body brushed against hers when he passed.

He moved around the dark kitchen with a grace to be admired. At least she assumed he moved with grace since she didn't hear any of the bumps or knocks that accompanied her own clumsy movements. The basement door was to the side, behind the farmer's table. She was walking cautiously in that direction when she heard the scraping of a chair being dragged across the floor.

"What are you doing?"

"The flashlight's in the back of the cupboard. With my cast, I can't reach it flatfooted."

"Then let me." Making her way back toward his silhouette, she took the chair from his grip. "It's pitch black in here. Break your other arm and I'll be here till Christmas."

"By all means then, be my guest. We wouldn't want that."

Even though he couldn't see her, Kelsey smirked in his direction and stepped up. A warm sturdy hand pressed to her back. "I'm steadying you," Alex said from behind.

Steadying, huh? Then why did her legs feel shaky? Why did her spine feel like it had an electrical current running up and down it?

"There a problem?"

"No problem." It was the dark, she decided. It heightened everything. Turning something innocent, like a simple touch or Alex's low-pitched voice, into something sensual. Once the lights came on, the illusion would disappear.

All of a sudden, a pitiful wail sounded in the kitchen.

"What on earth was that?" Alex asked.

"I'm not—" The wail sounded again and recognition dawned.

"Puddin'!" She'd wondered what kind of shelter the cat had found to ride out the storm. He must have heard her drive up and was crying to come in the house. "Poor thing must be drenched to the skin."

"Who's Puddin'?"

Jumping down from the chair, she hurried to the back door only to have a jet-propelled streak of water rush past her legs when she opened it. Loud meows filled the kitchen. There was a click, and Alex, who'd apparently retrieved the flashlight, focused the beam on the sopping orange mass shivering under the kitchen table.

"That," Kelsey said, "is Puddin'."

"It's a cat."

An extremely sarcastic retort jumped to the tip of her tongue, but Kelsey managed to bite it off. "A very wet one at that. Would you hand me the dish towel?"

"For what?"

"To dry him off, of course. Or would you rather he drip water all over the floor?" Alex sighed, but she heard him move toward the kitchen sink. All the while keeping the light shining on Puddin''s waterlogged form.

"Poor baby, he's trembling." She reached out her hand, letting the scared animal sniff her fingers. "You're okay now. I think he's been living in your garden. He showed up on the terrace the other morning and has been keeping me company since."

"You mean you've been encouraging him?"

Don't tell her, she broke another rule. Taking the towel Alex draped over her shoulder, she gently wrapped the stray up. The cat barely protested, an indication of how wet and miserable his state was. A low rumble sounded deep in his chest. "See, he's happier already," she said.

"Bully for him," Alex grumbled. "Now that he's happy, what are you going to do?"

"I—" Good question. She hadn't thought much further than rescuing the little guy. "Well, we can't very well put him back outdoors," she said.

"We can't?"

"Look outside. It's raining cats and dogs."

"Then he'll be right at home."

"Very funny. Why can't he stay the night in the house? He's not causing any trouble." She lifted Puddin' a little closer. The cat immediately curled into her, seeking warmth and attention. "See?"

Alex flashed the light at her. "He doesn't belong here."

His words pushed a button inside her. How many times had she heard that same disinterested tone? "Says who?"

"Says me, the owner of the house."

Didn't matter. She looked at Puddin' who was flexing his front paws, oblivious to the debate around him, and felt frustrated anger swelling in her chest. Suddenly this wasn't about keeping a cat dry; it was about being wanted. About having someone want you. "I'm not putting him outside in this weather. He'll catch cold."

"He's a cat, not a child."

"So what? He still has feelings. Don't you?" Looking up, she found herself staring directly into the flashlight beam. "Surely you don't hate the world so much you'd send a defenseless animal out to drown."

She could hear his exasperation, and while she couldn't see his face, she could picture the irritation clouding his expression. Okay, maybe that last remark crossed the line.

"The way I feel about the world, you're lucky I don't make both of you sleep in the rain."

Kelsey was pretty sure he meant what he said. She clutched Puddin' a little tighter.

Alex turned around, taking the light with

him. As she blinked the spots from her eyes, she heard the sound of a door opening and for a wild second, she wondered if he planned on carrying out his threat. That is, until she heard him heading downstairs.

"Just make sure he's gone by morning," he grumbled. "And if he leaves any kind of thank-you present on my doorstep, I'm holding you responsible."

A smile tugged the corner of her lips as she savored the moment of victory. A small victory, but a victory nonetheless. Maybe Alex Markoff wasn't as hardhearted as he'd like the world to believe.

While she may have won this particular battle for Puddin's rights, there were only so many times she could push her luck before Alex tossed her out, Stuart Lefkowitz's threats be damned. By her count, she'd already pushed twice. Three times if she counted using the breach of contract threat as leverage. Therefore, Kelsey made a point of bringing Puddin' to her room for the night, making sure the cat stayed out of Alex's way.

"The less he sees of you, my friend, the better," she told him. Puddin', naturally, didn't mind. He simply sprawled across her comforter and started bathing.

Next morning, she woke at the crack of dawn

and deposited the now indignant Puddin' on the doorstep before heading into town. The latest Grandma Rosie payment was due and she wanted to make sure the check went out registered mail. The storm had ended a few hours earlier, leaving only a few downed branches and puddles as evidence it existed. Pulling onto the main road, she saw a power truck restringing the line and was surprised at the small stab of disappointment. Surely she didn't want to spend another night in the dark with Alex, with its odd mixture of intimacy and mystery. Did she?

She pulled onto Main Street, grateful the early hour meant an abundance of parking. Stockbridge was one of those sleepy towns that exploded in summer. Once a Gilded Age playground, the area had reinvented itself as an arts center featuring everything from symphony orchestras to offbeat art galleries. City dwellers flocked to the region, eager to soak up the pastoral atmosphere even as they disturbed it. For the residents, she imagined the crowds were a double-edged sword, simultaneously welcome and disdained.

Except for Alex. He simply disdained.

A sign on the post office window told her she had another fifteen minutes so she made her way down the street to the Leafy Bean. Farley's grocery store captured the area's atmosphere in one eclectic building. Part grocery, part café, part gourmet haven, the place featured everything from imported almond oil to homemade pastries served with a healthy dose of local color. And, as Kelsey discovered when picking up her grocery order, the store boasted an amazing selection of brewed coffee.

A brass bell announced her arrival. Farley was behind the counter, a large green apron covering his burly frame. His gloves and wrists were covered with flour.

"Morning, Farley," she greeted him, getting a grunt in return. "Some storm last night, huh? Nuttingwood lost power."

"Whaddya expect, up there in the middle of nowhere."

Alone, where no one could find him. "That's what Mr. Markoff likes about the place. It's private."

"Private like a hermit," Farley muttered back.

The Hermit of Nuttingwood. The moniker fit. It was sad and enigmatic. Now that she knew his story, or part of it, she couldn't blame him for wanting a little privacy, although retiring to the side of a mountain for five years still seemed a bit extreme. After all, she knew as well as anyone that life was seldom fair. The letter tucked in her satchel proved that. People used other people all the time. You learned to adapt.

Not to mention keep your distance. Mind your own business. Don't get too attached and think too far into the future. For people who didn't have the luxury of hiding on a mountainside, those rules were the key to survival. She knew because she'd been following them since she was four years old.

Except for this week. What was it about Alex Markoff that made her forget the rules?

"Better get your coffee while you can," Farley said, coming around to pour himself a cup as well. "Once the tourists wake up, they'll clean the place out."

She took it as a supreme compliment that he didn't lump her in with that group. "Isn't business a good thing?"

"Pain in the neck is what it is," Farley replied. "Always looking for some fancy flavor or asking if my beans are 'fair trade'. Says right there on the sign clear as day. Can't they read?"

Kelsey smiled over the rim of her coffee. "Guess not."

The older man was about to add more when the doorbell jingled. A group of two men and three women, clearly tourists, entered. The men wore pastel island shirts and khaki shorts—an outfit that was nearly uniform among visitors—while the women wore various forms of linen. All of them wore some kind of hat—either straw or baseball—perched on their heads.

"Do you have cappuccinos?" one of the women asked as they approached the counter.

"Everything we've got is on the counter," Farley replied, shooting Kelsey a look as if to say "see what I mean?"

"Who needs lattes, just give me a straight shot of joe," one of the men said. He was tall and athletic looking with sandy brown hair. Smiling at Kelsey, he added, "Too bad you can't hook up an intravenous line."

"Then how would you add sugar?" Kelsey asked.

"Who cares as long as it's going straight into my veins." The stranger grinned, then after a pause, pointed a finger at her.

"Nels Bïrdgarten's gallery showing, right? I was trying to think where we met. You look familiar."

If she had a nickel for every time a stranger tried that come-on, she wouldn't have to worry about paying off her debt. "Maybe our paths crossed somewhere in the city," she suggested.

"Could be. Or it was a cheap excuse to introduce myself. Tom Forbes."

At least he admitted the line was cheesy. Kelsey shook the hand he offered and introduced herself.

"So you're from New York," he continued. "Come to the Berkshires often?"

"First time. I'm here for the summer for a work assignment. You?"

"Every summer since I was eight. My parents have a place on the lake. Not a bad locale if you don't mind quiet."

You don't know quiet, Kelsey thought to herself. "I don't. Besides, you can't beat the coffee."

"Not New York standards, but it'll do, I suppose." Over at the register, Farley coughed. Oblivious, Tom raised the cup to his lips.

"Tom!" the female ringleader called over. "We're heading to the arts and crafts store."

"You go ahead, Moira. I'm going to finish my coffee, unless—" he flashed a bright smile "—I can talk you into breakfast at the Inn."

Kelsey chewed her lower lip. She should head back to Nuttingwood. On the other hand, it felt good to have someone want her company for a change. What she wouldn't give to have Alex toss even a hint of a smile in her direction.

She reached for a plastic to-go lid. "Why not?" she said, smiling back. "Breakfast sounds nice."

She got back to Nuttingwood far later than planned. Tom turned out to be pleasant company: charming, talkative, entertaining. A tad pompous but nice enough. He described himself as a social gadfly, doing a little bit of everything. "You know," he'd said when she asked, "a freelance project here, a blog article there."

In other words, he was rich enough that he didn't need to work.

When they parted company, he insisted on taking her cell phone number and made no bones about wanting to see her again. Had she been in New York, maybe she'd consider the offer, but here, under the circumstances, she wasn't so sure.

And her reluctance had nothing to do with her antisocial boss, she insisted to herself. Even if she did spend a good portion of the meal wondering what sharing breakfast with Alex would be like.

True to form, Alex was nowhere to be found when she returned, but Puddin' was. Someone had left the garden door unlatched and the cat had ensconced himself quite comfortably on her desk chair.

"And I thought I was pushing my luck," she said. "You know that nine lives thing is a myth, right?"

Puddin' rolled onto his back, exposing his belly.

"Easy for you to say. You're not the one with a negative checking balance." She'd made an extra large payment this month. It drained her account, leaving her barely enough to cover expenses. And Grandma Rosie's debt still loomed as mountainous as ever.

So while Puddin' might be willing to risk Alex's wrath, Kelsey wasn't. She needed this job.

"Sorry, pal, but I used up my defiance last night." Since Puddin' didn't care to cooperate by moving on his own, she gathered him in her arms. "Now," she said, walking outside and setting him gently on the stone terrace, "why don't you go find a nice bush to sleep under before the boss sees you."

"Too late." Alex appeared out of nowhere, brandishing a walking stick.

How on earth did he manage to sneak up on her like that? It was like he really was some kind of ghost. He glowered at Puddin', who appeared unimpressed.

"That thing's still here, I see."

"Good morning to you too," she replied. In addition to his specter-like approach, he managed to look uncommonly good this morning. Those khaki shorts and hiking shirt suited him way more than Tom. Probably, she stole a glance at his toned calves, because he actually hiked. "And this 'thing' has a name. Puddin'."

"You named a stray cat?"

"Even strays deserve an identity." She knelt

down to scratch Puddin's head. "Everyone wants to know they matter a little bit."

"As long as you don't mislead them or make them think they mean more than they do."

"Because they might get too comfortable."

"Or burned."

Were they still talking about the cat? No longer sure, Kelsey fell silent, letting the sound of Puddin's purring fill the void.

"Where did you go this morning?"

"Are you keeping tabs on me?"

"I saw you drive away."

Kelsey wasn't sure if she should resent or be flattered by the close attention. "I had some errands to run in town," she replied.

"Errands."

"Yes." She did know she resented the skeptical way he repeated the word. "You know, post office, grocery store... Farley had fresh baked apricot turnovers. I brought back some if you're interested."

Alex appeared to be only half listening, too busy was he rubbing the back of his neck. His eyes were half-closed, and he twisted his head back and forth like it needed loosening.

"Stiff neck?" Kelsey asked.

Naturally he gave her a suspicious look. "Why do you ask?"

"You're rubbing your neck same as you were last night. I made the assumption."

"You shouldn't make assumptions."

"And you shouldn't rub your neck so hard if you don't want people to make them."

Her comment earned a grimace. "I have a headache. Nothing I can't manage."

"Are you sure?" Upon closer inspection, she could see dark circles under his eyes and that his normally ruddy skin had a slight pallor. The sight kicked her maternal instincts into gear. Without realizing, she reached out to feel his forehead. His skin was cool and smooth. Touching it made the pads of her fingers tingle. "Did you take anything?"

"I'm fine." His expression remained guarded, but a note of tightness managed to creep into his voice. It was that note that drew her closer.

And closer. Until she'd practically eliminated the space between them. Her hand was still brushing his forehead. "You look pale," she murmured.

"You don't need to be concerned."

"I know I don't *have* to. Maybe I—"

The low sound of jazz music interrupted. Her phone. As expected, the moment the song rang out, Alex backed away leaving her hand hovering in the air. Balling her still tingling fingers into a fist, she reached into her skirt pocket with the other and fished out the phone.

"Frutti de Mar."

Between the static and the non sequitur, it took her a moment before she recognized the voice. "Tom?"

"Looks like I made as good an impression as I thought."

"We parted company less than an hour ago. Kind of hard not to remember."

She turned her back. Feeling Alex's probing stare burning holes in her spine, she tried her best to sound casual. "What can I do for you?"

"I told you. Frutti de Mar. Best gourmet seafood around, at least for this area. I find myself with a table for two and only one chair filled. I was hoping you could fill the other."

"You want to have dinner? Tonight?"

From the corner of her eye, she saw Alex walk away, their moment from before a distant memory.

If there had even been a moment. She could have imagined the whole thing. Just like last night's spark in the dark.

Or the way she was imagining the air cooling with his departure.

"Seven o'clock okay?"

"What?" Her attention had been on the man disappearing into the trees.

"For dinner. Does seven o'clock work for you?"

"I, uh…" It's not like she had any other plans. Tom was a nice guy. A pleasant guy who wanted to take her out to a fancy restaurant for dinner. But for some reason, she couldn't work up the interest.

Her eyes drifted back to the tree line. "Can I take a rain check?"

She'd give him credit. The rejection barely fazed him. "Sure. But so you know, I have every intention of holding you to it. We will have dinner one of these nights."

"If you say so." But she already knew she'd turn down the next invitation as well.

They talked for a few more minutes, basically polite chatter so her refusal didn't feel too unfriendly, before Kelsey went to work. For the next few hours she immersed herself in transcription until her brain couldn't take the dark subject matter any longer and screamed for a break. Then, unable to look at the screen another second, she saved her document, grabbed her coffee cup and headed into the great room.

What she saw stopped her in her tracks.

CHAPTER FOUR

ALEX sat by the French doors.

Actually slumped was a better description. Kelsey rushed towards him.

"Are you all right?" she asked, already knowing the answer. Eyes closed, face paler than before, he was leaning forward with a hand cradling his forehead. His walking stick lay discarded by his feet. "It's your head, isn't it?"

"Go away," he groaned through motionless lips. "I'm fine."

"Liar. You look like you're ready to pass out." He looked up at her with glazed eyes, proving her point. "I'm calling your doctor. What's his name?"

"No doctor."

"Are you crazy? This could be a complication from your injury." Like a blood clot or something. Her insides froze at the thought he could be seriously hurt and she hadn't realized.

"It's not a complication, it's a migraine." His eyes closed again. "I just need to sit for a while. Regain my equilibrium."

From the looks of him, that might take a while. Kelsey didn't think a person could look more miserable if they tried. She remembered when Rochelle, her second foster mother, would get migraines. She'd kick all the kids outside for the day, no matter the weather. "And no making noise either," she'd order.

At her worst, Rochelle had never looked as miserable as Alex.

Remembering Rochelle made her think of something else. "Do you take anything? Some kind of prescription?"

Alex made a rumble deep in his throat. "Upstairs. In the bathroom." He continued speaking that stiff-jawed manner, as if the mere act of talking hurt.

"Do you want me to help you upstairs," she asked, reaching for his elbow, "so you can take—"

"No!" He said the word forcefully, so much so he winced immediately, and dropped to a whisper. "I just need to sit. Alone. Please leave."

"And let you suffer? I don't think so. Where upstairs do you keep your prescription?"

"My bathroom medicine cabinet."

"Don't move. I'll be right back."

She dashed upstairs, making her way to the bedroom next to hers. Alex's room was exactly as she expected, chic and dark and very masculine. Rust, beige and brown, like a fall landscape. Magazines and books covered what looked like an expensive, king-size bed.

She walked into the bathroom, momentarily envious of the airy modern style. The scent of wood and clove hung in the air telling her Alex had been there recently. A plastic sleeve, presumably worn to keep his cast dry, hung from the shower rod and the mat in front of the shower stall was still damp. Suddenly she was assaulted by the image of Alex standing under the stream, water cascading down his body…

Blushing from the inappropriateness, she shoved the image away. Now was not the time to start some kind of weird, useless fantasy. She found the prescription bottle in the medicine cabinet. Grabbing it and a glass of water, she headed back downstairs.

Alex hadn't moved. If he hadn't shifted uncomfortably when she walked back into the room, she'd have thought him asleep. "Probably a little late for this to kill the pain completely, but it might help a little. Hold out your hand."

He grumbled, but did what she asked.

Kelsey smiled at her victory. "Now, how about

you lie down? Do you think you can make it to the sofa?"

"I've got a headache—I'm not paralyzed."

Good to see the headache didn't spoil his charming demeanor. She watched as he eased himself into an upright position. Body bent, shoulders and head stiff, he shuffled across the floor like an arthritic old man. It was all she could do not to wrap her arm around his waist and help him. In fact, if she wasn't certain he'd bite her head off, she would have.

Instead, she followed quietly while he made his way across the room and eased himself onto the sofa.

"Are you sure you don't want to go to your room? You'd be more comfortable in a bed."

"Too many stairs," he mumbled. "I'll be fine here."

The couch was too small and too pillow-laden to accommodate his lanky frame, so he'd ended up with one leg propped on the floor. His cast rested on his chest, while his good arm lay slung across his eyes. The helplessness of his position tugged at her heartstrings.

"You can leave now," he said.

She could. But she didn't. Drawing closer, Kelsey noticed his skin was covered with gooseflesh. In spite of the fact the afternoon sun poured through the windows heating the room, he was shivering.

"You're still here," he said in a low voice.

"And you're cold," she replied back. "Would you like a blanket?"

"No."

God, he was stubborn. What was he going to do, lie there and shiver? Did he know how pathetic that looked? She looked around for something she could use as a blanket. A dozen pillows and no throw. Remembering the extra blanket in her room, she ran up and got that, tucking it gently around his torso, being careful not to jar him too much.

"Why are you doing this?" he asked.

"Because you're shivering."

"I mean, why are you sticking around?"

"Oh, that." Why indeed? Truth be told, she couldn't explain, other than it hurt her to see him suffering. "What can I say? I have a rescue complex."

"In other words, I'm another cat."

The medicine was starting to kick in. Still, even thick with sleep, there was no mistaking the resignation in his voice as if he didn't believe someone could sincerely care. It made Kelsey think of the other night, when he was watching the rain.

Her heart ached a little more.

"Do you need anything else?" she asked. "Water? A phone?"

"I'll be fine. You can leave with a clear conscience."

"Thanks for the permission."

He didn't respond. Sleep had claimed him. Kelsey watched as his breathing slowly evened out.

Two hours later, she was still sitting in the living room, watching. She'd told herself she was only going to stay a few extra minutes. To make sure he was truly asleep before heading up to her room. But the longer she sat, the more she couldn't tear herself away. Couldn't stop studying his face. The way his brow smoothed in sleep or how his lips parted ever so slightly. Nestled among the pillows, he had a gentle serenity about him that, when awake, he hid from the world.

Unable to help herself, she tucked the blanket around him a little tighter. He smelled of clove and woods and sleep, and she had the overwhelming urge to lean closer and bury herself in the scent. Her fingers longed to stroke his cheek. Dear Lord, he was beautiful. She couldn't deny her attraction if she tried. But beneath the attraction, she sensed something else. Something she couldn't quite put her finger on. The sensation stirred inside her, faintly, tentatively, afraid to make itself fully known. She was afraid too. Because she wasn't sure if she wanted the sensation to go away.

Alex slept through the rest of the afternoon and into the evening. At some point, Kelsey considered waking him so he could go to his room, but she didn't. He looked too exhausted to disturb. Plus downstairs she could keep an eye on him.

At least that's what she told herself.

She'd been joking about the rescue complex. Truth was, she didn't know where this maternal streak of hers was coming from. As a kid, she sometimes helped the younger children with homework and stuff, but that was expected in a large household. But since moving out on her own, she'd focused solely on taking care of herself. Clearly something about Nuttingwood brought out her nesting instinct.

Something or *someone*?

After dinner, which she was pretty sure didn't come close to Frutti de Mar standards, she returned to the great room to find Alex beginning to stir. "Hey," she said softly, as his eyelids fluttered open, "you're awake." And feeling better, judging by the clarity in his gaze.

"You're still here," he greeted back, his voice still a little thick. "I thought you had dinner plans."

That's right, he walked away before the end

of her and Tom's conversation. "I took a rain check."

"Oh."

His response had a queer-sounding note she couldn't pinpoint. "Good thing too," she told him.

"Why's that?"

Slowly, he shifted himself into a sitting position. With his hair matted on one side and a crease on his cheek, he looked perfectly and adorably tussled. Kelsey's stomach twittered. "Well, for one thing, you'd have woken to a dark and empty house."

"News flash—I've done that for years. Goes hand in hand with the hermit thing."

The medicine still had a hold; his words were slurred and punchier than normal. Try as she might, Kelsey couldn't help a smile. "Funny, that's what Farley called you."

Sleepy cuteness turned sullen. "I'm sure they call me lots of things."

"What makes you think they talk about you much at all?"

"Try four hundred thousand, ninety-four search engine hits," he replied. "Or have you forgotten already?"

"No, I haven't forgotten," she snapped. When Alex sat up, the blanket she'd tucked over him slid toward the floor. Instinctively she picked it up. "But not everyone is as—"

"Nosy?"

"Curious," she shot back, "as I am." Her cheeks warmed remembering the whole exchange. Was he right? That once a victim of gossip, always a victim of gossip? She draped the blanket back over his legs. "Though if you ask me, moving up to a castle in the middle of nowhere, you're kind of inviting speculation."

"I'm here because I like my privacy," he replied in a clipped tone that said the conversation was over.

Kelsey noticed him rubbing his eyes. "Head still hurt?" She remembered Rochelle's migraines sometimes lasted for days, once getting so bad she ended up in the hospital on a morphine drip.

Alex grabbed the change of topic. "Some, but it's definitely better. The medicine helped. Along with the sleep. A few more hours and I should be fine."

Meaning she should take her cue and leave? "Are you heading upstairs?"

He shook his head, while at the same time closing his eyes and burrowing into the throw pillow. "Not yet. I'm comfortable right where I am."

"Very well then, I'll see you in the morning."

"Kelsey?"

He reached out and caught her wrist, an unnecessary gesture since she stopped as soon as he called out. "Yes?" she asked.

"Thank you."

That was it. Two words and nothing more, but Alex's expression was soft and sincere, and his eyes turned from metal to dove-gray, making the sentence sound like volumes. His grip stayed on her arm, simultaneously gentle yet firm. Kelsey could feel the pulse of each individual finger beating against her skin. Their cadence echoed the heart in her chest. A slow honey-coated sensation began twisting deep inside her, and she smiled.

"You're welcome." Reluctantly, she slipped her wrist free and headed upstairs.

"Did I really expect anything to change?" she asked Puddin' the next morning. "I mean, so I helped him with a headache. Big deal." One second of gratitude hardly changed anything.

"It was just for that one moment—" her skin tingled, remembering how his fingers encircled her wrist "—I felt like we understood each other, you know? That we connected.

"I should have realized it was my imagination." For starters, she didn't make connections. Not that kind anyway. And second, this morning Alex was still the dark, aloof man he'd been since her arrival. Worse, if that was possible.

"The guy's been through the wringer, that's for sure," she said, hitting the save button. "I'd probably do the same thing if I'd been ripped apart like that. Makes you wonder what he'll do when this book comes out."

If the book comes out. Her gaze traveled back to the dwindling stack of yellow pads. This morning Mr. Lefkowitz sent an e-mail requesting a progress report which she was avoiding answering. With all the cross-outs and redirection, she'd transcribed maybe a third of the book. Certainly not a complete novel by any means. The editor wouldn't be happy.

"If Alex doesn't start producing soon, I'll be stuck here till Christmas," she said to Puddin'.

Did Alex even celebrate Christmas anymore? The image of a somber, undecorated Nuttingwood popped into her head, breaking her heart. Didn't seem right he should spend the holidays isolated and lonely.

"Will you listen to yourself?" she said aloud. "What do you care how Alex Markoff spends his holidays?" This was a perfect example of why she didn't do connections. Connections started you down the road toward foolish, elusive concepts like home and family and holidays…

And kindred spirits with stormy gray eyes.

"That's it. Time for a break." Her thoughts were getting way too out of control.

On the terrace, Puddin' stretched and started to get up. Grabbing her empty mug, Kelsey sent a mock glare at the feline through the open French doors. "Don't even think about coming inside while I'm getting coffee," she told him, knowing full well he wouldn't listen.

Coffee was the one area where she and Alex had an automatic accord. Apparently they were both caffeine addicts so by unspoken agreement the pot remained full and fresh all day. Usually Alex made the first pot, then midmorning it was her turn.

There was only one problem. Alex had put the coffee grinder on the top shelf. He had been leaving the machine on the counter, but today he must have forgotten. Too much on his mind, perhaps?

She set her mug on the counter, then dragged a chair from the table, making a mental note to remind him he promised to keep the machine within her arm's reach. Not everyone loomed over six feet.

"You're standing on my counter," Alex said from behind her.

"What the—"

She nearly dropped the grinder. Worse, she nearly knocked her cup off the edge.

"One of these days I'm going to buy you a bell," she grumbled.

"I didn't realize my comings and goings were so important to you."

"They are when you insist on scaring the bejesus out of me every time you show up."

Coffee grinder in hand, she hopped off the chair, bringing Alex closer than she expected. Cloves and wood and awkwardness packed the kitchen. For what felt like minutes, neither of them moved, their bodies and gazes stuck in place. Kelsey found herself suddenly painstakingly aware of the stubble on Alex's cheeks and the way his lips were dry but soft-looking. Eyes traveling upwards, she realized he was studying her too. Or so it appeared. His eyes had an expression she'd never seen before.

"I'm—I'm making fresh coffee," she finally managed to stammer. What was it about his proximity that made her brain short-circuit? "How's your head?"

His hand touched his temple as if remembering what she meant. She had the crazy urge to do the same. "Better. Nothing left but a dull ache."

"Have you had anything to eat? An empty stomach doesn't help."

He broke the moment, moving away. "Are you always this concerned about other people's welfare?" he asked, opening the fridge, "or just mine?"

"Are you always this suspicious of people's motives? Never mind. Pretend I didn't ask," she added as he glanced over his shoulder.

With the atmosphere less charged, she returned to the task at hand, carefully measuring the beans into the grinder. A flick of a button filled the kitchen with a loud whir.

"Clearly you have no idea how awful you looked yesterday," she continued over the noise.

"I've been having migraines my whole life. Last time I checked, I survived them all. Besides, I didn't ask you to stay."

"Silly me, putting your health first." She turned off the grinder. "Next time I'll leave you to suffer all by your lonesome."

"Thank you."

"You're wel—watch out!"

Everything happened in slow motion. Alex had moved to her section of the kitchen and was reaching up to retrieve a cup from the cabinet. As he turned toward her, the outer edge of his cast smacked her coffee mug. The faded floral cup wobbled back and forth, then tumbled over the edge. Kelsey reached out to catch it, but moved too late. With a crack, the mug hit the floor and separated into three large pieces.

"No!" Her stomach churning, Kelsey dropped to her knees. Not her mother's cup. She blinked, hoping when her eyes opened, the cup would somehow reassemble.

No such luck.

Alex's legs appeared at her side. "I didn't realize the cup was so close to the edge."

"It's ruined." She looked up. His face was too blurry for her to read his reaction.

But she could read his voice. "It's just a coffee cup."

Just a coffee cup? Of course, that's how he saw it. As just another old piece of kitchenware.

"I'm sure you can find a replacement—"

"How? Go back in time?" If she paused a second to think rationally, she'd realize Alex had no idea what the cup represented. How could he know that the last tangible piece of her childhood—her real childhood with her real mother—lay in pieces on his kitchen floor? Moisture burned her eyes. She was going to cry, and she didn't care.

"Don't you understand?" she snapped, swiping at her cheeks. Of course he didn't understand. Living up here as a hermit, not caring if anyone cared about him or not. Why would he understand losing something precious? "It can't be replaced. It's gone. Ruined." A tear escaped down her cheek.

Angrily, she wiped it away. Dropping the pieces on the floor, she stormed from the room before she crashed completely.

"Kelsey!"

She ignored him. Nothing Alex could say would make a difference. All she could hear in her head were his words from before. "Just a cup, just a cup." They echoed with each step on the stairway.

Once inside the sanctuary of the guest room, she slammed shut the door, pressing her back against it. *Just a coffee cup.* Alex was right. What was a faded, chipped-up piece of stoneware anyway? So what if she'd carried the stupid thing from foster home to foster home? So what if...

The floodgates opened as everything hit her at once—her solitude, her past, her grandmother's crimes. Why didn't anyone want her? Was she that unlovable?

Out of answers, she sank to the ground and gave in to self-pity.

How long she stayed there crying, she wasn't sure. Thirty minutes. An hour. Eventually she stopped sniffling. What was done was done, she told herself. No amount of wallowing would change anything. There was nothing else to do but pick up the pieces and move on. She done so her entire life; she would do so again.

Swiping the moisture from her cheeks, she sniffed back the last tear and pushed herself to her feet.

The house was unusually quiet when she came down the next morning which, given its usual silence, said a lot. Perhaps yesterday's outburst scared Alex out of hibernation, and he was, at that moment, in town looking for men in white coats to carry her off. A fresh night's sleep made her realize how disproportionate her reaction must have looked to him. Of all her missteps, this might be the one that finally helped him get rid of her.

Puddin' was in his regular spot when she entered the office. She gave the napping cat a quick glance, sat at her desk, and while she waited for the computer to boot, drank coffee from a substitute mug, telling herself the change in flavor was all in her head. As usual, Alex's writing sucked her in, chasing away other thoughts. She welcomed the distraction, losing herself in today's words. It wasn't long before her absorption made her oblivious to anything but the story.

She didn't hear the door push open or the footsteps approach the desk. In fact, she didn't notice a thing until she heard a thump on the wood in front of her. Pulling herself out of her typist's trance, she looked toward the desk and blinked. There, in the middle of her papers, sat her coffee mug. Chipped and cracked, but whole again nonetheless.

"I doubt it'll hold liquid," Alex said. "But you can put it on a shelf or something."

She ran her finger along the rim, feeling the gaps where the pieces were unevenly glued together. If the thing looked like a battered piece of junk before, it looked like a pre-schooler's craft project now. A lump stuck in Kelsey's throat. Unable to trust herself with words, she settled for raising her gaze.

Alex's face was soft, reminding her of the day before. In the entranceway. "The cup means a lot to you."

Throat constricted, she nodded.

"I thought so. Consider it payback for the migraine."

"It was my mother's," Kelsey called out. She found her voice as he reached the door. Though he hadn't asked for an explanation, she wanted to give one. Wanted to explain why she'd reacted so poorly. "She died when I was four. This mug is the only thing I have that belonged to her."

Kelsey imagined him wondering what kind of family left a child nothing but a battered coffee cup, but he said nothing. He simply nodded in a way that told her he understood. At least the gratitude filling her insides made her feel like he understood. "Then good thing I had glue."

"Yes," she said, smiling up at him. "A very good thing."

CHAPTER FIVE

STOP being a coward.

Kelsey stood outside Alex's bedroom door for five minutes with her hand poised to knock. Much as she didn't want to, she couldn't put off this conversation any longer. Mr. Lefkowitz wanted a status report. After days of dodging his e-mail requests, she got a phone call. A very testy phone call. "I hope the reason I haven't heard from you is because you're too busy typing," he said as soon as she answered. That had been the high point of the conversation.

She knocked.

Alex's answer came back deep and distracted. "Yeah?"

Pushing open the door, she poked her head into the room and saw him seated at his desk near the window. Dozens of crumpled yellow balls littered the floor around his feet. He was working. A good sign. "Sorry to bother you."

"But you're going to anyway. What is it?"

"Mr. Lefkowitz called. He wants to know how the book was coming."

Alex didn't look up. "I'm sure you filled him in on all the details."

"Actually I told him you were making great progress and were almost finished."

That got his attention. He turned sideways to look at her. "Did you now? And why would you say something like that?"

Kelsey shrugged. Why indeed? She wasn't quite sure except as soon as she heard Mr. Lefkowitz's irritated voice, she felt the overwhelming urge to take Alex's side. True or not.

"Are you making progress?"

"Depends on how you define progress."

"Moving forward." Having pages to type. The last notebook was nearly transcribed and still no new ones had appeared. Which wouldn't be so terrible, if he was busy editing what had already been written, but as far as she could tell that wasn't happening either.

"Interesting definition." Tearing the top sheet from the pad, he added it to the collection of yellow wads on the floor.

Kelsey watched it arc and drop. "So I lied to Stuart."

"If you say so. Why would you tell him something you didn't know for certain?"

"I thought I was doing you a favor."

"A favor?"

"By keeping your editor off your back." His suspicious tone made her bristle. "You sound like I have some ulterior motive."

He shrugged. "Maybe you do."

Jeez. And she thought relations between them had thawed over the last couple days. Ever since he'd repaired her coffee mug, albeit poorly, she'd felt closer. So much for that illusion. "What could I possibly be after?"

"You tell me."

"Oh, brother." Shooting him a dramatic eye roll, she leaned against the door frame. "You caught me. Getting your medicine, lying to Stuart—they're part of a grand ploy to soften you up. Really, you should hear yourself sometimes."

"Do you blame me?"

The truth? Not really. But they needed to get past this issue. "You're not the first person to get burned by the people around him," she replied in a gentler voice.

"What's that mean?"

"Nothing." She wasn't about to get into a contest over who had suffered a bigger betrayal. "Look,

I thought I was helping. Next time I'll tell Mr. Lefkowitz the truth. That better?"

"Better would be not telling Stuart anything at all."

"I have to tell him something."

"Why?"

"Because it's my job, and he needs to know." She let out a long, calming breath. "Not everyone is out to get you, Alex, or get something from you."

"Could have fooled me."

"Wow." She understood his bitterness; she really did. But why couldn't he see she wasn't the enemy? Hadn't they made any headway over the past few weeks? "I'm beginning to see why he's paying me extra to work here."

Not wanting to wait to hear his response, which wasn't going to be something she wanted to hear anyway, she went to her room. Sometimes she wanted to kick Alex Markoff for his obstinacy. All she wanted was to be his friend.

Really, that's what you want? His friendship?

Yes, that was all. Sure, she was attracted to Alex. Incredibly attracted. But hit and run affairs weren't really her style. Affairs weren't her style, period. And neither was acting on her attraction— assuming Alex was remotely interested. Which, seeing as how he trusted no one, wasn't likely.

Screw it. She peeled off her cotton tank top and

threw it on the bed. If he didn't care about his manuscript getting done, why should she?

A knock sounded on her door. "Kelsey?"

What now? Grabbing her tank, she thrust it back on and opened the door. "What?"

A pair of very contrite eyes met hers, killing every ounce of her earlier acrimony. "Is Stuart really paying you extra to work here?"

"If I say yes, will you use it against me?"

His mouth had come dangerously close to curving into a smile. "I'll try not to." He looked around at the bare bones bedroom, checking out the setting like it was the first time he'd been there. "You're very neat," he said all of a sudden.

"Makes packing easier." As well as moving on.

Alex nodded, and in her mind she wondered if he wasn't agreeing with both points.

The coffee mug he had repaired sat crookedly on top of the bureau. He walked over and picked it up. "Not my best repair job in the world, that's for sure. I notice you don't use it, so I was right—it doesn't hold liquid."

"I didn't try." She'd been afraid to find out lest it fall apart again. After seeing it smashed to bits, she wasn't about to take any chances. Even now she was fighting the urge to slip the mug from Alex's grasp. "Why are you here? Did you knock on my door merely to confirm my pay rate?"

"Ah, so he is paying extra." Setting down the mug, he continued his tour, stopping at the window. His broad shoulders filled the frame. "How much?"

The appropriate answer would be "none of your business," but the truth came out without second thought. "Triple."

"Triple." He took a moment to let the answer sink in. "Says it all, doesn't it. That why you took the job? For the money?"

"Yes."

The look crossing his face as he turned was a mixture of surprise and admiration. "I appreciate the honesty. Though I have to say, you don't strike me as the mercenary type." He cocked his head to study her better. "What's your story, Kelsey Albertelli?"

Now was the time to tell him to bug off, same as he did whenever she asked a personal question. "It's complicated."

"How so?"

"Now who's prying into whose private business?"

"Point taken," he replied with a nod. Sincerity marked every feature and Kelsey realized, with more than a little admiration, that he wouldn't press her for more. He was respecting her privacy.

Her chest swelled. She wasn't used to respect. The notion that someone would honor her privacy made her feel…well, special, she supposed. She stared into Alex's eyes, feeling herself being drawn in.

The two of them were a lot alike, weren't they? Both keeping the world at arm's length, rather than offering or asking more than necessary. Her chest went from being tight to feeling warm and full. The feeling grew bigger and started inching its way outward, down her limbs and to her toes. A nebulous longing to be closer gripped her. Suddenly sharing her story didn't sound all that horrible.

"My grandmother, she—"

"No need to explain." He held up a palm. "You're right. I was prying."

Kelsey smiled. Again she appreciated the respect, despite the fact it restored their distance to arm's length.

"And thank you," he continued, "for covering with Stuart. I'm not used to—well, it's been a long time since someone did me a favor for no reason."

"I understand."

"I know." His long assessing look reached

deep inside her, stirring emotions she couldn't identify.

And wasn't really sure she wanted to.

A week later, Alex had a doctor's appointment to check out his arm. Since he couldn't drive his stick shift, Kelsey drew chauffeur duties. Normally she wouldn't mind, but she'd failed to factor in what it would be like sharing an enclosed space with Alex. His long frame mere inches from hers. His body heat mingling with hers the entire trip, filling the air with his scent. His hand rested on the armrest, close enough to her that when she touched the gearshift, the underside of her forearm would brush across his knuckles. Thank goodness, she chose to take her car rather than Alex's sports car. Driving a standard, with the distraction of continually touching him—no matter how lightly—would result in them ending up in a ditch somewhere.

Since silence only exacerbated the situation, she forced conversation. Fortunately, Alex was in a talkative mood. At least, talkative for him. After exhausting the weather and road conditions, she decided to take a risk and ask something she'd been dying to know since her arrival. "May I ask you a personal question?"

Of course, the moment she said *personal*, wariness crept into his expression. "What do you want to know?"

"How did you break your arm?"

"Oh, that." Relief returned to his face. "Stuart didn't tell you?"

She shook her head. "He only said you broke it."

"Well, score one for discretion." He sounded surprised. "I tripped over a root and fell while walking in the woods."

"You were by yourself?" Obviously. "How did you get help?"

"I broke my arm, not my leg. I made my way back to the house and called an ambulance."

Somehow Kelsey doubted the scenario went quite as smoothly as he described it. Navigating a wooded path with a broken arm… Poor man must have been in tremendous pain. "And you had no one to help you."

"You're assuming I wanted help."

She thought of the other day. "No, I'm assuming you could have used help."

"Didn't we cover the problems with assumption the other afternoon?"

"Was this before or after you were lying inca-pacitated on the sofa?"

"I would debate your use of the word *incapaci-*

tated, but in this case I got myself to the hospital just fine."

And came home by himself to an empty house. She knew Alex chose to live that way, but the idea of Alex alone and in pain made her sad. "What about painkillers and medication and all that?"

"I managed."

"I'm sure you did." Managed. It sounded so... lacking. Like he was getting by with the bare minimum.

You should know, Kelsey. Manage had been the story of her life. Manage and adapt.

Why then, did *manage* suddenly feel inadequate?

"So is that when you started writing longhand?" she asked, pulling herself back to the conversation.

"No, I've always written by pencil. Started when I was teaching and would scribble notes between—"

"You were a teacher?" She nearly hit the brakes.

"High school English."

"Unbelievable." She shook her head.

"What, you can't picture me as a teacher?"

"In a word, no." She couldn't picture him interacting with people, let alone teaching teenagers.

"It didn't last long. I was far more interested in

my own work than *A Tale of Two Cities*. But writing longhand stuck. You never know when some detail or passage will spring to mind." His mouth came dangerously close to curving into a smile. At least Kelsey thought she caught a glimmer before it disappeared. "I once wrote an entire short story during a dinner party."

"Really?" Now that was an Alex she could picture, hiding out from the crowd, lost in his work. "I finished your last notebook yesterday," she told him.

"Is that a not so subtle way of reminding me Stuart wants his book?"

"Yup." She smiled.

"Spoken like a true babysitter."

"Speaking of not-so-subtle reminders," she murmured.

"Hey." A hand touched her forearm. A rush ran up her arm and she had to squeeze the steering wheel to keep it from traveling further. "As babysitters go, you aren't that bad. Stuart could have foisted far worse on me."

"Wow." A sideways glance showed Alex's expression was sincere. "A girl could get a big head from that kind of sweet talk."

"I'll keep that in mind."

Meanwhile the memory of his touch remained

on her skin, a warm, firm pressure far more reassuring than it should be.

She cleared her throat, hoping to clear away the sensation too. "Since we've established that I'm the official whip cracker, will I be seeing more pages soon?"

Alex turned his face to the scenery. "Eventually."

There was little enthusiasm to his answer. In fact, if she didn't know better she'd say he actually sounded sad. Now she wanted to give him the reassuring touch.

Something inside made her refrain, settling instead for a smile and a change of subject. "Just planning my schedule. If I don't have anything to type, the more time Puddin' and I have to work on our tans."

"Puddin', huh?" There was a satisfying note of relief in his voice. "That mangy cat of yours still around?"

"Whoa, he's not my cat. Puddin' is strictly a free agent."

"Says the woman who named him."

"I told you, everyone deserves an identity. The world has enough faceless orphans."

"Orphan?"

"Stray, orphan. Same thing, right?" Kelsey brushed her hair behind her ear. She could feel

Alex studying her, wondering about the slip. He wouldn't ask though. He'd leave it up to her to explain or not, respecting her right to privacy. It was one of the traits she loved—

Check that. Admired. It was one of the traits she admired about him.

Love was nowhere in the picture.

Kelsey thought forty-five minutes flipping through gossip and consumer magazines would clear the queer thoughts from her head, but no such luck. The second Alex appeared in the doctor's reception area doorway, her pulse quickened. He was gorgeous no matter the setting, but the contrast between the institutional décor and his dark virility was awe-inspiring. She wasn't the only one to notice either. The nurses and receptionist all perked up upon his appearance too. Kelsey wasn't sure, but she swore one woman actually licked her lower lip.

Oblivious, Alex's eyes sought her out. "Dr. Cohen got tied up with another patient so I had to wait," he said in the flat, semi-annoyed voice she'd come to expect.

"No harm, no foul," she replied. "Gave me time to catch upon the latest gossip. Oh, and how to evaluate flat-screen TVs," she added quickly when she saw the disdain crop into his expression. "Are you ready to go?"

"Don't forget your appointment card," the receptionist called out.

Kelsey bit back her smile at Alex's rolled eyes. The receptionist was painstakingly scheduling his appointment, leaning forward a little more than necessary in her opinion. The woman shot her a jealous glare when she joined Alex at the check-in desk. Again, she controlled her urge to grin. Did her hermit have any idea how many heads he was turning?

Whoa. Her hermit? Where did that come from?

"Did Dr. Cohen say when the cast would come off?" she asked, shaking off the thought.

"End of summer. Same answer he gave me last time. I'm beginning to think he's incapable of giving an exact date."

"Probably because you'd hold him to it."

"That's a bad thing?"

"It is if your arm hasn't healed by then. Or maybe Dr. Cohen simply wants to string you along because he enjoys your company."

Alex made a noise deep in his throat and took the appointment card. This time Kelsey not only smiled, she giggled. Lately she'd been finding Alex's grumpy demeanor more amusing. Guess because he'd slipped enough times for her to know he actually had a heart underneath.

"While we're out, are there any other errands you need to run?" she asked while they made their way through the parking lot. "Bank? Library? Groceries? We were low on coffee this morning."

We? Again with the possessiveness. What was with her today?

Thankfully Alex either didn't notice or care about the slip. "Coffee would be good. Milk too. And maybe," he paused, as if unsure about his next words, "maybe some of those apricot turnovers."

Was that pink coloring his cheeks? Kelsey couldn't believe it. Dear Lord, he couldn't look cuter if he tried. Insides fluttering, Kelsey grinned. "All right then, we'll stop at Farley's."

CHAPTER SIX

SHE hadn't given it much thought but being lunch-time, the Leafy Bean was filled with customers. To a person, heads turned the second the doorbell announced their arrival. Turning not, she was certain, because they recognized the famous author, but because Alex commanded attention.

"Would you rather come back another time?" she asked.

"I thought you said we needed coffee."

"We do, but I forgot about the noontime crowd."

"I like privacy, Kelsey, I'm not sociophobic."

"I only meant…"

"I know what you meant, and," the corner of his mouth quirked ever so slightly, "I appreciate the gesture."

It felt like he'd verbally squeezed her hand. A blush warmed her cheeks. She gave him a half smile of her own. "You must really want those apricot turnovers."

"Hey, never underestimate the lure of coffee and pastry. Where does Farley stock the beans?"

"There's an entire display at the back of the store. You grab a couple bags and I'll get your baked goods."

He gave her a nod and headed off while she made her way to the crowded bakery counter, trying to shake off the weird domestic sensation surrounding the task.

"It's only coffee and turnovers," she reminded herself.

Farley was running around behind the counter, grumpy as ever as he accommodated orders and questions. When he saw Kelsey, he gave her a quick wave followed by a dramatic roll of his eyes when a customer asked if he used organic flour. Kelsey waved back. "Popular today," she commented.

"Big fund-raiser's kicking off at the Music Center this weekend. Everyone and his second cousin's in for it. And every one of 'em's got special orders," he added, slapping the cutting board with a loud, overly enthusiastic whack of his knife.

Kelsey shared a smile with the young girl at the counter. "I'll take a half-dozen turnovers," she said.

"Kelsey, is that you?"

She was taking her bag from the clerk when she spotted Tom Forbes coming towards her, charming smile firmly in place. "What a pleasant coincidence. I was going to call you this afternoon."

"You were?"

"I'm here for the concert this weekend. I thought maybe you'd like to join me." The smile got a little wider. "You still owe me that rain check."

"Right, rain check." She thought that had been a way to save face, she didn't really think he would follow up.

"So what do you say? Think you can get away?"

"Well, I…"

"Please don't say no." He flashed her an exaggerated pout. "My poor heart won't take a second rejection."

Kelsey laughed. Somehow she doubted that was the case. "Are you trying to make me feel guilty?"

"Whatever it takes," he replied. "Do we have a date?"

One dinner wouldn't hurt, right?

She was about to say yes when suddenly she caught sight of Alex at the other end of store. Dark and serious, he was studying a bag of coffee beans like it contained the secret to life incarnate. A small piece of her insides tumbled.

Dragging her attention back to Tom, she gave him a polite smile. "Flattering as the guilt trip is, I'm going to have to pass."

"Even if it means breaking my heart?"

"'Fraid so."

Tom shook his head, and shook off the rejection like she expected he would. "Guess I'll simply have to drown my sorrows alone."

"Somehow I don't think that's going to happen," she replied with a smile.

A shiver of awareness passed over her. Looking up, she saw that Alex was looking in their direction. "My boss looks ready to go," she said. "I better catch up."

Tom glanced over his shoulder. "Alex Markoff? That's your boss?"

"Yes." His instant recognition took her aback.

"You said you worked for a writer, but I had no idea…." Tom drifted off in thought for a second, before adding, "I thought he was holed up somewhere like a hermit."

"Never underestimate the lure of coffee and turnovers."

"He doesn't look happy that we're talking. In fact," Tom said, pursing his lips, "if I didn't know better, I'd say he looked jealous."

As if. More likely it was his suspicious nature coming home to roost. "Impatient," Kelsey answered. "I told you, he's ready to go."

"Is he the reason you can't have dinner?"

Although asked with a smile, the question had

a pointedness to it that she didn't like. "I have to go," she said. "Enjoy your concert."

Alex was lost in thought on the drive back to Nuttingwood. So lost, Kelsey wanted to squirm from the uncomfortable silence. If it weren't so Alex-like, she'd think Tom was right and he was jealous.

The silence was deafening. A hundred and eighty degrees from the rest of their day. Do not chatter, she chided. Just go with the silence.

"Turnovers smell good. The clerk said they were fresh out of the oven and still warm. Maybe I should have gotten more than a half-dozen."

So much for going with the silence.

"That guy from the store a friend of yours?" Alex asked.

"Acquaintance." She could hear the suspicion in his voice.

"Your rain check from the other night."

"Yes. He wanted to know if I would attend the concert at the Music Center with him."

They reached the large pine tree. Kelsey turned to the right, pleased she was finally recognizing landmarks.

Too bad she didn't feel as confident regarding the man beside her. "Would that be a problem?" she asked.

"What you do on your spare time is your business," he replied with a shrug.

Her insides tumbled again, only this time the fall was heavy and hard. Of course he didn't care. Why would he? Tom's comment simply put thoughts in her head. "Thank you for respecting my privacy."

"No problem."

They drove the rest of the way home in silence.

Kelsey assumed Alex would disappear as soon as she put the car into Park. To her surprise, he didn't. He stayed in the passenger seat, his long fingers tracing the hem on his hiking shorts. "You going straight to work?" he asked suddenly.

What work? She still hadn't gotten any new notebooks. "Why? You need me to do something?"

"No." Some kind of conflict seemed to play across his profile, as if he were having an internal war. She figured he was debating asking a favor. Never in a million years did she expect his next question. "Do you want to go for a walk?"

"A walk?" she repeated. With him?

"It's a hot day. The woods are cooler and you're right about the turnovers smelling good and since it is lunchtime..."

"Wait." She had to make sure she wasn't hearing

things. "You want me to go on a picnic with you?"

"I thought I might eat the turnovers in a cooler location and figured, since you did all the driving today, I'd ask you to join me. But," he shrugged, "if you've got other things to do, or get ready for…" He reached across his body for the door handle.

"No, I'll go," Kelsey said, stopping him. "Give me a minute to change first though." She flicked the edge of her peasant skirt. "This isn't the best outfit for walking in the woods."

As he looked her up and down, she told herself the flutter of excitement in her stomach was unnecessary. "Fine. I'll meet you at the edge of the garden in five minutes."

With more enthusiasm than she should have, Kelsey raced upstairs to her room. Since she preferred skirts and sundresses, she didn't have a lot of clothes suitable for walking in the woods. She settled for a pair of royal blue track shorts and a bright pink tank top. Her hair, she fished in a ponytail through an old baseball cap she wore when running. Hardly the most stylish of outfits.

Then again, like Alex said, it was simply turnovers in a cooler location. He wouldn't even notice. That is, if he was still waiting. She'd taken longer than five minutes. Snagging two bottles of water on her way through the kitchen, she headed toward the garden.

Alex was leaning against the garden shed when she arrived, looking like a slinged sentry. He looked so comfortable standing there she had to, yet again, quell her insides. Especially when she imagined his eyes scanning her appearance.

"Lead the way," she said with a smile. "I'm starving."

While she'd known there was a path leading up the mountain, she didn't anticipate how picturesque or how well traveled the path would be. Pine tree branches formed a canopy that shielded them from the sun while brown needles formed a soft carpet beneath their feet. Occasionally light would break through a gap and a white shaft would beam down on the ferns and underbrush that littered the ground. It was an otherworld of coolness, lush and green.

Kelsey had never seen anything like it, not Central Park, not even the view from her window, though that came close. No wonder Alex disappeared into here every morning.

"Is this where you fell?" She was afraid to speak too loud lest she disturb the tranquility.

Alex pointed to a bend in the path. "Up there.

I was watching a red squirrel jumping around the branches and caught the toe of my shoe."

The idea of somber Alex Markoff distracted by a squirrel made Kelsey giggle, earning her a questioning look. "Do you think the squirrel realized he nearly derailed the year's biggest literary comeback?"

"Is that what Stuart's calling it?"

"Among other things. A lot of people have been waiting for a follow-up to *Chase the Moon*."

"Good old *Chase the Moon*." Reaching up with his good arm, he pulled back a pine branch blocking their path. "My prize-winning albatross."

Kelsey ducked beneath the needles. "I'm sure there are a lot of writers in the world who wouldn't mind bearing that kind of burden."

"They can be my guest." Alex let go of the branch. It whipped into place with a loud thwap. "Sometimes I wish I'd never written the book. Life would be a lot easier, that's for sure."

The last sentence wasn't directed at her, but to the trees. Kelsey thought of the notepads that weren't appearing on her desk and of the dark, pain-riddled pages that had. "You don't want to write this book, do you?"

"Writing isn't the problem. It's publishing I hate. Publishing and everything that goes with it."

Remembering those articles, she understood

his reluctance. "Surely this time will be different though."

"Why? Because this time I'm not married?"

The bitterness in his voice didn't escape her. "I mean this time you'll know what to expect."

"Forgive me if I don't take comfort in the thought."

They resumed walking in silence, albeit more weighted than before. Every so often Kelsey stole a glance in Alex's direction. She wished she could read his thoughts but like always, they were shrouded.

Then, suddenly, as if reading hers, he spoke. "It's funny how life works. You start writing because you have stories you want to share with the world. Once you get your wish though, everything changes, especially if your story becomes The Next Big Thing." He announced the words to the air with his hand. "Suddenly, life stops being about the words and more about you. What you did, where you went, who you were with. What you can do for them. It's easy to get lost."

"I can see why a person can become jaded," Kelsey replied carefully.

"Jaded is the tip of the iceberg." He stopped suddenly, and setting the paper bag on a nearby rock, turned to face her. "I know full well I'm a nightmare to share a house with."

The admission, a blip compare to his other admissions, went straight to her heart. "Really?" she joked. "I hadn't noticed."

He met her attempt at deflection with serious eyes. "Most people would have told me where to go by now."

"Don't think I haven't been tempted."

Alex reached out and plucked a pine needle from her hair, his touch soft as a whisper against her cheek and setting off a freefall inside her. "Then I guess I should be grateful you're so patient."

Unsure what else to do, she tucked her hair behind her ear while Alex retrieved the turnovers and led on. Compliments? Openness? This couldn't be the same Alex Markoff. Suddenly, in this magical forest, he was different. They were different. Something was pulling them together. Connecting them.

But she didn't do connections.

What was going on?

The question dogged her for another quarter mile. Until Alex paused and held up his hand. "Hear that?" There was a soft rumble in the distance, like wind gathering speed through the trees. "We're here."

He led them up and around one final bend, to where the path opened. Kelsey's eyes widened and all her questions vanished in a fog of wonderment. "Oh my," she whispered.

They were at a side of a mountain river. The rumble she'd heard was the water racing down the slope, splashing over rocks in a rush to reach the end.

"Pretty amazing, isn't it?"

"Amazing doesn't begin to cover it," she replied, awestruck.

To her right, a pair of large flat boulders formed a natural ledge on which a person could perch overlooking the current. She watched, impressed, as Alex made his way across to the edge and sat down, his long legs dangling above the water. For a one-armed man, he was amazingly agile. Then again, he spent all day in these woods; he probably knew every rock and crevice by heart.

Suddenly she realized where they were. This was his sanctuary. She picked her way toward him, each step feeling like she was traveling sacred ground. That he would share this place with her of all people… Why, she wanted to ask.

Instead she sat down beside him. "Is this where you write?"

"Sometimes. Other times I head a little further upstream. The sound of the water drowns out my thoughts."

"Funny, I would think you'd need your thoughts to write."

"Not all of them."

Kelsey could buy that. Lord knows she had thoughts and feelings she'd like to drown out herself.

Alex dug into the bag and handed her a turnover, and she handed Alex a water bottle. They sat and ate, swinging their feet in the air, the cadence instinctively in sync. There was something very childlike to the moment, and Kelsey suddenly felt more carefree than she had in years. Maybe ever. She studied the pattern made by the water swirling beneath their feet, imagining Grandma Rosie and her debt being swept away in the whitecaps. "Is the water cold?"

"Stick your feet in and see for yourself."

"Is that a dare?"

"I don't do dares."

"Right. That's why you won't answer my question."

"I'm not answering because you might have a different assessment."

In other words, see for herself. Which meant yes, the water was cold. Different assessment her foot. It was a dare.

Feeling him watching her out of the corner of his eye, she slipped off her sneakers and socks. Then, scooting as close to the edge as she could without falling, she carefully, slowly dipped her toes in the water.

"Holy cow, that's freezing!" Felt like she stuck her foot in a bucket of ice.

"I take it back, we did have the same assessment," Alex remarked.

Damn if his eyes weren't sparkling. If she hadn't a good grip on the rock, their impact might have knocked her into the water. "You could have simply told me."

"You would have stuck your foot in anyway."

"No, I wouldn't."

"Yes, you would. Because I would have."

"That your way of suggesting we're alike?"

"Aren't we?"

She'd recognized that fact days ago. Seemed unlikely. After all, they were from completely different ends of the spectrum. Rich and successful versus poor and rootless. Hermit versus nomad. And yet, here they were, sitting on a rock in a world that, to Kelsey, felt suddenly very small and right.

She drew her knees tight. "Sure don't get to see sights like this in Throg's Neck."

"That where you grew up?"

"Among other places." She waited, grateful he didn't ask for a list. "How 'bout you? Did you always live in L.A? The clippings, remember," she added when she shot her a sideways look.

He shook his head. "I grew up in New York. We moved to L.A. a few months before…"

Kelsey didn't need for him to finish. She knew what he meant. "Do you miss it?"

"L.A.? Hardly."

"Sorry, dumb question, right?"

"No. There were parts of California I loved. Like driving along the coastline and watching the ocean." Looking at the cascades swirling below them, Kelsey could easily see him doing just that. "But I guess I'll always be a New Yorker at heart."

"Have you been back? I mean, since your marriage…"

"No."

"What about your family?" She was probably pushing her luck asking such personal questions, but the intimacy created by their surroundings made her press anyway.

"My father was in the Twin Towers. My mother followed a year later."

Leaving him alone. "They weren't there to see your success."

"No," he answered, his voice wistful and heavy.

"I'm sorry."

He shrugged. "Life happens."

"To some more than others."

"Ain't that the truth." Kelsey watched as Alex took a long drink, withdrawing into his thoughts. What goes on in that head of yours? she wondered. It felt like such a lonely place.

So much silence gathered between them that for a moment, she thought he forgot her. That is, until he spoke again. His voice was low, barely audible above the rushing water.

"She thought it would make her a star."

The comment wasn't what Kelsey expected. He had to be talking about Alyssa.

"I'd sold the movie rights to *Chase the Moon*. She figured my wife would have the inside track for the lead. I was foolish enough to think there was affection behind the ambition. But then I had a lot of misconceptions about people. Like I said, it's easy to get lost."

His confession broke her heart. He was, in her mind, being hard on himself. A man alone, without family or anchor to celebrate his fame, pursued by a sexy desirable woman. No wonder he got caught in her web. She wanted to reach out, cover his hand with hers and tell him he wasn't alone, but she refrained lest she scare away this rare show of vulnerability. "What made you realize—"

"That Alyssa was just using me?" He paused, chewing the inside of his cheek for a second. "I think I always suspected, I simply didn't want to see it. Alyssa was always about going out and being seen. At first it was novel, and of course, I wanted to make her happy, but I never enjoyed it."

Thinking back to the photos on the Web, Kelsey could see it. The discomfort behind his sober expression. "Guess she didn't think much of you writing a short story during a dinner party."

"Oh good Lord, no," he said with a laugh. "That, I think, might have been the final straw. That and the fact *Chase the Moon* got stalled in preproduction. Hard to piggyback on your husband's fame if there's no part."

So she left and used the divorce to piggyback instead. Her and his so-called friends. Leaving Alex alone again.

Her heart broke a little more. Yet at the same time it somehow managed to swell. She didn't know why he chose her to hear his story, but she was honored and humbled that he did. A sense of something deeper than companionship wrapped itself around them. At this moment, in this place, she felt closer to Alex Markoff than she'd ever been with a person. It was like they belonged together, sitting here on this rock.

"Do you have any idea what you'll do when you go back? Once this job is over?"

And like that, the illusion fell away.

"I don't believe in thinking too far ahead," she said, chasing away the dullness in her stomach. "Plans have a way of changing." Or getting yanked out from beneath you. "There are always temp jobs available. I'll find something that interests me."

"Another difficult boss that pays extra?"

"Hopefully I won't need to." When he cocked his head, she added, "I have a debt I need to pay."

"May I ask why?"

Maybe the tranquil setting lowered her defenses, or maybe she was feeling the remnants of closeness from before, but like the other night, Kelsey found herself wanting to share her own story. "My grandmother forged my signature on a loan application that she never paid back. And before you ask, no, she didn't have a good reason." Unless lack of a moral compass counted.

"Don't," she said cutting off what she knew was coming. She recognized the emotion in Alex's eyes. She hated that look, hated being seen as some pathetic orphan. Especially by him. "She'd never been much of a grandmother to begin with. The loan thing wasn't a big surprise when I found out."

"You know that legally, you don't have—"

"To pay? I know, but then I'd have to turn her in to the authorities for fraud."

"And you don't want to."

She gave him a weak smile. "Lousy grandmother

or not, she's the only family I've got. Besides," she looked away so he wouldn't see the shame in her eyes, "she's already a guest of the state. Check kiting."

A fish jumped in the stream, splashing water across her bare toes. Chin resting on her knee-cap, she ran a hand up and down her chilled leg. "Punishing her more felt petty."

Alex didn't respond. Kelsey didn't really expect him to. After all, how do you react when your assistant unloads that kind of information, other than be sorry you asked? From the way he folded into himself at her last comment, he definitely regretted asking. She never should have shared in the first place. Now every time he looked at her, he'd see poor little Kelsey whose grandmother ripped her off.

Instead of what? Kelsey the employee? Or Kelsey the woman?

"Just goes to show you really can't trust anyone, doesn't it?" she forced herself to say lightly.

"No, I guess you can't." His words, flat and far-away, made her sad.

"Anyway, thanks to you and Mr. Lefkowitz's increased pay rate, I'll have most of the debt paid by the fall and I can put the whole debacle behind me."

Unsure what else to do, she reached for her shoes

and socks. The movement pulled him back to the present and he looked up. "So my…temperamental behavior serves some purpose after all."

"Looks that way."

She tied her sneaker and together, they scrambled to their feet. Once again, Kelsey marveled at how effortlessly Alex maneuvered. He must be a sight to behold when he had two working arms.

"I don't know why you're complaining about waiting a month," she said, nodding at his cast. "You move pretty well."

"Move, perhaps. But I'd give my other arm to be able to scratch again. Do you have any idea how much my arm itches? And don't get me started on having to shower with my arm wrapped in plastic."

She held her hands up in surrender. "I take back my words. Your suffering knows no bounds."

"Thank you."

A crumb from a turnover clung to the hem of his sling. "Looks like we should have brought you a napkin." She reached out to brush it away.

The charge started as soon as her fingers touched the heavy canvas. The pull of a connection completed. Without thinking, she traced along the hem, running her fingers downward until they touched the hard plaster. From beneath her lashes, she saw

Alex watching her, his eyes bright like silver as they scanned her face. Looking for something.

The surface beneath her hand went from hard to soft. A couple brushes of her index finger and she realized she was touching Alex's skin. Color flooding every inch of her, she yanked her hand away.

"We—we should probably head back." She balled her fingers into a fist, blasting herself for the slip.

But Alex simply continued to study her, a new layer marking his inspection. Some new facet in his silver-gray eyes Kelsey couldn't describe. "There's a hogback another half a mile upstream with an amazing view," he said, tucking a stray tendril behind her ear. "Interested?"

"Sure." She had no idea what a hogback was, but at that moment, with him watching her like that, she'd follow him anywhere.

It was dusk by the time they returned. Impossibly, the second location was more idyllic than the first. A space among the trees where the rock formed natural stairs and you could sit and see the green valley below. Together they'd sat and watched the raptors catch thermals while finishing the last of the turnovers. The birds were, of course, captivating, but she'd found herself more captivated by the man whose knees provided her backrest. He was a presence that was impossible to ignore. A brush of his elbow, the whiff of his scent. Dear Lord, if he ever were to smile—really smile—in her direction, she'd be a goner. As it was, her pulse quickened every time he so much as looked in her direction.

"Thank you," she said as they climbed up the stairs to their rooms that night. "Today was…" She didn't have the words.

Turns out she didn't need them. "Yeah, it was." Alex leaned against the balustrade, his perpetually intense eyes dark and smoky in the dimly lit hall.

Kelsey's pulse skipped a beat. Her first instinct was to break his gaze and focus on something else. The energy in the air reminded her of a first date, although though they were a million miles from such a scenario. But still, a note of expectancy hung in the air. Like those nervous last minutes, right before the good-night kiss, when your mouth runs dry.

She bet Alex kissed wonderfully.

Alex pushed himself away from the rail and moved slowly toward her. Kelsey's insides started to spin. Her mouth went dry.

Seeking ballast, she reached for the doorknob behind her. "Good night."

He didn't miss a beat. In fact, he'd been reaching

for his own door. But his eyes were still smoky and dark when he looked in her direction. "Good night, Kelsey. I'll see you tomorrow."

The heat that night was oppressive. Or so it felt to Kelsey. Long after she said good-night to Alex, she lay on top of the covers, heat pressing down on the thin cotton T-shirt she wore as a nightshirt. That her sleeplessness was related to anything other than the heat, she didn't want to consider, even if images of Alex appeared every time she closed her eyes. *Alex sitting by the river. Alex's eyes as he said good-night.*

Speak of the devil. In the next room she could hear his bed creak and the sound of footsteps on the floor. Apparently she wasn't the only one having trouble sleeping in this heat as well. Interestingly, the humidity didn't feel nearly as strong earlier. A weather front must have moved in.

Maybe if she opened the window wider the air flow would improve.

With a sigh, she eased herself off the bed and padded to the window. At first, she was surprised to see a soft light spilling out onto the pine trees, till she realized the moon was directly overhead, lighting the yard like a spotlight. She heard the scrape of a window opening to her left. Then a second. Alex? Curious, she raised her window screen and looked out, coming face to face with her neighbor.

"Shhh," he admonished when she opened her mouth to speak. He pointed toward the trees. Kelsey followed his finger, wondering what he was doing.

Then she heard it. A soft, distinct hoot-hoot coming from the tree. A second later, a giant owl swooped down past her window, gliding low over the ground and disappearing into the shadows.

"Wow." In the night air, her stunned whisper sounded loud.

"Beautiful creature, isn't she? Usually she hangs out deeper in the woods, but she must have decided to do a little exploring tonight."

Kelsey looked down at the shadows, to where the bird vanished. She'd never seen anything like that before. "Think she'll be back?"

"Not tonight anyway."

"Isn't there some kind of rule about owls outside your window being bad?"

"Only if she shows up three nights in a row. I think you're safe."

"Good. I'd hate to have more bad luck."

"You and me both."

His comment only fueled her unsettled insides. What was it about his sadness that touched her so deeply?

"Still," she said, keeping the subject light, "she was beautiful." She turned her head to look at him. "I'm glad I got to see her."

"Me too."

And then, to her surprise, he smiled. A real, honest-to-God, full smile that put the owl's beauty to shame. It lit up his face and melted her insides. *Breathtaking.*

Fifteen minutes later, Kelsey was back on her bed counting sheep. This time she didn't even try to blame her sleeplessness on the heat.

CHAPTER SEVEN

SINCE she was awake early anyway, Kelsey decided to head into town for more pastry. She and Alex had eaten the entire batch on their hike. A thrill passed through her remembering the feel of his body shielding hers on the trail, another still as she recalled his smile last night. Then she firmly pulled herself together. It was just a hike and a bird-watching moment. Don't read too much into it. After all, who said the smile was directed at her? Maybe he was simply happy to see the owl up close.

Like it had been the day before, the Bean was jammed with customers, most in line for gourmet takeout. Here and there she caught snatches of conversation, all excited commentary about the gala concert that night. Farley, meanwhile, held court at the register, grumbling and grousing with each sale he rang up. Kelsey chuckled.

"If I didn't know any better, I'd say you were stalking me," a voice said in her ear.

Startled, Kelsey jerked her cup away from the coffee she was pouring, splashing it on the counter. She turned around to find Tom standing behind her wearing another of his ubiquitous tropical shirts. "Sorry," he said handing her a napkin. "I didn't mean to startle you."

"Since you're the one who's always walking up on me, shouldn't I be the one worried about stalking?" she asked, mopping up her spill.

He smiled. "Good point. Why don't we chalk it up to a mutual love of caffeine."

"Sounds good to me."

He reached past her to grab a cup. As he did, Kelsey got a whiff of flowery aftershave. Pleasant, but nothing like Alex's earthy scent. That, of course, conjured up another memory from yesterday. Without meaning to, she sighed.

"That was a pretty contented sound," Tom remarked. "What's got you in a such a good mood?"

"Who says I'm in a good mood?"

"For one, the sparkle in your eyes. Along with that smile."

"Just enjoying the beautiful weather."

"And here I thought it was my charming company."

Kelsey kept quiet while he prepared his coffee.

She didn't mean to be coy, but Tom's comments left her unsettled. Despite his jovial tone, she sensed an edge. Probably wasn't used to women turning him down, she imagined. Reaching for the half-and-half she shot him a smile, silently letting him know her lack of interest wasn't personal. He just wasn't her type.

"Do you have any potato salad with fat-free mayonnaise?" a woman at the counter was asking Farley.

"We got two types of potato salad. With and without egg. You want nonfat, you have to make it yourself."

Both Tom and Kelsey snickered. "Will you listen to him?" Tom chuckled. "You'd think he doesn't like making money."

"Nah, it's all show for the customers. I bet he'd miss them if they left."

"Unlike your boss."

Kelsey's smile faltered. "What's that supposed to mean?"

"Nothing. I only meant Farley pretends to not like crowds, while Markoff really doesn't."

"Al—I mean, Mr. Markoff, likes his privacy." And she wasn't about to betray it now with Tom. She turned to leave.

"Hey," he said, catching her shoulder. "I didn't

mean anything. I can appreciate the quirks of creative genius, and God knows, Markoff is a creative genius. I hope I didn't tick you off."

Some of her annoyance faded. "No, you didn't. I simply—well, my job requires discretion."

"Of course. I understand." He started to sip his coffee, then stopped suddenly with a thought. "Hey, you still not interested in the music festival?"

Kelsey had to hand it to him; he had perseverance. "Thanks, Tom, but I think I'll pass."

"Oh, no, I didn't mean come with me. I, uh—" he blushed "—already found another date."

"Good." It was Kelsey's turn to blush.

"Some friends of mine from New York bailed at the last minute and I have a couple extra tickets. If you're interested, you can have them."

"Really?"

"Sure. I'm not one to hold a little thing like rejection against a fellow coffee lover. You can take a friend. You interested?"

Despite knowing better, an image of Alex and her sipping wine in the moonlight flashed into her mind. She imagined him smiling again, only this time maybe standing a little closer.

It was a fantasy.

On the other hand, what would it hurt to take the tickets? She could always go alone.

"Sure," she answered. "I'm interested."

* * *

The local radio station talked of nothing but the upcoming event as she drove back to Nuttingwood. A gala like none the Berkshires had ever seen. Kelsey got a thrill listening to the buildup. Moonlight and music. Sounded like a wonderful evening.

Alex was already out on his walk when Kelsey got to the house. Leaving the turnovers she bought on a plate next to the coffeemaker, she filled her new green coffee mug and took it, along with her other surprise, into the office.

"Hey, Puddin', look what I brought home for you."

The cat meowed hello and trotted out to greet her. Or more accurately to greet the plate of fresh tuna she brought with her. "Everyone gets a treat this morning," she said, scratching his head. "You can have the rest before we go out tonight."

Her hand reached into her pocket and felt the tickets Tom had given her. What did one wear to a gala like none had ever seen? All she had was a pink cocktail dress left over from New Year's Eve. It had cost too much to donate away or stick in storage, so she'd brought the garment along. She loved the dress, but was it glamorous enough? Alex would know; he had far more experience with society events than she did.

With that one thought, reality regained control. All this thinking about Alex and his smile. And the concert. Why would Alex go to an event like that in the first place, let alone go with her? It wasn't like they had some kind of relationship.

But you'd like to, wouldn't you?

No, she wouldn't. She didn't want a relationship with Alex other than the one they had. They weren't even relationship material. He was too busy being angry with the whole darn world and she... she was temporary in every sense of the word. In a few more weeks, she'd be out of here, and they'd never see each other again.

Besides, she knew better than anyone that any feeling this good could never last.

"Tell me that cat isn't eating tuna fish from a plate."

She looked up in time to see Alex step onto the terrace. Their gazes locked, and he stopped in his tracks. Kelsey's insides, on the other hand, went into free fall. All of a sudden she felt very shy.

"Morning," he said, his voice dropping to a hon-eyed baritone that sent the free fall into overdrive. "You were up and out early."

"So were you."

"I couldn't sleep. The heat."

"I know. I mean, about the heat." In the early morning light, his eyes glinted like polished silver.

Unable to hold his stare, Kelsey looked to

Puddin'. "I couldn't sleep either so I went to Farley's for coffee. Brought back some turnovers."

"Pastry and tuna. That's quite a combination."

"Well, Puddin' didn't think humans should have all the fun."

"Interesting. I didn't realize you and he were on such intimate terms." Hearing the word *intimate* slip off his tongue so easily, Kelsey's breath hitched. It caught again when Alex grinned. Not as wide or bright a smile as the night before, but every bit as breathtaking.

"He's a very good listener," she replied, unable to stop herself from nervously tucking hair behind her ear.

"I bet. Any topics I'd be interested in?"

"I'll never tell."

"Ahh," he said, grinning wider. "You might not, but I know your partner's weakness." He leaned down to look at the cat licking his whiskers. "From the looks and smell, I'd say albacore white packed in water."

"You wouldn't sell me out for a serving of tuna, would you, Puddin'?"

The glint that had been shining in the sun grew hard. "People will always sell you out, Kelsey."

Ouch. The lightheartedness began to fade.

She was struggling with how to rescue the atmosphere when Alex turned to head inside. "I have two tickets to tonight's fund-raiser," she said in a rush, stopping him in his tracks. "Would you like to go?"

Alex didn't answer. He simply stared, looking as surprised as she felt.

"Never mind." Please say her face did not look as shocked yesterday as his did now. Why didn't she keep her mouth shut as she planned? "It was a silly thing to suggest. I don't know why I even suggested the idea." *Other than the fact you were getting that forlorn look and were walking away and I wanted to keep you with me.*

"What happened to your 'friend' from the store? I thought he invited you."

Who? "Oh, you mean Tom." She'd completely forgotten about both the invitation and the fact she'd told Alex about it.

"Won't he mind?"

"He and I aren't going together." She left out that he was the source of the tickets.

"Really?" She had to be imagining the interest in his voice.

"No." Although he wasn't asking for an explanation, the gleam in his eye, the one she was imagining along with the interest in his voice, compelled her to offer one. Or at least a partial one. "He's a nice guy, but not really my type."

"You have a type?"

Yes, you. She chased that thought away as fast as it formed. "Doesn't everyone?"

Alex nodded. "Sometimes. Other times a person catches you off guard."

She knew what he meant. "Anyway, never mind my suggestion. I can go alone."

"I'll go."

"You will?" Her voice traveled up at the end of her question, betraying all her surprise and excitement. Never in a million years did she expect him to accept. "Why?"

He went back to staring, this time actively searching her face as if the answer were contained there. "A woman like you shouldn't have to be alone."

For the rest of the day, Kelsey tried to keep her enthusiasm at bay. *Go alone,* she would remind herself whenever she started to get too excited. He meant a woman like her shouldn't have to *go* alone. A small slip of semantics, but important nonetheless. One version referred to escort status; the other implied…well, it implied arrangements she already knew weren't realistic.

Of course, neither version explained why he was suddenly shedding his hermit mode. She decided not to go there. Thinking about that only brought her back to the illusions she knew weren't possible.

And yet, despite all her self-lecturing, she was a bundle of nerves by nightfall. Sometime during the day, she realized tonight would be the first time Alex had ever seen her truly dressed up. As a result she spent what felt like hours getting ready, lying to herself that the effort was so she wouldn't embarrass her boss and not because she wanted to impress him.

Surveying her reflection, she offered herself a nervous smile. "Not bad." Her dress swirled about her calves; the shimmering pink made her look like a bright flower, and her makeup was more dramatic than normal. Nothing excessive, but enough that it played up her blue eyes. Deciding casual was best when it came to her hair, she clipped the front of her curls in a rhinestone clasp and let the rest tumble down her back.

A lot of work for a non-date, she thought with a sigh. And this wasn't a date.

Another point she spent the day reminding herself.

She headed downstairs to the great room where she found Alex staring out at the garden. That he looked great didn't surprise her. She'd long ago concluded he would always look great. Tonight, he wore a black suit. Long, lean and simple, the ensemble fit him both literally and figuratively. Even with his sling, the jacket somehow managed to drape seamlessly over his shoulders and down his back, with just enough snugness to hint at the muscles beneath. He looked a million miles away. Regretting his decision?

Softly, she cleared her throat, alerting him of her presence. "Hi."

He turned and his expression went from thoughtful to something darker but far from somber. His eyes swept the length of her, the appreciative glint leaving shivers in its wake. "Hi back."

"Are you ready to go?"

"Almost."

At first, Kelsey couldn't decide if his immobility was from reluctance or something else. He stood there studying her in that distracted way of his. Behind his eyes, wheels were turning, but about what he was thinking, she had no idea.

Then she noticed the tie in his left hand. Of course. "Need help?" Without waiting for the answer, she moved toward him. "Thank goodness it's not a bowtie. I'm only good with Windsors."

It wasn't the first time she'd tied a tie. But it was the first time the action felt so intimate. Worse, it felt natural. They stood mere inches apart, wood and spice drifting off Alex's skin. Kelsey struggled not to close her eyes and inhale, same way she struggled not to stare at his tanned skin or the hint of dark curls at the vee of his white shirt. "Can you button the top button?"

Part of her was hoping he'd say no so she could continue seeing his skin as well as touch him further. But, unfortunately, or fortunately, he did as she asked, and a moment later, she was looping the silk around his neck.

"Where did you learn to tie a tie?" he asked.

"School uniforms. In junior high one year, I was in charge of making sure all the kids in the house didn't look sloppy. Our foster mother—"

"Foster mother?"

Kelsey blushed, feeling the color all the way down her neck. "Grandma Rosie wasn't much of a guardian, I'm afraid."

"That's too bad."

Too bad indeed. She returned to somewhat lighter subjects. "Like I was saying, my foster mother was a stickler about appearance. She wouldn't let us leave the house unless we were all knotted and groomed. There was this one kid, Tyrrell, who couldn't stay neat if he tried. I used to tie his tie for him every morning."

"We had to wear ties with our school uniforms, too. Wretched things made it hard to do any kind of activity. I hated them."

Kelsey wasn't surprised. Men like Alex weren't

made for suits and ties inside. "I imagine Tyrell would agree. That's probably why his tie never managed to stay put for more than an hour."

She fished an end up and through. "I always wondered who took over fixing his tie when I left."

"How long were you there?"

"At that house? Eighteen months or so, I guess. I never really kept track." Knot complete, she drew it tight against his collar. "There you go. Not my best, I'm afraid. I'm a little out of practice."

"Good enough for me. Was it difficult?"

"Was what difficult? Tying your tie?"

Surveying her handiwork, she reached up and made a minuscule adjustment. It wasn't really needed; she wanted an excuse to keep her hands close to him.

"Moving so much," he replied quietly.

Her fingers paused in midaction. When did the conversation turn personal? "You get used to it," she answered with a shrug. "After a while, picking up and moving on becomes a lifestyle." Out of necessity, she added silently.

"Like temp work?"

Slowly, she looked up to find him looking down, his face serious and sincere. "Yeah, like temp work."

Time stopped for a second. Or so it felt by the

way the air grew thick around them. A dull thud vibrated against her fingertips. She realized it was Alex's heart, that her hands were pressed against his chest. The slow steady beat was nothing like the one racing inside her body.

"You're good to go." Needing distance, she backed away.

The radio station wasn't exaggerating when it said New Englanders were turning out in droves for tonight's fund-raiser. Celebrities, local leaders and every arts patron with access to the highway was in attendance. For Kelsey, entering the administration building was like entering a summer wonderland. The decorated room wasn't as colorful as Alex's garden or as tranquil as the cascades, but it was beautiful and elegant with its tea lights and floral topiaries. She felt like Cinderella on the arm of her handsome prince.

A handsome, silent prince. Alex barely said a word after they left Nuttingwood. He spent the drive staring out the window, his long fingers tapping the armrest. He was still a million miles away now. Although his face didn't show any expression, Kelsey knew he had to be tense. After all, there was a huge difference between stopping into the local store and attending a crowded gala full of New England's social elite. The night had to be bringing back memories of the world he thought he'd left behind.

"We don't have to stay long," she said to him.

The comment brought him back to attention. "What are you talking about?"

"The concert. I know you'd rather be somewhere else."

"Then you underestimate me."

"Are you telling me you'd rather not be hiking in the woods right now?"

His delayed shrug gave her his answer. "We're a little overdressed for rock hopping in the cascade, wouldn't you think?"

"Very funny," she said, rolling her eyes. "What I meant was that I appreciate you coming with me."

"Well, like I said, a woman like you shouldn't be alone."

There it was, that slip, again. Through she tried, the tremors of expectation running down her back made the remark hard to brush off. Perhaps he didn't know his word choice could be misconstrued. On the other hand, he was a writer so maybe he did.

"I—" Before she could say anything, a waiter approached bearing a tray of fluted glasses.

"Champagne?"

Kelsey shook her head. "Designated driver," she

lied, hoping Alex would follow his usual pattern and not press.

Unfortunately tonight seemed to be his night for behaving out of character. At least he waited until the server moved on before asking, "What's the real reason?"

"What makes you think there's a different reason?" She fiddled with the fringe on her shawl. *How did he know?*

"Your face. The corners of your mouth tighten when you're being falsely cheerful."

"They do?"

He nodded. "I noticed your first day, when you kept throwing me those fake smiles."

Feeling her skin getting hot, Kelsey suddenly regretted wearing a dress that revealed so much skin. The entire fund-raiser had to know she was embarrassed. "You noticed my smiles were fake?"

"I noticed a lot of things about you."

If the rest of the people in the room didn't see her blush before, they certainly did now. Alex's comment shot straight to her toes, its journey assisted by his tone of voice. A rough, gravelly tone that spoke of pleasure and more. Kelsey's insides turned to warm honey, and her knees threatened to buckle. Through lowered lashes, she watched as Alex raised his glass to his lips. "Wonder if

Stuart knew what he'd done when he hired you," he murmured over the rim.

"Done?" Distracted by how the champagne left Alex's upper lip shining, she'd missed his meaning. What did Stuart do other than hire a qualified typist? "He simply wanted the manuscript done on time."

"I wonder," was all Alex replied, and he took another sip. "Back to my original question, do you feel like explaining the designated driver excuse?"

"Who says it's an excuse? Oh, right." At his knowing smile, her fingers came up to touch her mouth. Very well, she might as well tell the truth. "Alcohol was the source of too many bad situations growing up." Hopefully her shrug looked nonchalant.

"With your grandmother?"

"Rosie had her share of drunken mishaps." So did one particular foster father, but she wouldn't go there. Not tonight. "Made me decide that when it came to drinking, avoidance was the best policy. For me anyway."

Those gray eyes softened. "I'm sorry."

"For what? You weren't there." She didn't want to talk about her past right now. The night was too beautiful to think about things she couldn't change.

Or things she couldn't have.

She drowned out the warning with a change in topic. "Did you see all these flower arrangements? I think there might be more flowers in here than in your garden."

"Hmm," was Alex's reply.

"You don't think so?"

"What I think," he said, leaning in a little closer, "is that you're an incredibly strong woman for having survived so much and coming out the other side so full of life."

"No stronger than anybody else."

"You sell yourself short. And as for the flowers…" He leaned in even closer. "You're far more colorful."

The air in the room shifted abruptly, becoming close and intense. Looking at Alex's expression, Kelsey saw that he felt it too. A bond of silent understanding formed between them. It felt like coming together at a center of a bridge from separate directions. Setting his glass down, Alex nodded toward a nearby exit. "Come with me," he whispered.

CHAPTER EIGHT

THEY managed to get as far as the exit before a large, blue-jacketed torso stepped in their path.

Tom Forbes smiled like he was greeting an old friend. "Kelsey! I thought that was you in the crowd." His eyes flickered from her to Alex and back. "And you brought a friend after all."

Not knowing what else to do, Kelsey smiled back. It was like being stuck in one of those movie moments where the heroine finds herself caught between two romantic rivals. Only she was caught between a guy with a bruised ego and… And she didn't know how to define Alex anymore. Didn't matter; the situation was still awkward.

"Aren't you going to introduce me?" Tom asked. He was still smiling, but the grin had a sharper edge.

"Of course." She tucked some hair behind her ears and found her manners. "Tom Forbes, this is—"

She didn't get any further before Tom stuck his hand out, completely ignoring the cast on Alex's right arm. "Alex Markoff. Big fan. I've followed your career for a long time."

Kelsey half thought Alex would ignore the handshake offer, but he didn't. He held out his left hand and allowed Tom to awkwardly pump it up and down. "Kelsey mentioned she was typing your manuscript," he continued.

"Did she now?" Alex slid his gaze toward her. She shrugged, knowing that wasn't what he wanted to hear.

"I mentioned I worked for a writer, and then he saw you the other day at Farley's."

"Can't wait to read it. Any idea when the book'll be out?"

"When it's finished."

Tom laughed, a little too affectedly for Kelsey's taste. The guy was trying too hard. "Hopefully that'll be soon. Been a long time since *Chase the Moon*. A lot of readers have wondered where you've been."

"Well, you can't rush the creative process," Kelsey piped up. Next to her, she could feel Alex's tension. The night was going well. She didn't want it spoiled because of Tom's overeager questions.

Meanwhile, Tom continued smiling that sharp smile. "No, I suppose you can't. Of course—" this time it was his gaze sliding in her direction "—having the right inspiration helps."

Okay, now he was definitely pushing his luck. Kelsey waited for Alex to refute him or cut him down with one of his cold stares. To her surprise, he did neither.

Instead, he took her hand. "Certainly does. If you'll excuse us, Kelsey and I want to get some air before the concert begins."

He pulled her toward the exit, not forcefully, but decidedly enough that anyone watching would know not to deter them.

"So, that's your 'friend'," he remarked, once they stepped outside.

"That's Tom." She knew he had an ego, but she hadn't expected him to act quite so...aggressive? She didn't expect Alex's behavior either. "Sorry about his questions. He really didn't know I worked for you until he saw you in the store. On the plus side," she added, "at least you know he wants to read your book."

"You're right," Alex replied.

She was confused. "About what? Him wanting to read your book?"

"Nope." Giving her fingers a squeeze, Alex

leaned in toward the crook of her neck and whispered, "That he's not your type."

Kelsey's pulse skipped a beat.

Outside the concert, on the grounds, organizers had forgone the standard spotlights in favor of lanterns strung from the trees, giving the grounds a romantic, amber glow. The early evening air still held the day's warmth, and the sky promised a clear, star-filled romantic evening. They walked the grass in comfortable silence. Every so often they would come across another couple who would nod hello as they passed.

Another couple. Kelsey knew she needed to correct her thinking, but with every step found it harder and harder to do. No sooner did she form the thoughts than they would slip away, lost in a haze of romance.

She stole a look at Alex. So tonight wasn't a date. They weren't a couple. But would it be so bad to pretend, if only for a little while? No one need know. She took a deep breath, savoring the scent of evening blossoms, and allowed herself a silent fantasy.

"Would you look at the view?" Kelsey said. They were toward the rear of the property, where the grounds overlooked Stockbridge Bowl. "Doesn't the water look beautiful?" Black and fathomless, with dapples of white, reflections of the lanterns dotting the surface.

She let out a soft sigh. "There's something very mysterious about dark water, don't you think? There's so much that you can't see. You have to look deep to really know what's there." She glanced over her shoulder at the man behind her. "Like people."

"That so?" His expression was gentle and tender. "And what do you think lies beneath?"

"More than meets the eye, that's for sure. Light. Beauty. Sensitivity."

"You sure? It could simply be more darkness."

"No," she said shaking her head. "The dark surface is simply camouflage. To protect what's underneath."

They both knew she wasn't talking about the water.

Alex reached over her shoulder to cup her cheek. Instinctively she nestled into his touch. His body drew closer, so close she could feel the straps of his sling through her thin silk wrap. Feeling them brush against her shoulder blades, she trembled.

"Cold?" Alex asked, his lips dangerously close to her earlobe.

Kelsey shook her head. "Not cold at all." In fact, she'd never felt warmer.

"Good." His hand slid downward slightly,

allowing his thumb leeway to trace her lower lip. "You know," he murmured, "the same thing can be said about flowers."

"Flowers?" Her body was too busy reacting to his touch to follow his comment clearly.

"Mmm. At first, all you see is an explosion of color and petals that won't last. But then they fool you, and you realize the blossoms are far sturdier and do a lot more than distract you with their beauty."

Gently, he urged her to turn and face him. "You, Kelsey, are a very sturdy flower."

That slow melting sensation grabbed hold of her spine, turning her insides soft. She could feel herself hovering on the edge of something. A shift between fantasy and reality that, if allowed to happen, might not be reversible. "Sure I'm not more a flowering weed?" she asked, seeking solid ground.

"Oh, but some of the sturdiest, prettiest, sweetest-smelling blossoms start out as weeds. They're also the ones you can't shake, no matter how hard you try."

"So I am a weed." Why didn't that sound bad to her?

"No, you're a completely original flower. One that's impossible to ignore. God knows, I've tried and failed all summer." He brushed the hair from her cheek.

Kelsey's mouth ran dry. Alex's words were touching a place deep inside her, a place she kept locked away from the world. The precipice loomed closer. Another step and she'd be lost to illusion and fantasy forever.

The fingers tracing her jaw reached her chin and tilted her face upward. She looked up and saw Alex's heavy-lidded eyes, as glazed and lost in the moment as she felt. "What would you do if I kissed you right now?" he asked.

"I—"

She didn't get the chance to finish.

Alex slanted his lips across hers. His kiss was like him: strong, confident with a hint of arrogant possession. As if he knew she'd readily submit. Doing just that, Kelsey wrapped her arms around his neck, and when she felt his tongue demanding entrance, she gave a soft sigh and complied. He tasted of mint and something more, something she suspected was uniquely Alex. It was heavenly.

The kiss ended far too soon. Alex was the one to break away, resting his forehead against hers. The air filled with the sound of their labored breathing.

"Well," he said once they'd regained their composure. "That—I—"

He was at a loss for words. Satisfaction filled Kelsey, that she could have that effect on him. "I know," she managed to whisper. She'd say more if he hadn't had the same effect on her. Although it was hardly her first kiss, it might as well have been. Her toes were still curling with pleasure.

There was an inevitability to the moment as well. Like they were simply coming to the end of a path they started back in June.

Alex's fingers were combing lazy lines through the loose hair on the back of her neck. Surrendering to the sensation, Kelsey closed her eyes. *I could stay here forever,* she thought, resting her cheek on his shoulder. "I hear music. Do you think the concert's started?"

"Don't know," he replied. "Possibly."

"Should we head back?"

He leaned back and looked her in the eye. "Do you want to?"

Something lurked behind his question—something important—but Kelsey was too lost in the moment to give it much thought. "Maybe in a few minutes."

"Just a few?" Alex teased.

"Maybe a little longer."

Alex cupped the back of her head. "Good answer," he whispered as he lowered his mouth to hers. "Good answer."

They never made it to their seats in the amphitheater. They listened from beneath a spreading oak tree at the edge of the lawn. Alex lay stretched on his side beside her. He'd shed his jacket, gallantly spreading it on the ground so her dress wouldn't grass stain. Every so often, she would look over and find him studying her with a contemplative expression. More often than not, he seemed to be studying her mouth which kept the memory of their kisses alive. Did he know her lips still tingled from the contact?

"What?" she asked finally, when his scrutiny became too much.

"Nothing," he replied. "Admiring the view is all."

He was lying. There was more to his gaze than admiration. She could see it pooling behind his eyes.

But, she didn't press. Couldn't press the issue, actually, because he leaned in and kissed her. A quick, chaste kiss, but enough to erase all thoughts.

The soloist, a pianist who really was quite good, switched from an overture to a ballad. Like the sultry music drifting into the night, Kelsey's insides slowed too. The whole experience was too dream-like to be real. It had to be a dream. Surely reality wouldn't feel this natural or this good. Would it?

Common sense told her to stop. That what she was feeling was nothing more than two people giving in to their attraction. But she didn't listen. As the music built to a crescendo, Kelsey drowned out the warning voice and let her feelings take charge. For the first time in her life she allowed herself to think that maybe, just maybe, she'd found where she belonged.

"What?" Alex asked.

It was her turn to stare at his mouth. How had she gone all summer without kissing them?

"Nothing," she said, bringing her lips towards his. "Enjoying the view is all."

Later that night, when Alex walked her upstairs, Kelsey couldn't feel her feet touching the ground. Come to think of it, she didn't remember feeling the ground since Alex kissed her. Had it dissolved away?

They stopped at her door. Pulse quickening, she leaned back against the wood and waited. Expectancy clung to the air. Only unlike the other night, she wasn't wondering about a good-night kiss, she was wondering if he would want more.

"Tonight was amazing," she said, looking up at him. "I can't remember when I had such a good time."

"Me neither. Hard to see it end, but—" he caressed her cheek with the back of his hand "—I think maybe it should. This time anyway."

Pressing her lips to the knuckles grazing them, Kelsey nodded. Even though her body was willing, taking things slowly was the right move. For now. And that Alex recognized that too only pulled her deeper under his spell. "Then I guess it's goodnight," she said.

"Guess so."

Neither of them moved, making her giggle. "Good night, Alex."

He grinned, looking so boyish and adorable she nearly had trouble breathing. "Good night, Kelsey."

His mouth found hers. What started out sweet and gentle soon became heated, until the only sound Kelsey could hear was her blood pounding in her ears. Her bedroom door opened and they both stumbled across the threshold locked in the kiss. But instead of moving toward the bed as she expected, Alex lifted his head. "You make a man forget his resolve," he whispered, lips grazing her skin. "I better say good-night while I still can act like a gentleman."

Gently he pried her arms from his neck, ignoring her soft whimper. His kisses were far too addictive; she missed them already.

Reading her thoughts, he pressed one more to her lips. "Sweet dreams, Kelsey."

Sweet dreams? Wasn't she already dreaming? How else could she explain this evening?

She closed the door with a happy sigh. Was it possible for a woman to float away? Why not? She'd been floating all night, hadn't she?

Pressing her fingers to her lips, she smiled. They still tingled from Alex's kisses. His taste still lingered. She ran her tongue across her lower lip savoring his flavor. Remembering the possessive feel of his mouth as it covered hers.

Listen to yourself, she chided with a giggle. When did you get so fanciful?

She already knew. The moment Alex took her into his arms. His embrace felt secure. Right. She'd never felt anything so perfect.

Through the walls, she heard the scraping of a chair, followed by the sound of Alex's footsteps. What was he thinking right now? Was he thinking of her? Did he regret saying good-night? Was he, like her, counting minutes until they'd see each other again?

Dear Lord, she sounded like a smitten teenager. More proof tonight had to be a dream, because she'd never acted like that. Not even when she was a teenager. Surely, she'd wake up in the morning and reality would come crashing down. It always did.

Except for this time. Come breakfast, Kelsey

was still floating. In fact, she swore her feet didn't touch the stairs as she headed downstairs.

As it was normally her routine—although this morning felt anything but routine—she headed toward the office to check her e-mail. With all the activity yesterday, she hadn't touched base with Stuart. The editor hated radio silence. Weekend, weekday, it didn't make a difference. He no doubt flooded her inbox with requests for an update. Though she hadn't looked, she bet her cell phone inbox was full too.

Reaching the office, however, she paused. A soft, low voice drifted from the terrace. Looking out, she saw Alex, his back to her, his head focused on his lap.

"You're a mangy son-of-a-gun, you know that don't you?" He spoke in a singsong voice, like what you'd use to address a child. The rhythm washed over her, making her smile. "A big fat mangy thing."

A flick of orange flashed by his elbow revealing his conversation partner. Where she'd been floating, she now tumbled, her insides turning in a weightless free fall. That he could be so sweet with a cat he supposedly didn't like...

"Careful," she said, "he might get insulted."

Alex turned and flashed a brilliant smile. So brilliant Kelsey had to grab the door frame. To wake up to that smile every day. The thought popped into her head so quickly that for a second, her heart stilled. Surely she didn't really think this could be something permanent, did she? She wasn't a permanent person. Alex wasn't either. Was he?

"I don't think he cares what I say as long as I rub his belly," Alex said, still smiling. He looked back to his lap. "Unfortunately, pal, our moment is over."

He rose, the motion causing the cat to slide unceremoniously from his lap. "How about you?"

"Are you asking if I want my belly rubbed?"

"Mmm, interesting idea." A sultry sparkle appeared in his eyes. The free fall inside her gathered momentum. Doubly so when he crossed the space and slipped his good arm around her waist. "However, I'll settle for a good-morning kiss."

Their bodies molded together as if they'd never said good-night. "Now that," Alex said when they finally broke for air, "is how a morning should start. Who needs coffee?"

"Unfortunately I do," she said with a smile. His kisses were as wonderful as she remembered. So wonderful she still couldn't believe this—they—were real. "Once a caffeine addict, always a caffeine addict, I'm afraid."

"Cast aside for a cup of Italian roast. I should be insulted. Though I guess I can forgive you. This time." He punctuated his answer with a kiss to her nose.

"You're so generous."

"Plus, I already had a cup."

"Cheater!" Kelsey gave his arm a playful slap, which he laughed off.

"Tell you what. Why don't we go get you a travel mug, refill mine, and have breakfast on the rocks? I feel like playing hooky today."

"You do, do you?"

"Uh-huh. Think your boss will let you come play with me?"

"I don't know. He's pretty tough."

"Don't worry. I'll persuade him. I can be very persuasive when I try."

She'd been expecting him to release her so they could head to the kitchen, but he didn't. Instead, he nuzzled the crook of her neck.

"So I see," she replied. He was nibbling a path across her skin, his nose nudging the strap of her yellow tank top. Kelsey arched her neck allowing him better access. Her fingers slipped up to tangle his dark curls. A soft moan left her lips.

Alex swirled his tongue across the hollow above her collarbone. "That a yes?"

Yes, yes, yes. Right now she'd say yes to everything.

He gave her one more deep, toe-curling kiss before letting her go. "Good. Hold that thought. I'll grab some breakfast and we'll be on our way."

"Can I help?"

"Nope. I've got everything under control. You can think of other things you might need persuading about. And you, pal—" he turned to Puddin', who had reclaimed his spot on the abandoned chair and was waiting expectantly "—will have to find someone else to rub your belly. Kelsey and I have petting of our own to do."

Though outwardly she giggled, inside Kelsey shivered with excitement. Glancing up through her lashes, she whispered, "Can't wait."

"Me neither." He kissed her again and disappeared into the office.

Too full of anticipation to simply wait, she headed into the office herself and fired up her laptop. Might as well do what she started and check in with Stuart before he started sending telegrams or something.

Sure enough, there were close to a dozen messages from the man dating back over the past couple days. "Human grain of sand," she murmured to herself. He could wear down the President of the

United States. But it was his last message that caught her eye first. Marked urgent, the subject line read HAVE YOU SEEN THIS?!! Intrigued, Kelsey clicked open the link.

In a flash, her dream became a nightmare.

CHAPTER NINE

"But the biggest surprise of the evening was the reappearance of prize-winning novelist Alex Markoff, who let slip he's working on his long-awaited comeback novel. From the looks of things, the novel isn't his only comeback."

Alex slapped the blog printout on his desk, his palm landing on the photo of them kissing during the concert. "How did they—?"

"Camera phone most likely," Kelsey replied. Unfortunately paparazzi technology had become more advanced during his hermitage.

Upsetting as the photo was, however, it wasn't nearly as disturbing as the blogger's byline. Tom Forbes. Kelsey felt sick. "When I asked him what he did for a living, he said a little bit of everything. I swear, if I had known…"

Alex wasn't listening. He'd moved away from the deck over to the garden windows. Staring out at the tree line, he looked so worn down it hurt to look at him. "I should have known. What made me think the world—people—had changed."

The defeat in his voice killed her. She didn't have to see his expression to know it was shrouded in darkness. He was folding into himself. Retreating.

Kelsey's stomach churned. She might as well have really crashed to earth, the change was so sudden and sharp. Only ten minutes ago they were in each other's arms.

Damn Tom Forbes for using them like that.

You mean using you. God, what an idiot she'd been. The one thing Alex feared more than anything, and she led it straight to his doorstep.

She made her way to the window and placed a hand on his shoulder. A pang stabbed her heart when he flinched. "I swear, Alex, I didn't know. When he offered me the tickets, I thought—"

"He gave you the tickets?"

It was her turn to flinch, from both the harshness of his voice and the memory. It was supposed to show there were no hard feelings. A friendly gesture. "He set me up. He saw us at Farley's and he set us up. I had no idea he would misuse our friendship for a story."

"People use people all the time."

"Including me?"

He didn't answer, which hurt more than if he had. "I don't know what made me think the world would change. People are as miserable as they always were. Concerned only with their personal agendas, ready to sell you out at the first opportunity. You can't trust anyone."

"You can trust me."

Again, no reply. He was slipping away with each passing moment, letting the betrayals of the past take over. She could feel the gulf widening and her words couldn't reach across the chasm. Reaching out, she tried one more time. "It's one blog, Alex. One of a million. He's probably got no more than a dozen readers." But even as she offered her reassurance, she knew audience size wasn't the point. This was about the betrayal. A return to the world he left five years ago where his wife used his fame, and his friends sold him out to the highest bidder. "I know you're angry…"

"Angry?" He shook his head. "I'm not angry. How can you be angry at reality?"

"But it's not reality. Not everyone has an agenda, Alex, or is out to use you."

"Really? Name one."

"Me."

He looked at the hand she placed on his shoulder, then to her eyes. "Then you're the lone swimmer in a very cold ocean," he replied. "Not to mention naïve. You, of all people, should know I'm right."

Because of her grandmother. But this was

different. Surely he had to realize she wouldn't hurt him. *Except you already did.* "Face it, Kelsey, the world is never going to change." He shrugged off her touch. "I should never have thought otherwise. It was a mistake."

He was calling last night a mistake. Did that mean he considered her a mistake too?

Alex had pulled away and was heading toward the door. "Where are you going?" she asked.

"For a walk. I need to get out of here and get some fresh air."

"Good idea. Let's go to the rocks and you can clear your head."

"No."

Kelsey stopped. He'd said the one word she feared he would say. "But you just said—"

"I'm going alone. I need to be alone. The way I should have stayed in the first place."

Watching him disappear in the garden, Kelsey wondered if she'd ever feel this morning's joy again.

She should have realized a dream as good as this morning's couldn't last. By suppertime, she wondered if it ever existed. Alex still hadn't returned from his "walk." He was avoiding her. Kelsey sat in the great room, studying the garden. It was like the early summer all over again. Only this time

Nuttingwood felt colder and more empty than ever. Not even the insistent presence of Puddin' could dull the ache inside her.

Curse Tom Forbes and his blog. Did he have any idea of the damage he caused? She wanted to grab him by his tacky tropical print shirt and choke him until he apologized. Not that an apology would make any difference. Alex was gone. At the first sign of his precious privacy being invaded, he'd retreated into his woods. Into himself. Away from her.

Vision blurring, she blinked to keep the tears at bay. You'd think she'd be used to rejection by this point in her life.

That's what you get for growing complacent. Rolling to her side, she drew her knees to her chest. She should have stuck to her rules. Don't get involved. Don't form connections. But no, she had to let her guard down. Let herself fall for a man with stormy eyes and walls around his heart as thick as Jericho.

Fool. Thinking she was worth Alex dropping his defenses. Like the man said, she was a mistake.

She squeezed her eyes shut, blocking the tears. If only life came with do-overs. If it did, she'd push reset and never step foot on Alex Markoff's doorstep. Sadly, however, life didn't, and once again, she wasn't wanted.

* * *

When she opened her eyes again, morning was streaming through the windows. Still half-asleep she sniffed for the familiar smell of coffee, her insides dropping when she didn't find it. The great room was empty. A quick check of the kitchen and office revealed they were too. An empty glass in the sink told her Alex had come and gone. Still avoiding. Still retreating.

Well, no sense waiting for the inevitable. If Alex didn't want her around, she wasn't going to stay. Not where she wasn't wanted. Not anymore. Wiping a tear from her cheek, she headed upstairs to her room to pack.

Like moving in, moving out also came with a ritual. First the clothes from the closet were folded and sorted. When she got to the pink cocktail dress, she clutched the garment to her cheek. A faint trace of Alex's aftershave clung to the silk. Holding it close was like holding him. She inhaled deeply and wished she could hold on to the scent forever.

But nothing stayed forever.

Bureau contents came next. Underwear, T-shirts. The blue running shorts she wore their afternoon in the woods. She ran a hand across the cloth. She'd never felt more at home, more like she belonged than when she sat on those rocks with Alex.

"No crying," she told herself, swiping another errant tear. Tears were not part of the ritual. It was a rule. You left a place with your head held high, not looking back.

Lastly came the personal belongings. Gently she picked up her ceramic mug, cracked and crooked, never to hold liquid again.

Good thing I had glue.

Yes. A very good thing.

How could she ever look at the cup again without thinking of Alex? Her vision blurred. That was the problem with the rules. They didn't apply when your heart was being ripped from your body. A sob rose in her chest, choking off her breath. She tried to fight its release, but couldn't. Gasping for air, she finally let the tears break free. They ran down her cheeks in hot streaks.

Why couldn't Alex want her?

CHAPTER TEN

IT took a while, but eventually Kelsey regained her composure. Placing the last of her belongings in her satchel, she took one last look at the room she'd come to call home. Outside the open window, a breeze rustled the trees. She thought of the owl and said a mental goodbye. The bird would be forever linked in her mind with the image of Alex's smile. Both had looked so breathtaking that night.

Like so many other things, that night was part of the past now. She was moving on, like she'd done so many times before in her life, and as she swore a long time ago, under her own terms. Eventually the ache in her chest would fade. She'd grown attached to places before and recovered.

Except this time it wasn't just a place, and she was far more than attached to Alex. She was in love.

She left her mother's coffee mug behind. In its new form, it reminded her too much of Alex.

Looking at it no longer gave her comfort. Better to leave the cup behind and make a clean break.

"Goodbye," she whispered, tracing the faded flowers one last time. Her summer at Nuttingwood was over.

Wonder how long it would take for Alex to notice she was gone?

Turned out Alex learned her plans immediately. He was walking up the stairs when she opened the door. Dust and sweat streaked his clothes, and there were mosquito bites dotting his skin. He moved with slow, deliberate movements, clearly trying to keep his head still. It didn't take a genius to recognize what was going on. "Headache?" she asked.

He looked up, the pale skin and dark circles providing her answer. "Nothing I'm not used to."

Except he hadn't had one in weeks. Not since that one afternoon. "Did you take your medicine?"

He shook his head. "I was on the rocks all night."

Avoiding her. Part of her, the angry, hurt part, decided he deserved his misery. Unfortunately, the other part of her, the bigger part, couldn't leave him when he was in pain.

Setting down her suitcases, she took his elbow. Despite the circumstances, heat rose up her arm.

"Come on, let's get you lying down, and I'll get your pills."

His eyes dropped to her suitcases as they headed to his room. "You're leaving."

"If I'm not around, Tom can't blog about our so-called relationship, can he?"

"No, I suppose he can't."

"That way you can get your privacy back."

"Yes, I suppose I can."

She led him to his room and to the side of his king-size bed. His bed was still unmade from the other morning. He'd kissed her in this doorway. She bit her lip before the memory made her sigh. Instead she focused on the business at hand and said, "Pills are still in the medicine cabinet, I assume."

Alex had slid beneath the covers when she returned. Seeing him lying against the sheets, his skin pale, his breathing ragged, Kelsey's heart ached. Even miserable, he was still the most breathtaking man she'd ever seen. *Don't let me go,* Kelsey wanted to plead. *Ask me to stay.*

She held out the pills and a glass of water. "You should have something to eat. You'll keep your medicine down better."

"I'll be fine. I just need to rest. What are you going to tell Stuart? About leaving?"

"I'll call him from the road and explain. He saw

the blog. I'm sure he'll get it. He'll send another secretary."

"At four times the pay instead of three," Alex slurred. Suddenly his sleepy eyes widened. "Your debt. You were counting on the money."

"I'll figure something out. I'm very good at adapting."

"Still, it's not fair that you should suffer." His eyes grew heavy again. The medicine and his exhaustion were too strong to fight.

Kelsey's fingers itched to touch his cheek.

"Like I said, I'll figure something out."

"I could pay it off for you."

Charity. Kelsey bit the inside of her mouth. She wanted his heart; he offered charity. Story of her life. "No, I don't want your money."

"But—"

"You're not responsible for my problems, Alex."

"Aren't I?"

No. He couldn't help not wanting her. "You're exhausted, Alex. Stop fighting and go to sleep."

"In a minute. What about Puddin'? What will you do with him?"

"He's a survivor too," she replied. "Put out a bowl of food in the morning and he'll forget all about me."

"You assume you're easy to forget."

Wasn't she? *Easy to forget, and easy to let go.* "Go to sleep, Alex."

"Kelsey, I don't…" The sentence drifted off unfinished. Guess she'd never know what he was going to say.

Unable to help herself, she pressed one last kiss to his parted lips and headed to the door.

One thing about emotional goodbyes, they left you drained. Kelsey barely got to the bottom of the hill when her own head began aching. Not having had her coffee this morning wasn't helping. Along with feeling guilty that she left while Alex was sleeping.

She didn't have a choice. He would be asleep for hours, she rationalized. If she stayed, she wouldn't get to New York until late, and she still had to find a place to sleep. Or worse, she would have to postpone leaving until tomorrow.

That's really why you left. You didn't want to spend another night and relive the rejection again in the morning.

Would someone *ever* want her?

Her caffeine-deprivation too loud to ignore, she turned onto Main Street. She could stop at the Leafy Bean and grab a cup for the road, before leaving the town—and the stubborn, guarded man she'd fallen so disastrously in love with—far behind.

Farley was in between rushes and stocking shelves when she arrived. Spotting him by the canned fruit, she gave a quick wave before heading toward the coffee station, grateful he wouldn't ask about her red-rimmed eyes. "How's the hazelnut this morning?"

"Same as every morning," he grumbled. "Popular. You tourists and your fancy coffee flavors. Hazelnut, French vanilla caramel nut. Italian roast. Every time I turn around I gotta brew more."

It was his way of saying the coffee was fresh. "Is this the largest size cup you have?"

"Do you see anything larger?"

"Thanks." Hollowed out with grief as she felt, Kelsey still smiled. The old man might be a cranky curmudgeon, short on patience, but he was an original. "I'm going to miss you, Farley."

He looked up from the canned peaches he was stocking and gave her a curious look. For a split second, she swore it was gratitude and—dare she say—affection sparkling behind his glasses. "Can't miss me unless you leave," he replied in typical Farley fashion.

The doorbell sounded and a female voice called out, "Good morning, Farley."

"What's so good about it," he snapped back

before adding under his breath, "Stupid customers. How's a man supposed to get any work done with everyone yapping away at me."

Yup, definitely she would miss Farley. She turned back to the coffee station, thinking there was a lot about the town she'd miss. She'd felt comfortable here. Which was part of the problem, she reminded herself. She'd let herself grow attached to her location. *Another connection.* She'd really broken her rules left and right this summer, hadn't she?

Sighing to herself, she added a healthy dollop of cream to her coffee. Farley believed in strong coffee, stronger than what Alex made. Alex made coffee exactly the way she liked.

Stop thinking about him. He was in the past now. He had to be. For self-preservation's sake, she had to stop dwelling on memories. Before leaving, she would ask Farley to look in on Alex, and then she wouldn't let his name cross her mind again.

Behind her, the new customers debated about groceries. Kelsey was reaching for a travel lid when suddenly a familiar female voice rang out across the store. "Tom, do you think two pounds of potato salad will be enough?"

Tom. Her hand stilled. The son-of-a... Anger replaced grief, welling up inside her like a summer storm.

"You!" She stormed toward the group of tourists, straight to the blond man in his tropical print shirt. Oh, it would be so easy to grab that flowered collar and twist. Or better yet, slap that smug-looking face. Especially when he smiled like nothing had ever happened.

"Hello, Kelsey. You saw the blog, I take it."

"How could you?"

"How could I what? Report news?"

Like he was a reporter. He was nothing more than a sleazy bottom-feeder. "Alex and I are *not* news!"

"Then what are you?"

"We're—"

From the corner of her eye, she saw Tom's companions watching the exchange with interest. Behind her, Farley was no doubt doing the same. Whatever she said would clearly be gossip fodder for them all.

Well, to hell with them and their gossip. He'd already destroyed whatever it was she had with Alex. What did she care if they talked more? "We're none of your business, that's what we are."

As expected, he waved off the remark. "Come on, of course you're my business. Alex Markoff's one of this century's most influential writers. People are interested in his life."

"That doesn't give you the right to splash our private moments all over the Internet!"

"Hey, if you wanted privacy, you shouldn't have made out in public for all the world to see." He smirked. "Or maybe attention's what you were looking for. After all, you did take those tickets."

Thawp! Thirty-six hours of hurt and anger erupted in her palm connecting with his cheek. The force of the blow could be heard throughout the store. It left a bright red print on the side of Tom's face. "Never come near me again," she spat.

She left the store without another word. From the road, she'd call Farley to check on Alex. Right now she wanted as much distance between her and Tom Forbes as possible.

Her foot didn't touch the brakes until the Bean, the town center and most of the buildings were gone from her rearview mirror. Five miles after that, the shakes began. Pulling over, she tried to calm herself by taking a deep breath. It didn't work.

Her hand still stung from the contact. Way to make a bad situation worse, Kelsey. She'd just given Tom the perfect headline for tomorrow's blog. Writer's Gal Pal Goes Ballistic. She balled her hand into a fist.

And wished she'd thrown a punch instead.

CHAPTER ELEVEN

NEW York City was noisy. In only a couple months Kelsey had forgotten exactly how noisy. She hadn't had a good night's sleep since she returned a week ago.

Who are you kidding? It's not the noise keeping you awake. She missed Nuttingwood.

She missed Alex.

At least financially, she was close to solvency. Last night she wrote out her last loan payment. Grandma Rosie's debt was gone. As she addressed the envelope, she realized she didn't get the same pang in her chest she used to get when thinking of her grandmother. Guess she was finally letting go of the old woman.

Too bad she couldn't let go of other things. A lump stuck in her throat. Two weeks and Alex was as lodged in her heart as strongly as ever. Curse him. The lump grew a little bigger. Why wouldn't he get out of her head? Why did he have to go and lower her defenses in the first place, worming his way inside and making her dream stupid, unrealistic dreams?

Making her fall in love.

Worst of all, she had become stuck. With her debt paid, she should be focusing on where to restart her life. The future was a clean slate. She could do anything she wanted. Problem was, nothing felt right. Not any of the jobs her temp agency found her. Not with any of the apartments she looked at. For goodness' sake, she was still in extended-stay lodging. She needed to make some decisions.

She needed to let Alex go.

Well, to start, she could mail Grandma Rosie's check and cross that item off her to-do list. Grabbing the envelope and her sunglasses, she headed out.

The minute she stepped outside, the heat and noise wrapped around her like a loud oppressive blanket. The ache in her chest increased tenfold. Oh, to feel the soft Berkshire breezes again, and smell the sweet smell of trees.

Stop it! Stop dwelling on things you can't have. Why couldn't she let go?

"Excuse me." A young woman wearing a plaid mini jumper and designer sunglasses approached her at the bottom of the front steps. "Kelsey Albertelli, right?"

The hair on the back of her neck prickling, Kelsey dodged the question. "Do you need something?"

"Is it true Alex Markoff stopped work on his book after you dumped him?"

"Excuse me?" The question caught her off guard. Enough that she foolishly stopped walking, giving the woman time for another question.

"His comeback novel. Is it true his publisher's suing him?"

Suing? Dear Lord, no. That couldn't be true, could it? "I—I—"

"Why don't you mind your own business."

Her insides stilled hearing the baritone. It couldn't be. The timbre was merely similar. They were talking about Alex so her mind conjured up his voice. That's what it had to be, right?

The reporter meanwhile was smirking to land such an exclusive scoop. "Maybe you'd like to address the rumors yourself, Mr. Markoff."

Kelsey turned to find a pair of storm-cloud-colored eyes. Her heart stilled. "Alex?" This had to be a dream.

Though if it was, then her dream was taking her wrist and pulling her away. "Print whatever you want," he tossed over his shoulder. "We have no comment."

Fortunately traffic, not to mention Alex's expert car dodging, kept the reporter from following them across the street. He pulled her through the crowds of pedestrians and down a block before releasing her. "Sorry about that," he said.

Not as sorry as she was that he'd let go of her hand. He was as handsome as ever. Instinctively, her body swayed toward him, seeking contact again.

"What are you doing here?" she heard herself ask.

He smiled that familiar sad smile that was but wasn't. "You got time for a cup of coffee?"

They found seats in a nearby coffee house. Settling in by the window, Kelsey couldn't but think if the reporter walked by, she'd have a perfect view. It was, perhaps, the only coherent thought permeating her brain, everything else drowned in a fog of disbelief. Alex. Here.

"Stuart put me in touch with your temp agency. They told me where to find you," Alex explained, sliding into the seat next to her.

He tracked her down? Don't get your hopes up, Kelsey. Just don't. "So you talked to Stuart."

"Oh, he and I have had several conversations. Some more colorful than others."

She could imagine. The editor had been furious when she called to resign. "He still issuing threats?"

"Nothing I won't work out."

Silence settled between them. Kelsey used the moment to study Alex. He certainly looked better than when she left. He'd gotten a haircut. The curls didn't brush his collar anymore. And he was wearing a striped shirt she'd never seen before, the sleeves rolled to the elbow.

That's when she realized. "You got your cast off."

He wriggled the fingers on his right hand. "Yesterday. Dr. Cohen finally got tired of listening to me complain."

"Must be nice to have two working hands again."

"Feels a little weird actually. Driving here was an adventure. I'm not used to shifting gears again."

"You should have waited till you had more practice."

"But then I would have had to wait longer to see you."

Kelsey grabbed her latte with both hands, steadying herself against the skip in her heart.

Unfortunately she couldn't steady her voice. "You wanted to see me?"

"You left this behind." For the first time, she realized there was a plastic shopping bag by his feet. He must have carried it in with them, but she had been too stunned to notice. Reaching into it, he pulled out a bulky tissue-wrapped package.

Without unwrapping, she knew what the object was. Her mug. "Why'd you leave it?"

"I decided it was time to let some things go."

"I see. What else did you let go of?"

Him. Fantasies. Kelsey kept the answers to herself, settling for running an index finger along the tissue and tape. "You didn't have to drive all the way down here to return a coffee cup."

"Ah, but this isn't an ordinary cup is it? And I didn't. I drove down here to see you."

She closed her eyes. "Alex—"

"You left without saying goodbye."

Is that what his trip was about? Closure? "You were asleep." *And didn't want her.*

"I wish you had."

"Why?" To drag out the inevitable? So he could reject her face to face? "Didn't Farley come check on you? I called and asked him."

"He did."

"Good."

"I would have preferred it had been you."

"I don't know why. You made where you stood pretty clear the second you took off for the woods." Leaving her.

Alex nodded, his Adam's apple bobbing in his throat as he swallowed her words. "I was angry," he said.

"No kidding."

"When I saw that blog article, it was like being thrust back in time. Alyssa and all those articles— it all came rushing back and it hurt. It hurt so much I could barely breathe. I just wanted to be numb again. To find someplace to hide again."

"I get that. Believe me, if anyone gets self-protection, it's me."

"I know. I told you before, we're a lot alike. Defensive and stubborn, among other things. It's why I had to wait and see you in person, because I knew you wouldn't take my calls."

No, thought Kelsey. She wouldn't have, however much she would have longed to.

He reached across the table and covered her hand with his. The warmth ran up her arm, igniting the familiar and painful heat. "When I woke up and you weren't there... The house felt so big and empty. For the first time since I moved to Nuttingwood, I truly felt alone."

Kelsey watched the fingers playing with hers. Her heart was afraid to believe what she was hearing. Surely she was misreading the situation. Again.

"I miss you." With his free hand, he caught her chin, forcing her to meet his eyes. "I don't want to be alone anymore."

Before she could respond, he leaned in and kissed her. A slow, tender, toe-curling kiss right there in the window for all the world to see. When he finished, he pressed his forehead to hers. "God, I missed you."

Me too. More than she thought possible. But as beautiful and perfect as the moment felt, could she trust it? "What about Alyssa? The past?" How did she know he wouldn't decide to hide again, leaving her even more broken?

"You're not Alyssa," he replied. "What we have is completely different. Though if I had any doubts—" chuckling, he pulled a folded piece of paper from his breast pocket "—this would have convinced me."

It was a printout of Tom's blog, written the day after their encounter at Farley's. She'd been too afraid to search for the article herself. As predicted, the story portrayed her as an out-of-control madwoman, an image helped along by a camera-phone shot of her just after she slapped Tom's face. The wild look in her eyes made her cheeks burn.

"Do you have any idea what I thought when I saw this?"

"I lost my temper. I'm sorry."

"Clearly. And don't apologize," Alex said, slipping the paper from her fingers. "No one has ever fought for me when it came to the press. Used me, sold me out, but defend me? Never. Seeing the photo made me realize how lucky I was to have you by my side, and that only a fool would push you away."

"Of course—" he tweaked the tip of her nose "—if someone had stuck around, I would have told her I'd figured that out while in the woods that night. Seems I'm not the only one with a habit of retreating."

She had retreated. She'd hidden behind her temporary status the same way he used Nuttingwood. And what happened? She got hurt anyway. Alex got into her heart, and no amount of running would lodge him loose.

Now with his declaration, he was offering her a chance to stop hiding. If only she could find the strength to accept.

Please don't let this be a dream. "Are you saying…"

"I'm saying I want you to come back."

He wanted her. The words were more beautiful than any novel he could ever write. Still, she hesitated. It all sounded too good to be true. "You mean as your assistant."

"I mean as a lot more than that. I want you. I need you." He cradled her cheek with the palm of his hand, his eyes bright and moist. "That's what I realized sitting out on those rocks all night long. I've needed you since the first time you knocked on my door."

"Could have fooled me," she said, lip trembling. Was this really happening? "If I recall you turned your back and walked away."

"Because I was a jackass," he said with a smile. Kelsey's insides melted at the sight. "You scared the life out of me. You made me feel so much. I liked it. More than I wanted to admit."

The smile grew serious. "But I'm not walking away anymore. Not from you or the feelings. I love you, Kelsey Albertelli."

With those three words, the last of the fear in her heart faded away. No one had ever told her they loved her, and hearing the words come from Alex felt like a dream come true.

Covering his hand with hers, she gazed into his eyes. Eyes no longer stormy but shining like silver. Shining with love. For her.

"I love you too," she whispered. She pulled him toward her for a soul-searing kiss, one that conveyed every ounce of emotion she felt and never dreamed she'd be able to share.

When the kiss finally ended, she opened her eyes and saw the same emotion pouring off of Alex's expression. "What do you say, sweetheart? Ready to go home?"

"So what do you think?"

Kelsey wiped a stray tear from her cheek. "I think you're brilliant," she replied with a sniff.

"Thanks, but what about the story? Do you think it's too schmaltzy?"

Alex paced around the bedroom where Kelsey had camped out to read his finished manuscript. Puddin' lay sprawled by her side, holding down the pile of pages with his paw. Shortly after they returned to Nuttingwood, Alex had been gripped with a creative flash, spending hours scribbling away on his yellow pads. Kelsey didn't mind. Alex in the throes of a creative frenzy was a sight to behold, all brilliance and distraction. The story poured out of him and within a week he had a completed first draft. A beautiful, poignant tale of lost and rediscovered love. "I know Stuart's expecting the other book, but my writing reflects how I feel, and I just can't write dark right now."

"I'm flattered."

"You should be." He flopped down on the bed

beside her and planted a kiss on her nose. "My very beautiful muse."

She kissed him back. "The story's perfect," she told him. "People are going to fall in love with your writing all over again."

"I don't care if readers love me, as long as you do."

More than she ever thought possible. "I think you're safe there." Sometimes she thought she would burst, she loved him so much.

"Good, because I plan on loving you forever."

Manuscript forgotten, they reached for each other. Later, as Kelsey lay sated and sleepy in Alex's arms, she felt him nuzzle her forehead. "I was thinking," he murmured. "Now that I've met my obligations to Stuart, why don't we slip away?"

She smiled. "You mean like hide?"

"Kinda, though I was thinking more like a honeymoon hideaway." He fingered the wedding band on her finger. They'd gotten married in the local town hall, during a break in Alex's writing. "What do you say? We could do Europe? Or is that too far from home for you?"

"I say—" she rolled over, and wrapped her arms around his neck "—that as long as I'm with you, I'm already home."

FRIENDS TO
FOREVER

BY
NIKKI LOGAN

All the characters in this book have no existence outside the imagination of
the author, and have no relation whatsoever to anyone bearing the same name
or names. They are not even distantly inspired by any individual known or
unknown to the author, and all the incidents are pure invention.

First published in Great Britain 2011
Harlequin Mills & Boon Limited,
Eton House, 18-24 Paradise Road, Richmond, Surrey TW9 1SR

FRIENDS TO FOREVER © Nikki Logan 2011

ISBN: 978 0 263 88859 1

23-0211

Harlequin Mills & Boon policy is to use papers that are natural, renewable
and recyclable products and made from wood grown in sustainable forests.
The logging and manufacturing processes conform to the legal environmental
regulations of the country of origin.

Printed and bound in Spain
by Litografia Rosés S.A., Barcelona

Dear Reader,

When I set out to write *Friends To Forever* I wanted to tell a story as engaging and intense as fellow Mills & Boon® author Liz Fielding's fabulous *Wedded in a Whirlwind*, where virtually the whole story unfolded in total darkness over twenty-four hours. I was challenged by the extra emotion and pressure that comes with a heroine being forced into intimate quarters with the worst possible man for her.

Instead of the darkness I gave them icy waters, a sinking sun, and a stranded false killer whale to rescue. I wanted them cold, tired, and desperately afraid for this giant life they were trying to save. I wanted to give them all the reason in the world to lean on each other.

But I gave them one massive, blazing complication: addiction.

Beth Hughes is a recovering alcoholic, and her best friend from childhood is the person she's most afraid to reveal it to. With good reason. Marc Duncannon hardly needs any new ammunition to judge Beth after she tossed away his friendship and then disappeared from the face of the earth for ten years. Marc harbours some deep-seated wounds, Beth harbours the scars of a troubled marriage, and together they find themselves nurturing more than just a whale on the icy shores of Australia's southern coast.

I fell in love with bitter Marc and damaged Beth, and pulled them out of the water sooner than any of us had planned since they'd both been through so much already. But not before that flame of attraction, affection and admiration had well and truly rekindled.

I hope you enjoy reading their story as much as I did writing it.

Nikki Logan xx

www.nikkilogan.com.au

Nikki Logan lives next to a string of protected wetlands in Western Australia, with her long-suffering partner and a menagerie of furred, feathered and scaly mates. She studied film and theatre at university, and worked for years in advertising and film distribution before finally settling down in the wildlife industry. Her romance with nature goes way back, and she considers her life charmed, given she works with wildlife by day and writes fiction by night — the perfect way to combine her two loves. Nikki believes that the passion and risk of falling in love are perfectly mirrored in the danger and beauty of wild places. Every romance she writes contains an element of nature, and if readers catch a waft of rich earth or the spray of wild ocean between the pages she knows her job is done.

Visit Nikki at her website: www.nikkilogan.com.au

For the Garvey clan (two-legged and four). Thank you for your years of friendship and your tolerance of my weird writerly ways.

To Liz for setting the bar so inspirationally high.

And to Rachel for keeping me sane and on the right path with this one.

PROLOGUE

Ten years ago, Perth, Western Australia

'MARC, have you got a minute?'

Beth Hughes caught up with her best friend between classes and steered him away from the teenage throng doing a fast book change between fourth period and fifth. The rock that had taken up residence in her gut since she'd spoken to his mother seemed to swell in size.

Marc looked at her in surprise. Understandable, given the past few weeks of slow retreat on her part. If he'd refused point-blank to go with her she would have understood. A weak part of her wished he would. That would be easier all round.

'Three minutes, Duncannon.' Tasmin Major swanned past, a friendly smile on her Nordic face, tapping her watch. 'Geography waits for no one.'

'I'll be there,' Marc threw after her, trailing Beth around behind the water fountains, tension rich in his deep voice. She ducked between the back wall of the library complex and some badly pruned shrubs into a rubble-filled clearing she'd never visited before. The place others came to do their smoking. Their deep-and-meaningful conversations. Their making-out.

The location got Marc's attention completely. His steps slowed.

'Beth?'

Her pulse beat thick and fast, high in her throat, reducing even further the space for her breath. She sucked in a few mouthfuls of air and forced them down as she turned to face him in the privacy of the little space.

'What are we doing, Beth?' His face was cautious. Closed. She curled her fingers into a ball behind her. 'Does your boyfriend know you're here?'

She stared at him, forcing air past her lips, hating how he'd taken to saying the word *boyfriend*. 'Damien's in fifth period.'

'Where we should be. Or do grades mean less to you now that you hang with the beautiful people?'

Her eyes fell to the dirt he scuffed at his feet, heat invading her cheeks. 'I needed to see you.'

'You see me every day.'

In passing. 'I needed to speak with you.' She lifted her focus. 'In private.'

A grey tinge came over him. His body straightened even more. Not for the first time, Beth noticed how broad he was getting. Those shoulders that had made the swim team captain seek him out a few months back. The way his jaw was squaring off. As if a switch had flipped on his sixteenth birthday and a man had started breaking out of the scrawny exoskeleton she knew as Marc. Maybe she'd left this too late…

Her stomach tightened.

'You have to hide out to talk to me these days?'

She could have pretended to misunderstand but Marc knew her too well. 'I don't want to make trouble with you and Damien.'

'I'm pretty sure McKinley's already aware that we're friends, Beth. I've known you since fourth grade.'

'I don't want… He might read into it.'

'Then you might want to choose another location for this conversation. You do know what The Pit gets used for, right?'

Beth swallowed hard, her eyes dropping to his lips for a second. She forced them up. 'I just wanted privacy.'

The second bell rang and urgent footsteps sprinting into classrooms petered out. Everything around them fell silent. Marc widened his feet and crossed his arms across his chest. 'You got it. Every other student at Pyrmont High is now in class.'

'I'm changing streams,' she blurted before she lost her nerve. 'I'm switching to B.'

Marc stared at her, his nostrils flaring. 'You're changing out of the classes we've been taking all year? Into McKinley's stream?'

'Not because of Damien—'

'Right.'

'I want less science. More arts.'

'Since when?'

'Since now.'

'B-stream is soft, Beth.'

'It has Literature and Philosophy in it. They're uni entrance subjects.'

'You're switching to avoid me.'

The rock in her gut doubled in size. 'No.'

Yes.

'Why?'

A throbbing started up behind her eyes. 'This has nothing to do with you—'

'Bull. You've been backing off from me since term

started. What's going on? No room for a mate in your busy new social schedule, Ms Popularity?'

'Marc—'

'I may not be as smart as you, Beth, but I can see which way the wind is blowing. Is McKinley threatened by me?'

She shook her head. Damien's field of vision was far too narrow for him to notice how Marc was filling out, growing up. He had way too much going on in his life, in his world, to worry about what some science geek was up to. It never occurred to him that Beth would see Marc as anything other than a buddy. An *old* buddy. The expendable buddy she'd had until *he* came along.

And now Damien just expected that she'd switch camps. Just like she switched streams. But since that fed right into what she knew she had to do…

'So that's it, huh? That's what you wanted to tell me—that you're switching classes?'

Beth struggled to take in a breath. He made it sound so minor. But still so ugly. Her words grew tight. 'It means we're only going to have one class together.'

'I know. The best thing about B is that it means only seeing McKinley once a week.' He glared at her. 'You're that desperate to get away from me?'

She would like nothing more than to have Marc Duncannon in her life for ever. But, as it turned out, that wasn't going to work. Guilt tore at her insides and thick shields shot up into place. 'The world revolves around the sun, Marc, not you.'

His face paled and the guilt turned inward, digging into the flesh around her heart. The truth was Marc Duncannon revolved around Beth Hughes and always had. Or, more rightly, the two of them rotated in a complicated, connected orbit. Something both their parents felt was unhealthy.

For him.

If it was just his nut-job mother who thought it, Beth wouldn't have given it another thought. But her own mother agreed and so did her father. And Russell Hughes was never, ever wrong. After a long and tearful conversation, Beth gave him her word that she'd cool things down with Marc for a while. See what happened. And she'd never broken her word yet.

'If you're not doing it to be closer to McKinley and you're not doing it to be away from me then why are you doing it?'

'Why can't I just be doing it for me? Because I want to?'

'Because you don't make decisions like that, Beth. You never have. You plan stuff. You commit.'

'So I've changed my mind. It happens.'

Not to you. It was written loud and clear all over his face. Could he tell she was lying?

'What about uni? Biology?'

A fist squeezed deep in her chest. Damn him for not just letting her go. Why was he pushing this so hard? Forcing her to hurt him more. 'That was your dream, not mine.'

He blinked, then stared. 'After all this time? You've been on board with that for three years.'

She shrugged, faking ambivalence she absolutely did not feel. 'Seemed like a good enough idea at the time.'

'Until something better came along? Or should I say someone?'

'This is not about Damien. I told you.' He stepped

closer and Beth retreated towards the library wall. When had he grown that big?

'I know what you told me. I just don't believe it.' He towered over her. 'We've been friends for eight years, Beth. Half our lifetimes. And you just disappear the moment a popular guy comes sniffing? Are you truly that desperate for affection?'

The library wall pressed into her back. She knew he'd be hurt, and she knew he lashed out when he was hurt. She'd seen him do it with his mother. 'People change, Marc. We all grow up. Maybe we've just grown apart?'

'I know you're changing, Beth. I've watched you.' His eyes glazed over, a deep russet brown, and skimmed her, head to toe. She'd never been more aware of the changing shape of her body. Then he sneered, 'I just never expected you'd change into such a cliché.'

'I'm just... I just need some space. We've lived in each other's pockets for so long we don't even know how to be around anyone else. Or who we are if we're not together.'

Lies, lies...

His snort was ugly. 'Don't dress this up as self-discovery. This is about the school jock making a play for the school tomboy. And you're falling for it hook, line and sinker.' He slammed two hands either side of her face and leaned into her.

She flinched and her heart raced at his closeness. *No, this is about your mother asking me to cut you loose. Begging me to.* She wanted to scream it into the face that she knew as well as her own. But she couldn't. It would kill him to discover what his only surviving parent thought he was worth.

'You could be anything you want, Marc. You don't

need me to be it with you. There's a whole world for us to discover.'

He leaned in further. The tightening in her body where he touched it wasn't fear. Marc was the only person on the planet she trusted implicitly never to hurt her.

'What's wrong with us discovering that together?' he ground, his chest heaving with restraint. 'We have history. A bond. What does McKinley have that I don't have?'

No rock-tight bond. No complicated history. No parents pressuring her to put some distance between them.

'I'm only asking for space, Marc. What's wrong with that?'

His face twisted and he swore. 'I've been giving you space for two years, Beth. Maybe if I'd done *this* back then I wouldn't be standing here now getting the brush-off from my best friend.'

And then suddenly his mouth was crushing down on hers, his body pressing her into the hard limestone of the library wall behind her. Shock stiffened her against the hardness of his chest as his hands slipped down to tangle in her hair and hold her face still for the assault of his lips. She swam in his scent, in his angry heat, in his perfect, practised kiss. The unfamiliar slide of a blazing hot mouth over her own and the furious press of his body. And then the dizzying sensation of their flesh melding into one, his enormous hands sliding around to protect her head from the lumpy wall behind her, his mouth shifting and softening on hers.

And then—somehow—she was kissing him back. Her own mouth moved tentatively against his and her body pressed forward. A choked whimper cracked

deep in her throat and Marc worked his tongue past
her uncertain lips coaxing them open. His furnace-
hot tongue twisted and danced around hers, intensity
pooling around her, engulfing all. Her body *whoofed*
to flaming life, hormones tangling and exploding like
kindling around them.

Overwhelming and unfamiliar, something she'd never
allowed herself to dream. To want.

Marc.

Suddenly Beth was free and Marc staggered back
against the force of her desperate shove. She held up
a shaking hand to stop him coming closer. His face
darkened as he looked at her.

'Does McKinley know you kiss like that?' His chest
heaved.

How could he know? They'd never kissed. She'd
never kissed anyone. Until today.

She dragged her fist across her lips. 'Don't ever—'
do that again, make me feel that again '—touch me
again.' Her voice was husky and low and appallingly
unfamiliar.

'Beth…'

A world of emotions surged up and spilled over.
'Don't *speak* to me…again.'

His frown doubled. 'You don't mean—'

She lifted tortured eyes to him. 'Why does it have to
be all or nothing with you? I just wanted some space,
Marc. Room for us both to discover who we are. That's
all. Did you think you could keep me all to yourself for
ever?'

'I know who I am. And I thought I knew who you
were. But I guess not.' He crossed the little clearing in
two steps. 'You want space, Elizabeth? Fine. Take as

much as you need. If you're that desperate, then have a good life with McKinley.'

And then he was gone.

Her best friend.

Like a kite in a wild wind, she'd tried to give him some rope, some height, but instead he'd ripped completely free and was gone. Her fingers trembled as they touched her swollen lips and she slid down the rough library wall until she huddled in a tearless, emotionless, empty heap.

CHAPTER ONE

Ten years later, south coast, Western Australia

WHO knew silence came in so many shades?

There was the deep, black silence late at night, under the West Australian stars, miles from anywhere. The earthy green silence of Beth's shambolic warehouse studio, only broken by the splashes of colour from her latest artworks. There was the newly discovered, beige-coloured silence inside her head, where voices and thoughts used to clamour but had now all eased into a comfortable hum.

And there was this one…

The simmering red silence of a man who was not particularly pleased to see her. Not that Beth had imagined he would be. It was why she'd put this off for so long. The awful sound of nothing echoed through the heartbeat thumping past her eardrums. She cleared her throat.

'Marc.'

He may have been half a house larger than the boy she remembered, but Marc Duncannon had two trademark giveaways and one was the way he stood when he was on guard, legs apart as if readying himself for a physical assault.

Muscular arms stole up to cross in front of a broad chest as he continued to stare wordlessly at her. Twisted humour raced in to fill the aching void inside where she wasn't letting herself feel. While he'd grown a kick-butt chest in ten years, she was no bigger in that department than when he'd last seen her. Yet another disappointment for him.

Coming here suddenly seemed like a spectacularly bad idea. 'Are you not even going to say hello?'

He nodded briskly, his lips tight, resenting opening at all. 'Beth.'

One stony word, but loaded with meaning and breath-stealing in its timbre. More than she'd had from him in over a decade. A total contrast to the way he used to say her name. Beth. Betho. Bethlehem. They'd had their short lifetimes to come up with stupid nicknames for each other. He'd only called her *Elizabeth* once. The day he'd kissed her.

The day she'd ripped out his heart.

She swallowed past the lump threatening her air supply. Past the welling excitement that she was here—with Marc—again. 'How are you?'

'On my way out.'

Okay... She'd prepared herself to be unwelcome but it still felt so foreign radiating from him. 'I just needed... I'd like a couple of minutes. Please?'

His hazel eyes darted away briefly but the miracle of any part of him moving seemed to thaw the rest of him out. His whole body twisted and he resumed loading equipment into his four-wheel drive. Beth risked closing the gap, but her breath got shorter with her distance from him, until she either stopped advancing on him or took her last living gasp.

Seeing him again would almost be worth it.

He threw words out like a shark net to entangle her before she got nearer. 'You could stand there gawping or you could help me load the Cruiser.'

Beth scrambled to help, stunned by the gift of so many words in a row. It wasn't friendly. But it wasn't silence. And, given it was possibly the only chance she was going to get, she took it.

'I went to your old house. Your neighbours told me where you were,' she started to jabber. 'I heard about your mum. What happened? You two were so close…'

Oh-so-familiar eyes lifted below hooded lids and glared at her. Intense and intensely…adult. 'That's what you've come all this way to ask?'

Her heart lurched. Marc didn't do sarcasm when they were kids but it seemed he'd perfected the fine art in the years since she'd seen him.

'No. I'm sorry…' It was lame but what else could she say?

He turned to face her and straightened, frustrated. 'What for, Beth? For turning up unannounced or for dropping off the face of the earth for a decade?'

How could she have forgotten what a straight shooter he was? She took a shaky breath. 'That's why I've come. I wanted to explain—'

He moved off again. 'You'll have to explain some other time. Like I said, I'm on my way out.'

She watched as he tossed a few final items into his dusty black Land Cruiser. A satellite phone. A first aid kit. A wetsuit. She frowned. 'Where are you going?'

The hard glare he shot her from under the broad ridge of his brow should have had her quailing, if not for the fact that she'd developed immunity long ago, from exposure to much worse. Courtesy of her husband.

'We've had a report of a stranding out at Holly's Bay. I'm going to check it out.'

'Stranding?'

'A whale, Beth. It needs help. I don't have time to entertain you.'

She fought the bristle his unkind words inspired. She was here to help her healing process, not to pass the time. Would she have put herself through this otherwise? 'I just need a minute...'

He ignored her and moved around to the driver's side door and yanked it open. 'The whale may not have a minute. You've already slowed me down.'

She made her decision in a blink. It had cost her too much to come here today; she couldn't let him just walk away from her. Who knew if she'd find the courage to try again? She sprinted around to the passenger side of the four-wheel drive and leaped in as he started it. Up close and in the confines of a cabin, he was bigger even than he'd seemed at a distance.

'Get out, Beth.'

His voice certainly fitted the new him. Deep, rough. But still essentially Marc. That part tugged at her. 'I need to talk to you. If I have to do that on the move, I will. Whatever it takes.'

He practically growled, 'You're wasting time.'

Anger finally broke through her carefully constructed veneer. 'No, *you* are, Marc. Drive!'

Marc Duncannon concentrated on keeping his hands glued to the steering wheel, cemented there harder than clams on a reef. The tighter he held them, the less likely they were to shake, to give him away. He didn't want her getting the slightest clue about how thrown he was.

Beth Hughes.

She was still the same lean, athletic build she'd been as a kid. It still suited her, even if it made him wonder how long ago she'd had her last meal. Same high brows, straight nose. Full coral lips. He would have recognised her even if she hadn't spoken and he hadn't heard again the soft tones he'd given up as a memory, but there was something very worn out about the way she held herself. The way her long dark hair hung, defeated, from a dead straight parting. As if she was doing her best not to stand out. Very un-Beth. She'd always been such a show pony.

Now she looked a little too much like his mother's tormented appearance the last time he'd seen her. He clenched his jaw and leaned on the accelerator harder, flying down the long track leading from the homestead to the coastal highway.

His vehicle now reeked of Beth's particular scent. That skin cream that, clearly, she still used after all these years. Coconut something. Chemical free. Cruelty free. The scent he associated with summer and beaches and bikinis…and Beth. The scent that would take weeks to fade from his upholstery.

The way it had taken months to finally force her from his mind. Or not, he realised as every bit of him tightened. Seemed it had only lain dormant. Buried deep. Two seconds in her presence and half a childhood of memories came flooding back.

So much for moving on.

He concentrated on the road ahead.

From the corner of his vision, he saw her twisted mouth, teeth chewing on her full lips. The old habit socked him in the guts. She used to do that when she was problem-solving or trying to outfox him. But back then she couldn't sustain it and they'd break apart into one of her heart-stopping smiles. Not today. Her lips opened and she took a deep breath, ready to hit him with whatever it was she wanted.

'Since when did you become a whale rescuer?'

Not what he was expecting. And why did she sound as rattled as he was? She had the upper hand here. It surprised him enough to answer. 'It's part of life on the south coast. And I'm the closest trained landholder.'

'You train for this?'

'Through experience.'

'How many times have you done it?'

'Five. Two last year. This stretch of coast is notorious for it.'

'Why here, particularly?'

Small talk killed him. Especially with the one person he'd never needed it with. This was what they were now? Maybe never seeing her again was the better option. He shrugged. 'No one knows.'

Silence fell, thick and muddy. He slowed the vehicle and yanked the steering wheel hard to the right. They bumped off the asphalt onto a badly graded limestone track and headed towards the massive expanse of ocean. The crescent bay opened out before them like an electric-blue half-moon.

'How long before we get there?' she asked, voice tight.

He could practically feel her brain turning over. Her heart thumping. It vibrated off her and slammed straight into the waves of tension coming off him. 'About one minute longer than you said you needed.'

She saw his sideways glance. Interpreted it correctly. 'I needed to see you. To explain.' She cleared her throat. 'To apologise.'

Apologise? 'For what?'

Her mouth thinned. 'Marc…'

'Friendships end, Beth. It happens.' He used the casual shrug to shake free some of his tension.

Her eyes flared with confusion but then they hardened and blazed with determination he'd never seen from her. Adult Beth had some balls, then. 'Nonetheless, I've come a long way to see you. I'd like to say what I need to say…'

The Land Cruiser bumped up off the track onto the small dunes and Marc manoeuvred them as close to the edge as he safely could. The white crescent shore stretched out before them, meeting the blue of the Southern Ocean. Next stop, Antarctica. Down on the sand, about twenty feet apart, two large, dark shapes rolled and buffeted in the shallows.

Two whales. Marc swore under his breath.

'Your explanations will have to wait, Beth. I have work to do.'

CHAPTER TWO

BETH took one look at the scene unfolding on the beach and pushed herself into gear. It had been two years; her needs could wait a little longer. Those animals couldn't.

Marc grabbed his satellite phone and started dialling even as he ran to the back of his vehicle, peeling off his clothes as he went. By the time he had his T-shirt and jeans off, he'd communicated their location and the number of stranded whales to someone at the Shire and asked them to rally assistance.

Beth did her best to get busy lifting items out of the car to avoid staring at him, open-mouthed. Once-gangly Marc Duncannon had spent some time in the gym, apparently. The weights section. Her belly flipped on itself in a most unfamiliar way.

He tossed the disconnected phone into the back of the vehicle and stepped into his wetsuit, hauling it up over muscular legs and then flexing his broad back as he shrugged it up over his shoulders and arms. As soon as it was secure, he snared up the first aid kit and a small bag of supplies and thrust the phone into it. He shoved a snatch-strap, rope and every ockie-strap he could rummage up in behind it. Then he threw his T-shirt, a hooded trainer and an old towel at Beth, saying, 'You're going to need this,' and was off, down the dunes, racing towards the water.

Beth did her best to keep up. She stumbled several times in the thick sand and paused to kick off her unsuitable shoes, losing more ground on Marc. But she didn't need to be near him to know what was going on; his stiff body language was as clear as a neon sign as he ran down the shore, close to the first whale.

The sleek, marble-skinned animal was already dead.

An awful sorrow washed over her: that she might have delayed Marc for the precious minutes that counted. That this enormous creature was already gull-food because of her.

Marc paused briefly, those magnificent shoulders drooping slightly, but then he kicked on, further down the beach to where the second body rolled in time with the surf. As he got closer, he slowed and took a wide approach, lifting his hands high in the air in warning. Beth instantly slowed.

It was alive.

By the time she caught up with him, he was on his second wide pass of the beleaguered mammal. It lay partially submerged in the quicksand where earth met ocean, every second wave high enough to wash gently over its lower half. But exposed parts of its upper body were already dangerously dry. Compared to the liquid mercury-looking surface of wet whale skin, the dry parts looked like the handbag she'd left in her hire car at Marc's farm.

That couldn't be good.

'Put the sweatshirt on, Beth.' He didn't bother with a please and she didn't expect niceties right now. But it didn't mean she was prepared to be dictated to. Not any more.

'It's thirty-three degrees. I'll boil.'

'Better that than burn to a crisp. We're going to be out here for some time.' He moved to her side and relieved her of his T-shirt and the towel. Then he zipped up the wetsuit more fully over his chest, fastened the neck strap and tugged a cap down hard over his shaggy hair. 'And you're about to get wet. You'll thank me in two hours.'

'Two hours?' They'd be out in the water for a couple of hours, with an injured dinosaur? Alone? But Marc wasn't worried; he ran headlong into the water between the dead whale and the live one and soaked the towel and his shirt.

His five-times experience certainly showed.

By the time Beth had wriggled herself into Marc's sweatshirt and pulled up the hood for some shade, he was already beside the dangerous giant. A false killer whale, Marc told her. The fact it was not a true killer whale didn't fill her with any confidence. It was still big enough to send them both flying with a toss of its wishbone tail, which bore an arrow-head-shaped scar. One enormous dark eye rolled wildly at his approach. Marc slowed and started speaking softly. Steadily. Random words that meant nothing.

The eye wasn't fooled for a minute.

But when Marc gently laid the saturated towel onto its parched skin, the eye rolled fully shut and the beast let off a mighty groan that vibrated the sand beneath Beth's feet. Her heart squeezed. It wasn't pain, it was sheer relief. She sprinted forward and met Marc in the water, hoping that he'd think the tears in her eyes were from the glare coming off the ocean.

'Around the other side,' he ordered brusquely, glancing up as she wiped a stray one away. 'Stay up-beach from that ventral fin; it's pure muscle.'

'The *what* fin…?'

'Underneath.' He threw the sodden T-shirt her way and she just caught it. 'The fin closest to her belly.'

The whale barely moved as they took it in turns draping the wet fabric over its parched skin. Within fifteen minutes, Beth's wrists ached from wringing out the water to run down the whale's hide and she moved to a slosh-and-drag technique instead. Brutal on the back, but the most effective way of keeping the poor animal wet. A fierce concentration blazed in Marc's eyes, a flush of exertion highlighting the familiar ridge of his cheekbone. Familiar yet unfamiliar.

Her mind bubbled with memories of a younger Marc studying. Or whipping her butt at chess. Or listening to her dramas. That same focus. That same intensity. No question that some parts of him hadn't changed.

Even if the rest had.

Neither of them spoke, their focus centred on the whale. Beth's reason for coming to the south coast flitted entirely out of her head, dwarfed in significance compared to the life and death battle going on in the shallows of Holly's Bay.

'You need a break.' Marc's voice was reluctant enough and firm enough to cut through the hypnotic routine of *slosh-and-drag…slosh-and-drag.* But it was also dictatorial enough to get Beth's hackles up.

'I'm fine.'

'You're parched. Your lips are like prunes. Stop and rehydrate. You're no use to either of us if you collapse.'

Either of us. Him or the whale. Beth didn't want to see the sense in that but he was right; if his focus was on rescuing her, the whale could die. She straightened and used the sleeve of his sweatshirt to wipe at the sweat streaming into her eyes.

'I could use a swig of water myself,' he said, clearly hoping she'd fall for the incredibly juvenile ploy, but she barely heard him, focusing only on four little letters.

Swig.

Her body immediately picked up and ran with the evocative image: an icy bottle straight from the cooler, the hissing sound the cap made twisting off. The clink of the cap hitting the sink. Her near favourite sound in the world. Second only to the breathy sigh of a cork coming out of a good bottle of Chenin Blanc.

A sound she hadn't heard for two years. Since she'd stopped drinking.

Her mouth would have watered if it hadn't been so dry. Like Pavlov's dog, just the thought of a particular spirit could still make her saliva flow. Despite everything she'd done to put it behind her, her body still compromised her from time to time. When she least expected it. It sure was not going to be happy with what was about to cross its lips.

She moved up the beach and hauled a two-litre bottle of still water out of one of Marc's supply bags and then cracked the cap. She suddenly realised how thirsty she was, but she was determined not to let Marc see that. She stood and jogged back to his side of the whale and passed him the bottle first. He glared at her meaningfully, but took it and helped himself to a deep, long draw of purified water. His Adam's apple bobbed thirstily with each long swallow.

'Once this is gone we can use the bottle to help wet the whale,' she said.

Marc shook his head. 'We're going to have to make this last. I only have one more.'

Four litres of water. Between two people, on a blistering Australian day, with reflected light bouncing up off the surface of the salty, salty water.

Oh, joy.

He finished drinking and passed the bottle straight back to her. Beth's pride had limits and watching the way the clean water had leaked down his throat had stretched it way too far. Every fibre of her being wanted to feel liquid crossing her tongue.

If that had to be water, so be it.

She didn't guzzle, though she well could have. At least AA had taught her something about restraint. Greedily sculling their precious water supply was not something she wanted Marc to witness. And a small part of her was afraid that once she started she might not stop.

She made herself lower the bottle after a few restorative swallows and, buoyed by the wetness coursing into her body, she jogged lightly back through the beach sand and knelt to slide the bottle into the shade of Marc's supply bag. As she did, she dislodged the other occupants. The satellite phone. First aid kit. A clutch of muesli and chocolate bars, a small hand-wound torch. The second container of water. And a—

Beth leapt back as if burned.

A large seventies-era silver hip flask tumbled out onto the sand. Ornate, neatly stoppered and probably his father's before it was Marc's, one of the few remembrances he might have of the man who had died when Marc was nine. The sort you kept whisky in, or vodka, or just about any liquor you didn't care to advertise. Beth didn't need to pick it up to know it was full of something bad. He wouldn't have thrown it in the emergency pack for nothing.

She shoved it back into the bag and rose to her feet, shaking. She hadn't worked this hard for two years to blow it now. She glanced at Marc to see if he'd noticed, but he was too busy gently rubbing the wet towel over the whale's bulbous face to notice.

She'd finally hardened herself against facing her demons on every street corner in the city. Every billboard. Every radio commercial. To encounter liquor on a remote beach in the middle of nowhere. In front of Marc... What kind of a sick karmic joke was this?

She stumbled as her feet sank back into the loose shore sand and water rushed into the twin voids around her ankles. As she went down onto one knee, a wave came in and soaked her to her middle, her pale blue jeans staining instantly darker with salt water, the cold assault shocking her mind off the hip flask and what it held.

But her sunken perspective was how she noticed something else. The whale's ventral fin was partly underwater, even after the wave washed back out. The one that had been high and dry a couple of hours ago when they'd arrived.

She scrambled to her feet, nearly falling across the whale in her haste.

'Marc...'

He looked up at her, fatigue in his face, and something else. Fierce determination. This whale was not going to die while he breathed.

'Marc...the tide's coming in.'

He turned his eyes heavenward and closed them briefly in salute. His lips moved briefly.

'Is that good?'

Hazel eyes lowered back to hers, clear and honest, as if they'd forgotten she was an unwelcome blast from the past. 'That's very good. Maybe we can refloat her.'

'It's a her?'

'You can tell by her short, curved dorsal fin.' His head jerked in the direction of the other whale. 'I think that one might have been her calf.'

The unfamiliar stab of grief slid in under her ribs and washed over her with another shove of the waves. This mum had followed her baby in to shore. Maybe she'd stranded herself trying to save her little one. Was that why her eyes kept rolling around—was she trying to find her calf? Empathy for the animal's loss nearly overwhelmed her, stealing the breath she desperately needed to keep her muscles working. But she embraced the pain and almost celebrated it. Two years ago, she wouldn't have felt such sorrow. Two years ago, she wouldn't have felt much of anything.

Her eyes fell back on the suffering whale. Her ire—and her voice—lifted. 'Where are they?'

He kept up the rhythmic sloshing. 'Who?'

'The rescuers. Shouldn't they be here by now?'

The sloshing stopped. He stared. 'We *are* the rescuers, Beth. What do you think we've been doing for the past three hours?'

'I meant others. People with boats. Shovels. Whale-rescue devices.'

The sun must have been causing a mirage… That almost looked like a smile. The one she'd never imagined she'd see today.

'Oh, right, the whale-rescue devices.' Then he

sobered. 'A big group of volunteers is about fifty clicks to the west, helping with another stranding. As soon as they have that situation stabilised they'll be out to help us. Our solo whale doesn't stack up against their entire pod, unfortunately.'

'A whole pod stranded?' Beth cried. 'What is wrong with these creatures?'

If not for the tender way she ran the dripping T-shirt across the whale's skin, taking unnecessary care to avoid its eyes, Marc would have read that as petulance. But he squinted against the lowering sun and really looked at her strained face. Much paler than when they'd started. Despite the blazing sun. Back to the colour it had been when she'd first climbed out of her rental car back at his property.

Beth was tired. Emotionally and physically spent already, and they'd only been out here a couple of hours. She looked as wretched as his mother when she was coming off a particularly bad bender. The bleached cheeks and shadowed eyes had the same impact on him that his mother's had.

Used to. Before he shut down that part of him.

Beth had much worse to get through yet. The rescue was only just beginning. Maybe he should have shoved her out back at the homestead. Done her a favour and sent her packing. If he'd left just five minutes earlier he would have been out here alone, anyway, so what was the difference if she left now? He had enough supplies to get him through the night.

Water for life. Food for strength. Potassium for cramps. Whisky and wetsuit for warmth. Enough for a day, anyway. Hopefully by then backup would have arrived.

'It often happens this way,' he said, taking pity on her

confusion. 'There's nearly forty volunteers at the other stranding, apparently.'

Beth stared at him between refreshing her whale-washer in the ocean and leaning towards him over the animal as the water ran down over it. 'Forty! Couldn't they spare us a couple of people?'

'Anyone spare is already on their way to other isolated strandings that the aerial boys identify along this stretch of coast. They know we've got this one in hand.'

Beth laughed a little too much and waved her paltry, dripping T-shirt around. 'This doesn't feel very in hand.' Marc dived forward and covered the whale's blowhole to protect it from the cascading water. The whale feebly blew out at the same time. At least she could still do that much.

He found himself suddenly possessed of very little tolerance. 'Hey, if you want to go, knock yourself out. I'll do better without your negativity anyway.'

Beth lifted her head and glared, the first sign of fire in those bleak eyes since they'd got out of his Land Cruiser. 'I'm not negative; I'm terrified. I don't know what I'm doing.'

The raw honesty spoke to some part of him a decade old. It triggered all kinds of unwelcome protective instincts in him. This really was more than she'd bargained for when she came cruising down his drive, looking all intense.

He sighed. 'You're doing fine. Just keep her body wet and her blowhole dry. It's all we can do.'

They fell to silence and into a hypnotic rhythm in time with the wash of the ocean, the groans of the whale and the *slosh...slosh* of their wet fabric. Marc did his best to ignore her, but his eyes kept finding their way back to her. To features drawn tight that had once shone with zest. Trying to work out why she'd come. Part of him was curious—the part that had always wondered what the heck had happened all those years ago. But the other part of him wasn't into lifting lids off unknown boxes any more. And he'd done far too good a job of driving Beth Hughes clear out of his memory. Until today.

'Do you need to contact Damien? Tell him where you are?'

Frosty eyes lifted to his. 'I'm not required to report in.'

'I didn't say that. But I figured he'd be concerned about you.' She looked as if a stiff breeze would send her tumbling. *I'd be worried if you were mine to worry about.*

Whoa. Thank God for inner monologue. Imagine if that little baby had slipped out. A blast well and truly from the past.

Beth dipped her head so the hood shielded her face from his view. 'He won't be.'

There was something in the way she said it. So final. So cold. He couldn't help himself, although he really didn't want to have any interest in her life 'Why not?'

Slosh…slosh. Silence.

'Beth?'

Even the whale seemed to flinch at the sudden outburst of skinny arms to its right. 'We're not together any more, okay? I no longer answer to anyone.'

Her marriage was over? The King and Queen of Pyrmont High were no more? A nasty imp deep inside him badly wanted to smile. But there was nothing satisfying about the pain on her face.

'I'm sorry, Beth.'

'Don't be,' she mumbled from down the tail end of the whale. 'I'm not.'

She moved like a car wash up and down the three metres of the whale's body, sloshing as she went. The animal was relaxed and trusting enough now to let her do it without fussing. Her hand trailed along the marbled mercury of its skin as she went and every now and again it shuddered as though ticklish. He empathised completely. There was a time he would have given just about anything to have her hands touch him like that.

He slammed a door on that memory.

So she'd married McKinley young but now she was single again. And hot on the trail of her old pal Marc. A light bulb suddenly came on in his mind. 'I hope you're not expecting to pick up where we left off, Beth?'

She froze and looked up at him. 'Excuse me?'

Ooh. He hadn't forgotten that arctic look. The ice princess. There was a masochistic kind of pleasure in having it levelled on him again after so long. 'Because as far as I'm concerned we were done that day behind the library.'

Even under the hood of her oversized sweatshirt he could see her nostrils flaring. About as wildly as the whale's blowhole. 'You think I'm here to come on to you?'

'I'm still waiting to find out why you're here. You came a long way for something. Go ahead and say what you wanted to say.'

Permission seemed to paralyse her. Her mouth opened and closed wordlessly several times. Whatever she was going to say, it wasn't easy.

Her hands stilled on the whale. 'I hurt you back in school and I wanted you to know I'm very sorry,' her soft voice began.

Every part of him stretched sling-shot taut. He cast her a sideways glance. 'You didn't hurt me.'

Her pretty face folded. 'That can't be true. I was there, I remember...'

'What do you remember?'

She blew air out of full lips. 'How you looked. How we left things.'

How badly he'd handled himself? He shrugged. 'Like I said. Friendships end.'

'Not usually like that. You kissed me, Marc.'

Right on cue, he got a flash of the wide-eyed awakening on her face. The coconut taste on his tongue as her mouth had parted with surprise. As he'd sunk into the heaven of her lips. He clenched his teeth against the bittersweet memory. Forced it back down deep where it belonged. His muscles clamped up again. He calmed himself for the whale's sake. It was stressed enough for all of them.

'That wasn't a kiss, Beth. I was trying to make a point.'

Confusion marred her pale skin. 'What point?'

A lip-searing, unforgettable point. A friendship ending point. 'That you would have kissed anyone offering at that point.' *That you didn't need McKinley for that.*

She disguised her sharp intake of breath behind loudly dumping her whale-washer in the drink and then she bought herself some recovery time by wringing the life out of his old T-shirt. For one second he felt like a heel for hurting her. But he pushed that away too. Best course now—like back when he was a kid—was not to let himself feel anything at all for Beth Hughes. Time had passed. They'd both moved on. In a couple of hours she'd be gone.

'It's been ten years. It's not like I've been sitting around obsessing about it.' *At least not for more than a few months.* 'What else is there to say?'

Slosh…slosh. Her eyes glittered as she measured what he'd said. 'Other than "Good to see you, Beth".'

Her tight words cracked and his stomach flipped fully over. He was still a sucker for those big brown eyes if they were awash. Either she was a master manipulator or this really was a big deal for her. But it was for him too, after years of not letting himself think about her. *Good to see her?*

'We never lied to each other before.'

Her face grew pale beneath his hoodie and he turned his attention back to the whale, unable to stomach her expression.

They worked silently for another twenty minutes until Marc couldn't stand the quiet. 'If you want to take the Cruiser back to my place, that's fine. I'll get a lift back when reinforcements come.'

She lifted tired eyes. 'No, thank you.'

No? 'Why are you still here? You've said what you came for. You're sorry for the hurt you imagine you caused.' He made his shrug much more casual than he felt. 'Doesn't that mean we're done?'

It should. If it was the real reason. He could see in her eyes it wasn't.

They flicked away and back in a blink. 'You haven't accepted my apology yet.'

That stopped his hands and he slowed his bend to re-wet his towel. 'Is that a requirement?'

Her eyes held his. 'I'd like you to.'

Which meant the apology was more about her than him. *Why does that surprise you? Just acknowledge the woman's apology and get her the hell off this beach!*

Yet something in him couldn't do it. 'I don't see you for ten years and then you turn up looking for absolution?' Uncertainty filled her eyes. 'Why would you expect it?'

'Because…' Her pale face scrunched up, confused. As if she hadn't thought about that until now. 'Because you're Marc.'

He had to take two steps back from the whale for that one. In case it felt his surging anger through his touch. 'That might have been our dynamic as kids, Beth, but a lot has changed in the years you've been gone. I'm not a gutless boy any more.'

She seemed shocked. 'You were never gutless, Marc. You always went straight for what you wanted.'

Not always. He struggled to get his temper under control, his hands back on the whale. 'Bully for me.'

'You don't believe me?'

'I don't believe that's why you thought I'd fall for your apology.'

Her colour started to rise. 'I just want to know that you forgive me for what I did.'

And here we go… 'Ah, now we're getting to it. So, in addition to accepting your apology, you want forgiveness? What is this, some kind of twelve-step programme?' He'd studied up on those back when he was researching his mother's condition. Back when he still gave a damn. 'Make good for all the people you've burned in life?'

It was Beth's turn to sway away from the whale. He crashed onwards, too worked up to give much care for her enormous eyes. 'Where did I fall on the list, Beth? How did I fare against your other screw-ups in life? I hope I was at least in the top half.'

Her eyes blazed and it was beautiful and awful at the

same time. Now that he was faced with opportunity, hurting her was not quite as satisfying as he'd imagined back when he was seventeen and holding all those feelings close to him.

She stood and stared, her head tilted, her eyes glittering magnificently. 'Thank you, Marc. This actually makes it easier.'

He was already frowning into the sun too much to do it further. 'What?'

'In my head you were still the old Marc—gentle and concerned about people. I was really anxious about facing that man. But the new Marc is just a sarcastic pig and much easier not to give a stuff about.'

He snorted. 'Story of my life.'

She shook her head, disgust all over her face. 'Oh, boo hoo…'

Only one person on this planet had ever spoken to him like this—cut-throat honest. Getting straight down to the bones of an issue. And here she was again.

He gave as good as he got. 'Last time I saw you, Beth, the only thing you wanted from me was a goodbye. Well, you got it. Don't kid yourself that I've been mooching over that all these years. It was a good lesson to learn so early in life. It toughened me up for the real world. It drove me to succeed at school and in life."

She forced her tiring body to scoop up more water and sloshed it all over the whale, but never took her eyes off him. 'Fine. Here it is, Marc. I'm sorry that I hurt you back in high school. I made the wrong decision and I've come to regret that in my life. I'm sorry that I bailed on our plans for uni, too, and that I might have contributed to you not going—'

Pain lanced through him. 'Don't flatter yourself.'

She persevered. 'But most of all I'm really sorry that

I came to find you today. Because, up until now, you were the person I held in my heart as the symbol of everything I wanted to be. Clever, loyal, generous. I've spent years wishing I was more like you and—finally—I see the truth. Beneath all those new muscles you're just an angry, bitter, *small* man, Marcus Duncannon. And I've been wasting my energy feeling so bad about what I did.'

She stood up straighter and looked around her. This was where she should have stormed off. He could see she was dying to—making that kind of spectacular scene just wasn't complete without a flounce-off. But she had nowhere to go and a whale to save.

He blinked at her. There was absolutely nothing he could say to an outburst like that, which was fine because he was having a hard time getting past one small part of the significant mouthful she'd just spewed. It clanged in his mind like a chime.

You were the person I held in my heart... Every part of him rebelled against the impact of those words on his pulse rate. His mouth dried up and he could feel his heart beating in his throat.

Ridiculous. Unacceptable. She didn't even know she'd said it.

But it burned like a brand into his mind.

They stood staring at each other, chests heaving equally. Then all the fight drained out of him. 'Don't dress it up, Beth. Tell me what you really think.'

She glared at him but couldn't sustain it. The tiniest of smiles crept through. 'It's taken me a decade, but I've learned to say what I think. I don't pull any punches these days.'

'You never had any trouble with confidence as far as

I remember. You were always brash, always willing to go headlong into something with me. With anyone.'

But particularly with me... Those days were some of the best in his life. Back when Marc Duncannon and Beth Hughes were interchangeable in people's minds. There was nothing she wasn't willing to try once.

Fearless.

Marc frowned on the realisation. No, she hadn't been fearless. There were things that had definitely scared the pants off her, but she'd done them. With him by her side.

She looked up at him earnestly. Pained. 'That is not something I count under my virtues, Marc. Being an enthusiastic follower is not the same as thinking for yourself.'

He snorted. 'You're not trying to tell me you were an innocent accomplice?' He wasn't ready for another woman in his life blaming everyone around for her problems.

'I was a completely willing accomplice. I lived to follow you into trouble. I was fully up for any crazy idea you had.'

'Then what...?'

'I hadn't learned yet to ask for what I wanted. To put myself first.'

His stomach sank. *McKinley.* 'Don't tell me... You developed that sense right around the final year of school.'

She stared at him. Hard. 'On the contrary. It took me nearly a decade.'

Somewhere in there was some hidden meaning he should probably have been seeing. He felt like he always used to with Beth, as if he was operating on seven second delay. Always the last to get it. Always needing things spelled out. He'd forgotten what that felt like. He used to think that he was just not bright enough for her but now, with adult eyes, he wondered if it wasn't just that she tended to be cryptic.

He blew out a breath. 'Okay, as much as I'm enjoying our little trip down memory lane, it's not helping this whale. I want you to take over on the wetting; I'm going to try something.'

'Wait! What?'

'You'll see.'

Beth shifted nervously. 'No, I… Will it take long?'

'Probably. Why?'

'I need to…' She looked around. 'Despite the heat…'

Understanding hit him. 'Oh. Well, you're in the ocean. Go here.'

The look she gave him was hysterical. 'I'm not going to pee in the water while you're standing in it. And while a whale's lying in it.'

'What do you reckon the whale does, Beth?'

'I'm not a whale!'

True enough. She was slight enough to be the krill that whales liked to feast on. 'Look, the tide's running diagonally from the south, so if you go over there—' he pointed to a spot about ten metres away '—then the whale and I will be safely upstream.' He grinned. 'As it were.'

Beth turned and looked at the spot, then back at him. 'I can't.'

'Bashful bladder?'

'You're not helping, Marc.' She started to search around the shore for another alternative.

'Before you even suggest it, the dunes are not safe. Tiger snakes. Up beach might be okay but it's a lot more exposed and it's probably safer if we stay fairly close together.' *If you stay close to me.* 'Besides, a swim first will cool you off.'

'Oh, my God…' She looked around one more time, desperately, as if a Portaloo might materialise on the beach if she willed it hard enough.

It was difficult not to find that panicked expression endearing. Despite everything. He tightened his jaw. 'Come on, Princess. When did you get so precious? The quicker you get out there the quicker it'll be over.'

'Are you laughing at me?'

He forced his face into a more neutral expression. 'I wouldn't dream of it.'

'I'm sure you'd have the same concern if you were in my situation.'

'I was in your situation, Beth. About an hour ago. I just didn't make a fuss about it.'

It took her about two seconds to realise he hadn't left the water. Or his wetsuit. She lurched away from the whale—and him—and waded hastily away. 'Oh, my God. Men are so disgusting!'

He just grinned at her, the years falling away. 'It's human,' he cried after her as she kept striding up-beach, slowly into deeper water. He kept poking, in the painfully reasonable tone he knew she hated the most, calling after her fleeing shape. 'We all do it.'

Her cheeks had flamed from a heap more than windburn. Watching the mighty fall should have brought him more satisfaction. But Beth's prudishness only served to remind him of the vast gulf that lay between them. That always had. In school, she'd always had an aura about her, a subtle kind of quality that set her apart from everyone else. Definitely from him. Her brains certainly had. She was by far the brightest person he'd known, but she didn't hang out with the brains. Or the geeks.

Or the beautiful people—until the end—though it was where she and her luminescence had truly belonged.

She'd pretty much hung out with him. Rain, hail or shine. And he'd pretty much lived for that back then.

When he was younger, he hadn't thought to wonder about it. It wasn't until he was about fourteen and some helpful jackass had pointed out the social differences between poor Marcus Duncannon and rich girl Elizabeth Hughes that it had started to niggle. But she'd been unwavering in her friendship, uncaring about the condition of his mum's ancient car, the shabby hems on T-shirts he'd been wearing for two years. Or the fact that she had to ride buses to hang out with him. Some deep part of him had feared she might bail on him like everyone else when his father's life insurance money had run out. But she hadn't.

Not for three years. On the other side of *that* day, it had all looked more sinister. Maybe slumming with the poor fatherless kid gave her some kind of weird social cachet, some intrigue. Maybe he propped up her ego daily with his sycophantic interest. Maybe she was just biding her time until someone better came along.

Or maybe she just outgrew him. She'd said as much. He just never would have picked McKinley as the sort of chump she'd grow towards.

At seventeen he'd thought about ditching school immediately. Lord knew his mother needed the extra income back then. And he certainly could have done without the daily taunts of the beautiful people that his Beth was now one of them. McKinley's Beth, in fact, but always *his Beth* deep in his heart.

And now the Princess of Pyrmont High was peeing in the ocean. In public.

There was a certain satisfaction in that. No matter

how belated. He hadn't let himself go over these memories for years. Call it a self-preservation thing. He didn't like the person he'd become in those final months of school.

Beth's discomfort at being so debased only birthed a raw, shining affection deep in his gut—a feeling he hadn't allowed for a long, long time. He laughed to dislodge the glow deep within, to sever the golden filaments that threatened to re-establish between them.

He laughed to save himself from himself.

Then he locked his jaw and forced his attention back onto the only female out here who deserved his sympathy.

The ocean was full of water. What were a few drops more? And Beth was incredibly overheated. The idea of taking a quick swim before... Well, it wasn't the worst idea in the world.

She waded out into the deeper water, waist height, and peeled off Marc's oversized fleecy sweatshirt before bundling it high above her head to keep it dry. Then she slowly lowered her body up to her neck in the cold Southern Ocean. The frigid kiss of liquid on parched skin made her shiver. Cool ocean water rinsed away dried sweat. She tipped her head all the way back until cold water washed around her ears.

Bliss.

'Turn around!' she shouted back to Marc, onshore. Yes, it was pointless but it felt very necessary. He complied, busying himself with the whale, but she was sure his whole body was lurching with laughter.

Sure, laugh at the spectacle. Nice. Her humiliation was probably a gift to him.

She swapped the sweater into a raised hand, carefully

unfastened her jeans with the other and tugged them down single-handed, muttering the whole time. There was no way she was going to repeat Marc's wetsuit trick. She may have done some low things in her life but there were some barrel bottoms even *she* wouldn't scrape.

Getting her jeans down single-handed was one thing but getting them back on when she was finished, wet and underwater…

'Oh, no.' Beth looked urgently between Marc and the great expanse of nothing around them and realised there was no way—nowhere—she was going to be able to get out of this water with dignity.

'Come on, Beth. I'm doing all the work here,' Marc complained from his side of the whale.

For crying out loud! She wriggled left and then right and eventually stepped free of her adhesive jeans, trapping them on the ocean floor between her feet and standing fully up. Then she slid Marc's enormous hoodie back on over her cotton blouse. Its thickness cut out some of the sun's glare and pressed her wet blouse more tightly to her, cooling her even more. With one hand, she held the sweater high of the waterline and then she hooked her jeans up out of the water with a foot, into her free hand.

Then she started wading back to shore, barelegged. Her underwear was no worse than a bikini bottom, after all. Just because it was flouncy…

Just because it was Marc…

Her heart fluttered wildly, imagining his reaction to her stick-thin legs. The last decade and the abuses she'd put her body through really hadn't done her any favours. She stiffened her spine and trod ashore as though this had been her plan all along, letting his sweater slip back down to mid-thigh, and then laid her wrecked jeans out to dry on the sand high above the tide mark next to their bag of supplies. Her eyes instinctively fell on it, knowing what lay within, pulsing like a dark heart. And what lay *within* what lay within.

Walk away.

The thickness of the sand hid the unsteadiness of her gait. Not that Marc would have noticed; he was looking everywhere *but* at her long bare legs. The whale. The horizon. The sky. The extra delay probably irritated him if he couldn't even meet her eyes.

That didn't help her mood any. 'Okay. I'm back. What was so urgent?'

He waited until she got behind the whale before letting his eyes rest back on her. Then he cleared his throat. 'I'm going to try and dig a trench around her,' he said, indicating the now dangerously still whale. 'If I can get my snatch-strap around her, maybe we can drag her out a bit further.'

'Will it hold?'

'It pulls my Land Cruiser; it should tow a small whale.'

Beth frowned. 'Is digging under her safe?'

'I'll trench in front, then we'll try and saw the strap through the sand beneath her.' His hands mimicked the action, the cords in his wrists and forearms flexing with the motion. It briefly flitted through her mind that those bulging muscles could probably tow the whale to sea all by themselves.

Beth shook her head. 'No way. She must weigh half a ton. That sand will be too compressed.'

For a tiny moment he looked at her with a hint of admiration. Pleasing him had always pleased her. Even now. The slightest of glows leached out from somewhere deep inside her. But then he dropped heavy lids down over his eyes and the connection was lost.

'I've been thinking about that. If we can time it with the suck of the wash back out to sea it might loosen the sand just enough. It's worth a try. But we need to be ready for high tide.'

'What happens then?'

'We try and refloat her.'

'By ourselves?' Her voice sounded like a squeak, even to her.

'If we get lucky, the cavalry will arrive with a boat to tow her back out.'

'And if we don't?'

Steady eyes regarded her. 'If we don't, I hope you're stronger than you look.'

CHAPTER THREE

SHE wasn't. Not nearly. But she was getting better.

It had been a long, uphill road recovering from being Mrs Damien McKinley, but she'd found the strength to try. And it appeared that strength begat more strength, because she'd found extra to come here today. To face Marc. Even though ninety per cent of her whispered not to bother. Not to risk it. The ten per cent of her that disagreed was noisy and shovey and refused to be ignored. It remembered Marc. It trusted him.

Looked as if it had just learned a powerful lesson.

Marc Duncannon was not the man she remembered. He'd grown up in so many ways and while his physical changes were an unarguable enhancement, she couldn't say the same for his personality. Then again, after the decade she'd endured, she was no prize either. Maybe losing his father so young had damaged him irreparably. So close to losing his best friend. And apparently then his mother.

She frowned. 'So, you didn't tell me what happened with your mum. You two were so close.' Each was all the other had left. Even if Beth had really struggled to like Janice by the end.

Marc's whole body straightened and turned to stone, halting his digging. His mouth set. His eyes darkened dangerously. 'Did you imagine I'd still be living at home with my mother at this age?'

Scorn like that would have hurt a lot more once, before she calloused up at Damien's hands. Still, the fact that it still managed to slice down into her gut said a lot about how she still felt about Marc. She took a controlling breath. 'Obviously I expected you to have moved out of home but I never expected you to have moved out of her life.'

The blizzard in his eyes reached out and lashed at her. 'You still like to research before you travel, obviously.'

The one trip they'd taken together, when Marc had got his driving licence at the start of their final year in school, had been an exercise in military precision, thanks to Beth's aptitude for planning. Anything to take her mind off the fact that she and Marc were going to be camping. Out in the sticks. Alone. Right about then, her awareness of him as anything other than her best mate had crashed headlong into adolescent awareness of him as *a* mate. As in biological. That had been an awkward, confusing feeling that had never quite diminished.

'I had to start somewhere to find you. Your neighbour remembered me.' The woman had been very kind and given Beth the information she needed to track Marc down. Albeit with a slight lift to one eyebrow. She tried again. 'I thought…because Janice was all you had…'

Marc resumed his powerful digging, the chop and slide of his body adding emphasis to his curt words. 'I hope you're not trying to convince me that you had warm feelings for my mother. I remember how fast you used to like to get in and out of my house.'

Beth flushed. She hadn't realised how poorly she'd been covering her dislike of Marc's mum back then. It hadn't always been that way. It was just that as Marc grew older, Mrs Duncannon seemed to grow more hostile. Almost jealous. Until that last day...

Marc stood in his trench and eyed her. 'After school I spent some time up north on the trawlers. When I got back, I thought it was time to get my own space,' he said. 'She liked the city, I wanted the country. It's as simple as that.'

Right. And this whale was made of Jell-O. But if he didn't want to talk about it...

On a non-committal *uh-huh*, she let her focus drop back to where her hands continued to slosh the whale with a T-shirt that was now mostly shredded fabric. Ten years was a long time. One-third of their lives. What else could have injured him in that time? A woman? He didn't have a ring—not even a tan mark; she'd checked that out while he was choking the life out of his steering wheel earlier. But there was no doubt he was harbouring some wounds.

The thought brought her a physical pain that somehow rose above the ache in her lower back. That anyone would have hurt him like that. Bad enough what she'd done...

She dragged a deep breath in and concentrated on what her hands were doing. But silence wasn't an option either. 'Ask me a question.'

'About what?'

'Anything other than Damien or that day at school.' *Or what I've been doing for the past ten years.*

He waved his whale-washer in the air and then complied, plucking a question from nowhere. 'Favourite colour?'

'Still green. Moss-green, nothing too limey. My whole studio is painted that colour.'

'You have a studio?'

'Sounds more glamorous than it is. It's a partially restored old warehouse belonging to my father. I suspect I'm not supposed to be living in it. Council rules.'

'What do you do there?'

'I paint. Oils. My work is all around me.' For better or worse. The images from her abyss period were dark and dismal. But powerful. Lately, new brighter themes had started emerging. 'When I changed to B-stream it gave me an art double and I discovered I loved it. And I'm good at it.'

Two confused lines folded across his brow. 'That's good. I'd like to—'

...*see them?* The way he cut himself off made her wonder. They fell to silence. 'Ask me about my first car,' she eventually said.

Cars. The great equaliser. He smiled slightly and shook his head. 'What was your first car, Beth?'

'Toyota. Right after school. God, I loved that beat-up piece of junk. First thing I bought and paid for myself.' Until she'd stopped driving it because of the drinking.

'First kiss?'

She shook her head. 'Nope. Not talking about that day.'

Marc's eyes flared. 'Hold on, sidebar for just one second. That was your *first* kiss?'

She stared at him. 'You were my best friend. You don't think I would have told you the second someone kissed me?'

His eyebrows rose in apparent disbelief. 'No one ever tried?'

Beth shrugged; the hurts that had meant so much when she was younger were insignificant in the light of everything that had happened since. 'Guess I wasn't all that sought-after in school.'

He opened his mouth to say something, thought better of it and then changed tack. 'Until McKinley.'

'Right. But that topic's off-limits too.' Then something occurred to her. 'Wait—it wasn't *your* first kiss?' Marc dropped thick lashes down between them. Her mouth fell open. 'Seriously? Who was it?'

He had to know she was going to keep nagging until he told her.

'Tasmin Major.'

'*Olympic Tasmin?*' Her voice rose an octave.

'She was only state level then.'

But a twice Olympic freestyle diver since then. Tasmin was one of the classmates Beth thought of when she was counting her own many failings. Pretty. Gentle. Athletic. *Olympic.* And now she'd been Marc's first kiss, too. Maybe more? That thought bit deep down inside. Right down deep where she always considered their kiss behind the library to be special. Even if it had led to the end of their friendship.

Her throat tightened up. 'Why didn't you tell me?' More importantly, how could she have not noticed? She'd been so attuned to Marc's every breath.

He sidestepped her outrage. 'Why would I tell you? It was just a kiss.' Beth gave him her most penetrating stare, straight out of childhood. 'Okay, a bunch of kisses, but it's not like we were dating or anything.'

'I hope not, because that would mean I really was oblivious to everything going on around me.' Curiosity got the better of her. 'Why were you kissing Tasmin if you weren't dating?'

Marc dragged his eyes off to the horizon. Back to the whale. Anywhere but on hers.

'Marc?'

He hissed and tossed his hands up. 'She volunteered.'

Beth blinked. Several times. 'Tasmin Major volunteered to kiss you? Did I miss some kind of recruitment process?'

Cautious eyes met hers briefly. 'Actually, we volunteered with each other.'

Beth's stomach compressed into a hard ball. An insane jealousy surged through her as she realised what that meant. They wouldn't have been the first kids in school to do it. 'You went to her for *kissing practice*? Why?'

The look he gave her took her back a decade, too.

'Okay, other than *practice*, obviously. I can't believe you went to Tasmin. I mean she's nice and all, but... What was wrong with me?' And why on earth was this hurting so much?

That brought his head up instantly. Hazel eyes blazed sincerity. 'Nothing was wrong with you, Beth. But we were friends.'

She thought of all the girls at school who turned their snooty noses up at Marc because of the way he lived and dressed. As if they would ever find a finer person. Her estimation of Tasmin rose a notch because she wasn't one of them, even if it also meant that she'd spent half their childhood with Marc's tongue down her Olympic throat.

Then something else hit her. 'Who were you practising for?'

He tipped his face back down to the whale, sloshed harder. Resolutely ignored the question. Beth waited. Silently. Her heart pounded. How far had she truly come if she was this frightened of finding out?

'It's old news, Beth. Hardly important now.'

Her frown threatened to leave permanent grooves between her eyes, encrusted in the salt. 'I thought I knew everything about you back then, Marc. It's thrown me.'

He waved his shredded towel. 'I just wanted to get the whole first kiss thing out of the way, Beth. Can we just leave it at that?'

She looked at the tightness of his lips, the shadow in his gaze. She softened her tone. 'That library kiss was pretty accomplished. You guys must have practised *a lot*.'

The corner of his mouth lifted. 'Good times.' Then he looked back up at Beth, his eyes guarded. 'Anyway, I thought that day was off-limits. Moving on…'

Right. Moving forward… The past was in the past… 'Next question.'

It took Marc nearly two hours to hand-dig a deep enough trench a metre on-shore of the whale and reinforce it with driftwood to hold back the collapsing sand. In that time, the blazing afternoon sun dipped its toes into the ocean on the horizon and the most magnificent orange light coated everything around them. Her artist's eye memorised the colour for future use. Beth sighed as much as the whale did as the scorching heat suddenly eased.

In the dying light of dusk, Marc laid the strap out and then asked Beth to take one eyeleted end. She mimicked his bent stance, her prune-skin hands pressed down to the shallow ocean floor and her back screaming its protest. Then they started sawing the strap under the sand, towards the whale.

Push…pull. Push…pull. A slow, agonising rhythm.

Beth felt the moment they got close to her because, exactly as she'd suspected, the sand compressed into a rock-hard mass under the whale's weight. But Marc's idea worked, though slowly. With every wave that ran in, the suck of the water rushing back out between every one of a million grains of sand loosened it just a tiny bit and they were able to saw the strap, inch by agonising inch, beneath the giant mammal. The tide had crept in so much and they bent over so far that Beth's lowered face was practically touching the rising water. Her muscles trembled with exhaustion, screamed with frustration, but she wasn't about to complain to Marc, even though every part of her felt as if she'd been hit by a truck.

Her back. Her skin. Her feet. Her arms. Even her head thumped worse than any hangover she'd ever earned.

Marc grunted as loud as she did. The whale did nothing but blow the occasional protest out of its parched blowhole. Finally, just when tears of utter exhaustion pricked, he called a halt.

Standing upright nearly crippled Beth after the abuses of the day and she cried out as her muscles went into full cramp, stumbling back onto her knees in the rising water, wetting the bottom half of Marc's fleecy sweat-shirt. It galled her to go down in front of him, but how much did he expect she could take? She caught herself before she sank completely down onto her bottom but she was incapable of getting back up. She froze in an odd kind of rigor where she was. Her hands shook as if they were palsied. Her head drooped.

Marc was with her in seconds, his strong arms sliding around her middle to keep her up out of the water. 'Beth, grab on to me…'

Tears came then. Angry. Embarrassed. Relieved. It had been so long since she'd last felt any part of Marc against her and it felt so right now. Safe and strong. Welcome and long-missed. Where she was bone and long hollow muscles, he was solid and smooth and rooted to the earth. Even in the water.

And he was her friend. At least he had been. Once.

He might have been stronger but he was just as tired as she was, it seemed. He needed her cooperation to get her back on her feet. Hours ago, he could have lifted her single-handed. 'Come on, Beth, pull yourself up,' he said, low against her ear.

If she turned her head just a bit she could breathe in his intoxicating scent. 'I'm sorry...' Her vision blurred.

His strong fingers tucked around her waist, burned there.

'Don't be. You did well. We got the strap around her.' His voice was tight as he steadied her back onto her feet but she let herself lean into him until the last possible second. He smelled of salt and sweat; an erotic, earthy kind of scent that elicited all kinds of tingling in her. Nothing like the over-applied, cheap colognes Damien liked to mask himself with.

She turned her face more closely into Marc and breathed in deep.

He pulled her out of the water, supported her long enough that they got up on the beach to where the supplies were. She collapsed down onto the sand, knowing she might never get back up but knowing she couldn't keep standing.

Even for him.

'Take a break, Beth. We've been at this for seven hours. No wonder you're exhausted.'

He didn't join her on the sand. Instead, he snagged up the supply bag and fished around in it until he retrieved two muesli bars, a chocolate bar, a banana and an unfamiliar packet of powdered mix. He offered her a choice. As hungry and tired as she was, the thought of putting food in her stomach did not appeal. There was only one thing in that supply kit that had her name on it. And she wasn't letting herself have that, either. She pushed his hand away.

'You have to pick one, Beth.'

She shook her head.

'Fine.' He tossed the chocolate bar at her. 'This will give you immediate energy and potassium for the cramping, but in one hour I want you to have this.' He waved the pouch of powder.

'What is it?'

'Sports mix. Endurance athletes use it. Just mix it with water. You need the fats and carbs if you're going to last.'

Was that a comment about her weight? 'I thought men liked women skinny?'

He looked at her, appalled.

Mortification soaked through her. *Oh, God, Beth. Don't speak.* Clearly, she was too tired to think straight. She shook her head again, incapable of an apology that wouldn't make things worse. Her mind's eye slipped to what was left in the supply bag. How had she dealt with this sort of moment before? She couldn't remember. Excruciating comments didn't feel so bad when you were blind drunk and so was everyone around you. You sure had less to regret that way.

Had she forgotten even how to feel shame?

'The powder's slow release energy, Beth. It'll get you through the next few hours.'

If she could just get through the next few minutes she'd be happy.

Marc crammed a muesli bar into his mouth on a healthy bite. Where Beth nibbled, he practically inhaled. Then he took one of the endurance pouches and filled it with water, shook and consumed it in a drawn-out swallow. Beth was too tired to drag her eyes off the long length of his tanned throat. How could even a throat be manly? But here she was, ogling it for the second time today.

She forced her eyes down to the half-melted bar in her hands. Chocolate was one of those foods she tried to avoid. Something she liked a little bit too much. Something that challenged her hard won willpower. But Marc was ordering her to eat it, and she was feeling so weak, so…what to do…?

She took a small bite.

She forced herself to go slow, not to wolf it down, although her blood and her brain screamed at her to. It was part of her process. If she gave in on something small, then what chance did she have over something big?

This was where the downward slide began. Her eyes went to the pack of supplies.

'Okay, come on.' Marc stretched out his hand to her, mumbling around the last crumbs of his muesli bar. 'If you don't get up again, you'll seize up and be here all night.'

The thought of rising was horrible. She groaned and stared at his extended hand. 'I can't…'

'She needs us, Beth.' His gentle words pushed every guilt button she had. Beth looked over to the dark mass half-submerged in the even darker waters of dusk. It may be cooler now that the sun had set—significantly cooler—but the whale wasn't in a position to wet her own skin. Or drag herself back out to sea.

And maybe *taking a break* was actually the start of the slide—insidiously disguised?

Beth forced herself over onto her side and then pushed painfully to her knees. It was the least elegant thing she could remember doing. Marc took her hand in his callused, strong one and pulled her the rest of the way to her feet. She stumbled against his neoprene hardness before steadying herself and pointlessly shaking the worst of the beach sand off her soggy sweatshirt.

His hands were high on her bare thighs, brushing more sand off before either of them realised what he was doing.

A rush of heat raged up her skin where his fingers touched and she leapt back with a speed she couldn't have found if he'd begged her. Marc stiffened and a pink flush showed itself above the collar of his wetsuit. God, that was one hundred per cent habit from the good old days. The days before gender was an issue. Now, having his hot hands on her icy skin was *absolutely* an issue. For both of them.

It had to be.

'Okay,' he said, clearing his throat and straightening to his full height. 'Back in the water.'

Beth willed her legs to follow him back down to the surf. How many hours had passed since she'd stumbled down the dunes this morning? As bad as she felt—and she couldn't remember a time she'd felt worse, even in the depths of her withdrawal—they'd achieved a lot. The whale was still alive, its skin was in reasonable shape, and they had implemented the first part of Marc's plan to refloat her.

Sure, tensions were high between them and, yes, maybe she'd rather be curled up by an open fire right now watching reruns of *Pride and Prejudice*, but she was hanging in there. She felt vaguely hydrated now that the scorching sun had eased off and the chocolate was doing its job and feeding energy directly into her cells. Their conditions could be much, much worse. That thought gave Beth's spine the tiniest of reinforcement.

And then the sun set.

CHAPTER FOUR

THE moon was high in the bitter night sky by the time Beth risked further conversation. She poured the last mouthful of the fresh water into the endurance powder Marc had nagged her to have and shook the pouch thoroughly, knowing he was monitoring her from the water to make sure she drank it. She managed not to gag—just—as she chugged the chalky banana-flavoured mix. Then she turned to look at Marc, still sloshing the whale.

That little moment on the beach had been a major slip. For both of them. She'd had two hours of dark silence in which to go over—and over—the events of the day, looking for the moment when something had shifted between them. The moment when time had unwound just a tiny bit and taken them both back to a place that meant Marc could make a mistake like touching her. A woman he barely knew any more. He barely liked.

It was the peeing thing. As though seeing her so reduced in front of him had gone some way to settling old hurts. Maybe the loss of dignity had won her a measure of forgiveness?

Lord, if that were all it took, she'd be in serious credit by the time the night was out. Embarrassment over a bodily function was just a patch on the hits her dignity had taken in the years since she'd last seen him. He'd be delighted if he knew.

She chewed her lip. Maybe that was what he needed to hear—that she'd suffered? Impossible to know—he was as mysterious to her these days as the darkening ocean all around.

She stumbled back to the water. 'That was quite possibly the most disgusting thing I've ever tasted.'

Marc answered as though it hadn't been hours since she'd last spoken. His twisted smile was reluctant. 'You get used to it. It'll keep you going.'

'I can see why they call it survival food. You'd really want to be lost at sea before you cracked open supplies.' She turned her eyes to the dark, still shadow further down the beach. 'Do you really think that was her calf?'

'Yeah, probably.'

'Did it die because it was so young?'

'It's not that much smaller than Mum. It wasn't a new calf, I'd say. Some whales last days, others only hold out for hours. Just like people, some are tougher than others.'

A deep sadness snaked out and tangled around her heart. She could identify with an animal that turned out not to be as tough as it might have thought. 'Poor baby.'

Slosh…slosh…

'You never had kids? You and McKinley?'

Beth was unprepared for the bolt of pain that question brought her. She turned her face away from him and busied herself around the whale's small parched eyes. It had finally occurred to her that a marine animal wouldn't object to having salt water around its eyes.

Marc's question hung unanswered in the night silence. He patiently watched her.

'No. No kids,' she whipped out.

'You didn't want them?'

I didn't deserve them. And they sure as heck didn't deserve to be born into a life as wrong as hers and Damien's. 'Not particularly, no.'

Let him think whatever he liked.

'Funny.'

That was it. Just that one word. She sloshed away for a bit longer, but then curiosity got the better of her. She straightened. 'What's funny?'

'I always pictured you as a mother. Deep down, I thought that might have been the attraction with McKinley. He seemed like he was raring to get straight into the family and kids thing.'

Beth snorted softly. He was raring to get into one part of it, at least, like most teenage boys. If he struck strangers as family oriented, it could only be because he'd grown proficient at maintaining the same illusion as his own parents.

'No. Damien didn't really have any drive regarding family.' Any drive at all. Except for drinking. When things had first started going wrong in their marriage, she'd briefly considered children, something to bring them together. But, as it got worse, she'd secretly made sure that was never possible. Even when she was in the deepest reaches of the abyss, she'd somehow managed to remember to protect herself against pregnancy. Not that the issue arose very often by that point.

Slosh...slosh.

'What did you end up doing?' Marc asked casually. 'For a career.'

Her shoulders tightened up immediately, which made

the sloshing even more uncomfortable. Embarrassment
surged through her. Not because she hadn't had a perfectly legitimate job but because it wasn't even close
to the glittering career he was probably imagining her
having.

'I worked in retail.' She cringed at the blush she could
feel forming and struggled to make working in a dry
cleaners sound more impressive. 'Customer service.'

He frowned. 'You didn't go to uni?'

Just one of the many lifetime goals she'd poured
down her throat. She bit back a testy response. 'No.'

He stopped sloshing to stare at her. Was that satisfaction in his eyes—or confusion?

'Damien didn't want me to start a career.' Lord, how
bad had her life become that admitting *that* was easier
than admitting she'd soaked her professional future in
alcohol before it began?

'But he let you work in retail?'

Let. She tightened her lips. 'I chose to work. I wanted
something that was mine. Something that didn't come
from Damien or his family.' And she'd had it…as long
as she could keep a job.

He shook his head.

'What?'

'You were so gung-ho about going to uni.'

For three years it had been their shared goal, one of
the things that kept them so close together, kept them
in the same classes. In the same lunch timeslot. Until
the conversation with his mother that had changed all
of that.

You're sucking him into your dreams, Beth, Mrs
Duncannon had whispered urgently one time she'd
visited the Duncannon household, her grip hard on
sixteen-year-old Beth's forearm. Her voice harsh. *He's*

*not bright like you, he's not suited to further study. He
needs to get a job and start making his way.*

That had struck Beth as an odd thing to say about
the boy who was already flipping burgers after school
to help out financially. Who'd done all the research on
the best universities. Picked up all the pamphlets, looked
into all the courses. Was making the grades. Who had a
plan for where he wanted his life to go and his compass
set to get there. But Mrs Duncannon hadn't bought a
word of Beth's nervous reassurance.

*As long as he's with you, he'll never go for what he
wants in life. He's not a pet to be trained and instructed.
He'd walk through fire if you asked him to, Beth Hughes.
And some days I think you really would ask, just to see
if he'd do it.*

She'd never visited Marc at home after that. The ugly
picture his mother painted of their friendship filled her
with shame and echoed in every event, every activity that
followed. It made her question their relationship. Marc.
Herself. She'd tentatively asked her own mother about it
and Carol Hughes's careful answer and sad expression
had told Beth everything she needed to know.

Both women thought she was dragging Marc along
with her. *Both women* wanted her to pull back from
their intense friendship. For his sake. She looked at the
capable grown man standing before her and struggled
to see how anyone could have worried about his ability
to speak up for himself. Even as a teenager.

The irony was that Mrs Duncannon and her own
mother had it all back to front. Beth would have followed
Marc into the pits of hell if he'd asked her. Because
she trusted him. Because he was like another part of
her. A braver, more daring part. The idea of studying
biology had never entered her one-track mind until

he'd mentioned it, but separating after school never had either. And so she'd thrown herself willingly into Marc's dream. Adopting his had made up for having no direction of her own. Until the day she'd cut Marc loose and was forced to face her lack of ambition.

Her shoulders tightened another notch. 'Goals change.' She shrugged. 'You went up north after school, you said.'

His eyes shadowed over. 'I lost my…enthusiasm… for further study.'

'Because of me?' *Or did Janice get in your head, too?*

He glared at her. 'Responsibility for your own actions is fine; stop taking responsibility for mine.'

'If your goals shifted, then why are you surprised that mine did?' she asked.

'Because…' Marc's eyes narrowed. 'Because it was *you*. You could have done anything in the world that you wanted.'

Silence fell. Sloshing dominated. When he did speak again, it was so soft he might have been one of the night sounds going on all around them. 'So, what *was* the attraction, Beth—with McKinley?'

He still thought this was about Damien. Why not—it was what she'd wanted him to believe at the time. She had to find a way to cool their friendship off and Damien had been her weapon of choice. She'd used him to put distance between herself and Marc.

Used with a capital U.

'Damien was harmless enough…' *At the beginning.* 'We were kids.'

Okay, it was a hedge. Maybe her courage was as dried out as the rest of her. Her heart hammered hard in her chest. The anticipation of where this conversation might lead physically hurt. What he might think. What he might say. She just wasn't good at any of it. She licked dry, salty lips and wished for some tequila to complement it. Then she shuddered at where her thoughts were taking her.

After all this time.

You wanted forgiveness. Maybe that started with a little understanding.

He shook his head. 'You weren't like other teens, Beth. You were sharper, wiser. You were never a thoughtless person.'

The use of the past tense didn't escape her. How could a tense hold so much meaning? She sighed. 'I was overwhelmed, Marc. Damien made such a public, thorough job of pursuing me, it turned my head.' *And I was desperately trying to recreate what I'd had with you. What I'd lost.*

Marc was silent. Thinking.

She beat him to the punch that was inevitably coming. 'That day behind the library. When I told you… When you kissed me. You accused me then of selling out to the popular crowd.'

A flash of memory. Marc's hard young body pressing hers to the wall. His hot, desperate mouth crushing down on hers. Terrifying. Heaven-sent.

He assessed her squarely. 'I was an ass. I accused you of being desperate for affection.'

Surprise brought her head up. 'You were angry. I knew that.' *Eventually.*

He studied her, his mind ticking over. 'That explains why you dated McKinley. Not why you married him.'

The very thing she'd asked herself for a decade. Even before times got really tough. She frowned into the darkness. 'Damien was like two people. At school he was a champion, a prefect. His parents rushed him into growing up.' The specialised tutors, the pressure to achieve at sports, the wine with dinner. 'But he was still just a teenage boy with the emotional maturity to match. Once I agreed to date him, he seemed to expect me to cave automatically in…other areas.'

And *expect* was the operative word. She'd never met another person with the same kind of sense of entitlement as her ex-husband. She swallowed past a parched tongue and remembered how desperately she'd tried to wipe the blazing memory of Marc's kiss from her mind. How she'd thrown herself headlong into things with Damien to prove that all kisses were like Marc's. Only to discover they weren't. How much leeway she'd given Damien because she knew she had used him and feared she'd done him some kind of wrong by kissing Marc. By liking Marc's kiss. How Damien had taken that and run with it.

How she'd just let him.

She shrugged. 'I married him because I slept with him.'

Marc's lips tightened and his hands scrunched harder in the wet towel that was becoming as ragged as her own whale-washer.

'And because he asked.' She let out a frayed breath. 'And because there was no reason not to, by then.'

And because she'd had no inkling about the kind of man he was about to become.

Beth held what little air she had frozen in her lungs. Marc had honoured her request that he not speak to her again after the day behind the library. His absence had ached, every day, but it made it easier for her to bury what she'd done. Both hurting him and kissing him. And to forget how that kiss had made her feel. The awareness doorway it had opened.

Knowing she'd done it for Marc had never really helped. Having the approval of both their parents had never really helped. But physical separation combined with a sixteen-year-old's natural talent for selective memory had made it possible to move on.

After a while.

The whites of Marc's eyes glowed in the moonlight. 'You didn't have to marry him just because you slept with him.'

She knew he'd see the truth in the sadness of her smile. 'I've always accepted the consequences of my actions. Regardless of what else you think of me, that hasn't changed. I chose to do something contrary to the values my parents taught me. My church.'

Marc shook his head. 'McKinley was a jerk. It always surprised me that he married you at all. That he didn't stop chasing you once he…'

His words dried up and Beth swallowed the hurt. 'Once he had what he wanted? Go ahead, say it. Everyone else did.' Marc frowned. She straightened her shoulders. 'I hadn't planned to sleep with him but once I did, turns out I was a…natural student.'

The irony wasn't lost on her. She'd spent all year trying to come to terms with the blossoming feelings that Marc was beginning to inspire in her, yet she'd barely touched him. But she'd slept with the boy she was physically immune to.

Or maybe that was why?

'And he was naive enough to make that kind of life decision based on one girl?' Marc asked.

She swallowed around the large lump in her chest. 'We both were. Except that Damien grew up a lot in the following few years,' she went on. 'Discovered that other women could be good in bed, too. Extremely good, if you knew where to look. And my one piece of power vanished.'

And hadn't he let her know it.

'So you left him?'

Beth stared. 'No. I didn't. Not until two years ago.'

He gaped. 'You cannot be serious.'

Heat chased up her icy skin. 'My *vows* were serious. I was determined to make a go of it, certain he'd grow out of his…phase and maybe we could turn things around.' Determined not to lose any more face with her family. Her few remaining friends. Having screwed up so much in her life. 'Then, somehow, years went by. Empty, pointless—' *passionless* '—years.'

Only it wasn't *somehow*. She knew exactly how, but she wasn't about to go there. Not with Marc. Telling a room full of strangers was one thing. Telling the man who'd been your closest friend…

He growled, his eyes darkened. 'Hell, Beth.'

Her laugh was bitter. 'I thought you'd be thrilled I reaped what I sowed.'

He blew air out from between his lips in a fair imitation of their whale. 'Look, Beth. Yes, at the time I was pretty much gutted that you chose that moron over our friendship. But I never would have wished that on you. No matter how angry I was. I…' His eyes flitted away. 'I cared for you. You deserved better.'

She straightened up, not ready to hear him defend her. Not ready to hear how short a time he'd been impacted. Not ready for all her angst to be for nothing. 'I think I got exactly what I deserved. Like I said, I always was prepared to accept the consequences of my actions.'

'For years? Wasn't that a little extreme?'

She stared at him warily. Better he thought her a martyr. 'Some lessons take longer to learn than others.'

She shrugged off the comment and the conversation. 'So...what did you do after we went our separate ways?'

Marc made busy with the sloshing. 'Kept a low profile.'

Super-low. He might as well not have existed. Which was pretty much what she'd asked of him.

He'd walk through fire if you asked him to...

'The national skills shortage hit during my summer job up north, right after graduation, and suddenly I was pulling in a small fortune for an eighteen-year-old. It set me up beautifully to buy an old charter boat the next year and refurbish it during the off-season. Now I have three.'

'So it worked out okay, then—even though you didn't make it to uni?' Relief washed through her.

His smile wasn't kind. 'Trying to decide how high up the list you need to put me?'

Her make-good list. If she was going to finish the job she'd come for, she had to be thorough. Confession time. She found his eyes and held them, took a deep breath. 'Top half.'

'Sorry?'

She cleared her thick throat. 'You asked earlier which half of my list you were in. I just wanted you to know you were in the top half.' She clenched her hands. 'High in the top half...'

His next words were cautious. Almost unwillingly voiced. 'You seriously have a list?'

She nodded.

His brows dropped. 'Why?'

Panic surged through her. What a stupid question

not to have anticipated. She swallowed hard. 'Self improvement.'

His frown looked like doubt. But he let it pass. 'How high was I?'

Somewhere off in the dunes, a bird of prey shrieked out across the night. Her voice, when it came, was hushed. Quiet enough that he'd have to hear her heart pounding. 'The top. Number one.'

It took a lot to shock Marc Duncannon. But she managed to pull it off. He had a few goes at answering before coherent words came out of his gaping mouth. 'I'm the first person you've come to find?'

Shaking her head made thick cords of salty dark hair, still a tiny bit damp from her dunking earlier, swing around her face. It had to suffice as a screen. 'Actually, you're the last.'

'But did you just say—'

'Top of my list, yes, but the hardest. I left you till last.'

God. Would he realise what that meant? It was screamingly obvious, surely? The silence was almost material. Even the whale seemed to hold her breath. Emotion surged through his eyes like the waves battering them both. Hope, hurt, anger… Then, finally, nothing. A vacant, careful void.

'You've held onto those memories all this time?'

Her stomach sank. 'Haven't you?'

He looked away and when his eyes returned to hers they were kindly. Too kindly. 'No.'

No? Beth blinked.

'Give yourself a break, Beth. We were kids.'

His unconcerned words struck like a sea snake. Bad enough to have sabotaged for nothing the only relationship of her life that meant something to her. Now she'd

wasted years of angst, endured a mountain of guilt…
and it had barely registered on his emotional radar.

'Losing our friendship meant nothing?'

He sighed. 'What do you want me to say, Beth? It cut
deep at the time but everything worked out. Life goes
on.'

Mortification streaked through her. She stared at his
carefully neutral face. Maybe Janice had been right?
Cut free of her, Marc had gone on to make a success of
his life—not what he'd always told her he would do but
then how many of her school mates had ever actually
grown up to do what they imagined they'd do for the
rest of their lives? She certainly hadn't. While she was
literally drowning in her regrets, Marc had rebounded
and done a fine job of getting by without her.

Everything she'd been through… For nothing?

'Beth?'

She shot her hand up and turned away from his indifference. She tossed her tattered whale-washer ashore
and turned to wade out into the deep, dark water. The
only place she could go. To let her heart weep in private.
She pushed her legs angrily through the water for a few
steps and let the angry ache fill her focus.

'Beth!'

She wanted to keep walking, to show him he meant
as little to her as, apparently, she did to him. But she
just wasn't that good a liar. She turned when the water
was thigh high.

'Not in the water,' he urged. 'Not at night. Go up on
the beach.'

Screw you. 'Why not?'

'Sharks will be drawn by the dead calf. They're
more active at night. We shouldn't go in deeper than
our knees.'

She practically flew back to the shallows. Survival before dignity. Marc didn't say anything further. It took her several minutes walking down the beach to reach a place she felt was sufficiently dark and safe. Safe from the dune snakes. Safe from the whale-eating sharks. Safe from Marc Duncannon and his awful neutrality.

She sank down onto the sand and let the tremors come.

Her life had changed direction that day behind the library and it had changed again eight years later and this man was central to both. A man who was so entirely unaffected by what had happened to them back at school.

Deep breathing helped. Plunging her bare toes into sand that was still warm from the day helped. Closing her eyes and imagining she was anywhere else but here helped.

Whatever it took to fool her body into thinking it wasn't facing an unbearable amount of pressure. Something she wasn't really used to having to face. As a rule, a drunk body didn't care what was going on around it. And she'd been drunk for the better part of eight years. Even when she wasn't.

In the early months of her marriage, she'd walked a careful line with Damien and his rapidly developing fondness for the bottle, keeping him just shy of the point where he liked to express his drunken feelings with his fists. But that line quickly got too hard to predict and so it was just easier to give in. To tumble behind him into the abyss where he was happiest and she was safest. The help she might have had evaporated. Friends. Her parents. They'd all stopped trying after her repeated assurances she was fine.

Why wouldn't they? She was Beth. Beth didn't make

mistakes. But Beth—as it turned out—was a gifted and convincing liar.

By the time they'd realised she wasn't fine, she was well and truly sunk. After a while, she didn't even hate it. The abyss was a pleasantly blur-edged place to lose your youth. And she'd learned how possible it was to function in normal society while artificially numb.

And then one day she'd woken up and looked around at the empty half of her bed, the total strangers dossed down in her living room and she'd seen, with awful clarity, the faces of all the normal people she'd thought she was cleverly keeping her drunkenness from. Their averted eyes. Worse—their pity.

For no real reason, she'd thought about Marc that morning. About the boy who'd had such faith in her. The boy she'd lived her life for as a teen. The boy she'd finally forced from her dreams—her marriage—after his memory had steadfastly refused to leave. And she'd realised she hadn't thought about him in years.

She'd sat crying in the shower long after the hot water ran icy cold.

Those convulsive shivers had been nothing on what was to come. The spasmodic wretchedness of weaning herself off the liquor, alone in her father's old warehouse, surrounded by the tormented images she'd painted in her darkest days. The destructive try-and-fail spiral that had made her feel increasingly bad about herself. Increasingly desperate for the unconditional acceptance a bottle offered. The only thing that had kept her going was painting.

Then one night she'd stumbled—drunk, to her eternal shame—into an AA meeting and found a room full of survivors who'd given her compassion and empathy and a path out of the abyss, not judgement.

Those strangers had saved her life.

Long before any make-good list, she held onto Marc's name as a ward against ever again forgetting someone who had represented such goodness in her life. She'd scrawled his name down on a scrap of paper that day she'd tumbled from the shower and she'd carried it in her wallet ever since, in lieu of the photos she'd thrown out years before in a fit of drunken heartbreak because looking at him had hurt too much.

She'd known that facing him today wouldn't be easy. But it had never—ever—occurred to her that he simply wouldn't care any more. If he ever actually had.

'Beth? Are you done?' His voice called her back from the darkness, just as it had two years ago that morning in the shower. 'I need you.'

There was urgency in his voice she couldn't ignore. And, in the face of what the whale needed, her decade-old issues could wait a few hours more. She quickly did what she'd come to do and then staggered, too sore and tired to run, back down the beach towards him.

The whale was thrashing violently in the water, the nasty arrow-head gash on its tail sawing back and forth, its whole body twisting.

'Is she having a seizure?' she cried as she neared.

'She can feel the tide,' Marc called. 'She's trying to move herself. We have to do it now.'

'You can't be serious?' He wanted to get into the water with a crazed half-ton animal? Immobile with exhaustion was one thing…

'She's too far on-beach. She won't be able to pull herself out. We have to help her.'

He had a loop of rope laid over his forearm and he was making darting efforts in between the wild thrashes of the whale, trying to snag the eyelet of the strap they'd managed to drag beneath her hours ago. But every time he got close, the insensible sea-mammoth twisted in his direction and he had to leap away, stumbling into the water.

With one mighty lurch, Marc plunged his arm into the water on the whale's offside and jumped back, bringing the strap with him. It took only a moment to push the rope through the eyelet like a sewing needle. Then he pulled half of it through and tossed it high over the whale to splash into the water next to Beth.

She knew what he needed her to do.

The whale had slowed its frantic efforts now, perhaps realising that it wasn't going to be able to do this alone. Beth made three attempts, feeling blindly along the sand in the dark shallows for her end of the strap, squinting against the salt water that splashed up into her eyes. Her careless groping meant Marc's entire sweatshirt was soaked in cold water, but she didn't care. She wouldn't be needing it for long now that they were going to free the whale, and her own temporary discomfort wasn't a patch on what this animal was going through.

On her fourth attempt, she emerged victorious. She clutched the strap tightly in one hand and felt around for Marc's rope. When she found it, not yet soaked, still floating on the surface, she shoved it with trembling hands through the eyelet and then walked backwards away from the whale, pulling the rope taut. Marc did the same.

The strap slowly emerged and rose, flexing and dripping, above the water line as it tightened around the whale's rounded belly.

'We need to walk behind her, Beth. It'll pull the ends together and tighten around her flank.'

Behind her? But that meant… She lifted wide eyes to him.

He was silent for long seconds. 'I know. But, sharks are survivors, too. We'll have to hope they're more interested in the dead calf than in its dangerously thrashing mother.'

Was that likely? Beth's skin burst into terrified gooseflesh all over.

His loud voice carried over the sound of the whale's writhing. 'I don't see that we have much choice, Beth.'

'There's always a choice, Marc!' she yelled back. AA had taught her that. They could both walk away from this animal and leave her to nature. Maybe it was meant to be.

He knew which way her mind was going. 'Is that a choice you could make, Beth? Because I couldn't.'

No. When it came down to it, neither could she.

He called out again. 'We'll try and twist her your way so you're pulling in the shallows. I'll take the deep end.'

'Oh, great, so I'll get to watch you be eaten by sharks instead. That'll be nice!'

She gritted her teeth and plunged into the deeper water. The adrenalin did its job and fed her a steady stream of power. They didn't waste any time, pulling their ropes hard and closing in until they stood side by side—mountain by waif—up to Beth's waist in water. It was a lot by her standards but not much for a whale. Hopefully, it would be enough. The manoeuvre pulled the snatch strap tight around the whale's bulging midsection. Marc moved them slightly to one side so that their rope wouldn't impede the thrust of her powerful tail.

'Ready, Beth?'

She wasn't. She never would be. But it seemed life was determined to plunge her back into the real world with a vengeance. She found his eyes, drew strength from them and nodded.

'Pull!'

She put her entire, insignificant weight behind her and leaned back hard on her rope. Marc immediately made more progress, his side of the rope vibrating above the waterline enough to give off a dripping, high-pitched whine. The whale groaned in harmony.

Beth's already damaged hands screamed as her end of the rope bit into them and she stumbled forward at the pain, losing purchase and crying out.

'Wait!'

Marc let his rope loosen and the whale heaved a sigh. Beth quickly stripped off Marc's drenched sweatshirt and wrapped it around her hands to protect them and then pulled her rope tight again. The salt water sluiced into open blisters, stinging badly.

'Okay…go!'

They heaved again and the whale slid slightly sideways, adding her remaining strength to their far less significant pulling power. But it was movement. And, after thirteen hours in the sand, that was not a small achievement.

'She's moving!' Beth squeezed out unnecessarily. No way would Marc not have noticed. 'Keep going!'

Adrenalin roared now through her body, warming her and giving her a capacity she never would have believed she had. She leaned hard on the rope and pulled with all her remaining strength, twisting her body and virtually walking—inch by inch—out into deeper water, up around her armpits, towing the enormous beast.

Marc was right there beside her, his neoprene muscles

bulging with the force of every pull. Neither of them was suffering quietly and their roars of effort merged with the whale's to disturb sleeping creatures for a kilometre. The whale suddenly twisted so that she was side-on to the beach, her tail now fully submerged, her body more torpedo-shaped in the water than it had been on the sand. Still rounded where the strap held her firmly. Beth and Marc changed their positions, widened out so that they could contribute to the whale's slow sideways thrash into deeper water. If the sharks wanted either of them they'd be easy pickings right now. The water lapped at Beth's breasts.

The whale battered her tail violently, slamming on the water for added purchase. But the miracle of buoyancy meant it was easier to tow half a ton of whale flesh. They did—slowly, painfully. And then—

'Beth, run!'

Marc dropped his rope and surged away from the manic animal. Beth stumbled and went under as her rope suddenly went slack and Marc hauled her up after him, her throbbing legs pushing against the pressure of the deep water.

The whale twisted and surged and turned the quiet shallows into a spa of froth and bubbles. The rope zinged out of its eyelets with an audible crack and the snatch strap dropped harmlessly away. In the time it took Beth to suck in a painful breath, the whale was free, half submerged, then fully submerged. And then—finally—it sank like an exuberant submarine, surfaced once to grab a euphoric lungful of air and then disappeared silently under the deep, dark surface.

Beth screamed her joy as she ploughed through the water, and then she lurched sideways as something harder and warmer than the whale slammed into her.

Marc swung her in a full three-sixty, hoisting her up in his arms and hauling her backwards out of the waist-deep water, whooping his elation. But their momentum and fatigued legs couldn't hold them and they stumbled down together into the shallows, Marc sinking to his knees and bringing Beth with him.

Tears of pain and exhaustion streamed freely down her face and she pushed uselessly against his body to right herself. But the natural chemicals fuelling her body drained as fast as they had come and left her shattered and shaking. The strength she'd miraculously found just moments ago fled. She sagged back against Marc's strength, useless.

He collapsed unceremoniously onto his bottom in the ankle-high surf and he dragged an insensible Beth between his wetsuit-clad legs. His hands pulled her more tightly against him. She crawled up into his rubbery shoulder.

'We did it,' he repeated hypnotically, as though reassuring a child, stroking her dripping hair and pressing her hard into him. As though she belonged there. Beth squeezed her streaming eyes shut and soaked up the gorgeous feeling of being this close to him. After so many years. She nuzzled in closer. A bad idea, no doubt, but impossible not to. Every accidental touch they'd shared as kids flashed through her mind and she saw, clear as day, how she had evolved from comfortable touching to flirtatious touching and finally experimental touching. Stretching boundaries. Testing boundaries. Testing him.

Their gasping breath was the only thing now disrupting the silence. Marc's murmurs softened further and started up a senseless whisper against her ear. Not even real words, just sounds. But they did their job; she sagged harder against him and let the trembles come. Elation this time instead of fear or anxiety or—worse— the DTs. A much better kind of tremor.

But they transported her exhausted mind immediately back to a perfect spring day behind the library when Marc had kissed her for the first and only time. His body wasn't this hard then, or his shoulders this broad, but he'd been on the verge of filling out to the potential she'd always known he had. She'd clung to him then just like this; as if he was saving her life with the hard press of his mouth on hers. The touch of his tongue against hers. And she'd shaken afterwards exactly the same. Except that time she'd been completely alone. The kiss was the last time they'd so much as looked at each other.

The cold water soaking into her body offered a splash of reality. That was a lifetime ago. Before the alcohol. Before she'd abandoned him.

He doesn't care, she reminded herself. She straightened slightly and went to pull away.

He resisted her pull. 'God, I've missed you, Beth.'

The words were so simple, so brutally whispered hard up against her ear, she wondered if he'd even meant to say them aloud. But he had, and his words screamed for acknowledgement. She let her body sag back into him and wriggled up until her face rested in the crook of his neck, her arm slung around his neck.

He wrapped his arms more firmly around her and just held her, cold and shaking, against his body. Rocking in the icy surf.

It didn't matter that she'd never been with him like this before—that she'd never let herself be vulnerable like this with anyone—it felt very, very right.

'I'm so glad you were here,' she said. 'I couldn't have even begun to manage this alone.'

He chuckled but even that seemed to hurt his aching body. It morphed into an amused groan. 'If it weren't for me, you wouldn't have been here in the first place.'

She lifted her head and looked at him seriously. Eye to eye. Their faces so close. Water still dripped down her skin. 'I could say the same.'

If not for her treatment of him in that all important final year of school, would he have gone on to study at uni like they'd planned? Would he have been living somewhere other than the remote south coast of the state running a charter company?

'It is what it is, Beth. You can't control everything.'

'Why not?' she sighed against the warm skin of his throat. Too tired to move and not particularly inclined to. 'Whose great idea was that? That we have no say in our destiny?'

'I didn't say that. Just that sometimes things just... happen. You can't hold yourself responsible for everything that occurs.'

She crawled in more comfortably. He took her full weight. 'That sounds an awful lot like you're accepting my apology,' she whispered.

His broad chest rose and fell beneath her torn-up hands. She held her breath.

'We were both kids,' he mumbled against her wet hair. 'We both did things we regret.'

She lifted her head to stare quizzically at him. 'What do you regret?'

His eyes darkened. Then blanked carefully over. 'I regret a lot of things.'

Stop talking, Beth. Now! That voice in her head seemed to know exactly where she was going next. She ignored its excellent advice. Her saturated chest heaved. 'Do you regret kissing me?'

Marc sucked in a breath, and she was too close to him to miss it. She wished she could see his eyes to gauge his reaction. 'I regret the manner in which I did it,' he said simply.

Pushing her hard up against the library wall and forcing her lips apart with his? She could see why he might regret that. If not for the fact that she'd been waiting years for him to take the initiative. She just didn't know it.

The sixteen-year-old tomboy deep inside asked the same honest questions she always had. 'How do you wish you'd done it?'

His thick voice was strained and it drew her eyes up to his. 'That's not a question you can ask me, Beth.'

She lifted her head. But the move cost her. She winced as her over-taxed muscles reacted sharply to the move. 'Why not?'

'Because of what you said afterwards. What you made me promise as you pushed me away.'

Don't ever touch me again. Don't speak to me again.

She closed her eyes. 'I was angry. And confused. It never occurred to me that you would actually honour that.' But he had. All damned year.

'Confused how?' His tired eyes took on a sharper edge.

'Because I…' Lord, how to get out of this one. 'Because it was *us*. Kissing. It threw me.'

He straightened. 'Because you hated it? Or because you liked it?'

For all her faults, she'd never been a liar. Not to Marc. But she was proficient at hedging. 'Are you seriously asking me to rate your kissing prowess?'

'Do I look like I have any doubts about that?'

Her mouth twisted. 'No. You always were infuriat-
ingly confident.'

His expression changed in a blink and then was gone.
Maybe the moonlight was playing tricks on her, making
her see vulnerability that couldn't possibly be there. Not
in that body. Not in this man.

'It matters to me, Beth. Whether you hated it. Whether
I actually damaged our friendship, too.'

Too. Misery came surging back in at the reminder
that she'd said the words that destroyed their friendship.
Even if she hadn't set out to. She was only going to ask
him to back off for a while. But he'd kissed her and she'd
panicked. Those soft lips pressing against hers, forcing
hers wider. The hands that had plunged into her hair to
hold her captive sent electric sparks through her body
and threw her into confusion. The press of his eager
body into hers had made her want things she shouldn't
want. The desperate, intense pain in his eyes echoing
hers. The thick smoke-like energy he'd been pumping
out all around them.

Did she like it?

Enough to rip his heart out with her reflexive over-
reaction. She took a breath. Held his eyes. Held her
breath. 'I didn't hate it.'

This was where he'd kiss her in a movie. The water.
The cold. The intimacy. The moonlight. And her admission practically cried out for his mouth on hers.

Instead, he nudged her head back down to his shoulder and rested his cheek against her wet hair. She felt
his low words against her ear, vibrating in his throat.
'Thank you, Beth. Deep down, I worried I'd struck the
death blow.'

No. That honour remains with me. Snapping on the
heels of that thought came another. He'd wondered about

his part in that kiss? That wasn't the admission of a man who'd never given it another thought…

Beth lifted her face to study his. A particularly full wave washed over them and buffeted Beth against him with its chilly brush. Waiting for a kiss was stupidly naive and impossibly romantic. Her heart squeezed hard. Had she been so starved for affection in her love-less marriage that she was finding it now in impossible places? Marc was just moved by their circumstance and harking back to better times. That was all.

Since there was to be no kissing, she needed, really badly, to get off him. But her body had practically seized up in the foetal position and straightening her limbs was a new kind of agony. Just when she thought she'd already met all the cousins in the Pain family.

'Easy, Beth. You need to walk off the ache. Your muscles will be eating themselves.'

Pretty apt, really. Starting with the giant thumping one in her chest cavity. Crawling into Marc's lap had not been part of her plan as she drove up the coastal highway this morning, but now that she had it was hard to imagine ever getting the sensation out of her mind. Her heart.

But she had to.

Her back screamed as she pushed against Marc's chest and twisted up onto her knees, between his. She gave herself a moment to adjust.

'Just one more thing…' he said before she could rise much further.

Those powerful abdominal muscles she'd spied back at the car did their job and pulled his torso up out of the splash and hard into hers. His lips slid warmly, firmly against her mouth and he took advantage of her shocked gasp to work them open, hot and blazing against her numb flesh. Her lips drank heat from him and came tingling back to life, startled and wary. His hands forked up into her wet hair and held her face while he teased and taunted her blissfully with his tongue, letting her breathe his air as though he were giving her the kiss of life.

Which, in a way, he was.

Relief and a decade of desire surged through her. Forgiveness tasted an awful lot like this.

He lifted his face and stared into her glassy eyes. 'This is how I would do it if I had my time over,' he said softly and then lowered his mouth again.

Whether he was making a point or making good on a ghost from his past, Beth didn't care. His mouth on hers felt as if it belonged there. Her nipples, already beaded from the icy ocean, suddenly remembered they had nerve endings and they sang out in two-part harmony from the pleasure of being crushed against solid granite. Heat soaked out from the contact even through his wetsuit.

Marc seemed to notice too, because he groaned against her mouth and let one hand slide down to where small waves lapped against her underwear, worked under her blouse and then surged back up, scorching against her frozen spine.

It was the only other place that her skin met his. Other than his amazing, soft, talented mouth. Maybe she just hadn't kissed enough men, but she couldn't imagine how a kiss could possibly be better. Or more right. It was every bit as confronting as their last one.

Only this time she was equal to it.

It was a weird kind of rush, kissing a total stranger and your oldest friend. The man who knew everything about you. And nothing at all. Exactly as that unwelcome

thought shoved its way to the front of her mind, she felt
Marc stiffen beneath her. He ripped his lips away and
turned his head. Disbelief painted his features.

'Stop…'

A rock lodged in Beth's chest. He tugged his hand
out from under her shirt and resolutely pressed her away
from him. She twisted sideways against the pain of his
rejection and found herself on hands and knees in the
shallows, undignified and lost. How must she look to
him?

But he wasn't looking at her as he scrambled to his
feet.

Beth followed the direction of his eyes up the beach,
where a dark mass lurched and twisted on the shore near
the calf.

'She's re-stranded,' he said, stumbling away a few
steps, his voice thick from their kissing. Or from the
agony of having failed to save the whale.

When he turned and reached out his hand, she waved
him off. 'I can't, Marc. I hurt too much. You go. I'm
going to need a second.'

It was a measure of their past friendship that he didn't
falter and worry about helping her up. If anyone had ever
respected her independence, it was Marc. Just another
way he used to show his belief in her.

Pain came in all shapes and sizes. As Marc found the
strength to run up the beach towards the beleaguered
whale, stooping to grab his whale-washer from the
shore, Beth knew she'd have to too.

They were in this together. Ready or not. And she
was not about to let him down for a second time. Not
when he was the only man she'd ever known who had
ever believed in her.

She cried out as she straightened her tortured spine,

an anguished mix of pain and frustration and self-recrimination. Then she lurched up the beach after him, the golden glow of his kiss feeding her the necessary strength.

Just.

CHAPTER FIVE

THEY hadn't spoken in an hour.

Not because they were angry with each other, Marc knew. Not because there was weirdness after their kiss, which had happened so naturally. And not only because their spirits were broken by the return of the whale they'd worked so hard to save. It was just that they were both putting all their energy into the endless drag-and-slosh—slower, shorter, choppier. Eternal. At least there was no blazing sun to contest with now.

The whale could see her calf from her new beach position and Marc wondered if the stillness of her body meant she knew it had died. Attributing human qualities to it was as pointless as it was hard not to. Beth's eyes followed his to the whale's small round ones.

'Why do they do it—strand themselves?'

Marc shook his head. 'No one knows for sure.'

She blinked her fatigue. 'Do they want to die?'

'I don't think so.'

'Can't they see the land?'

'Some blame our electromagnetic technologies which throw their guidance systems out of whack. Others say their inner ears are damaged by under-sea quakes which mess with their ability to navigate.'

'What do you think?'

'I don't know. I just know what it does to them.'

Beth stroked the whale's cool skin. 'I think she came back for her baby.'

Marc nodded. 'Could be. I've seen mothers and calves together in the deep water creches, the bond is definitely strong enough.'

'Maybe she just wanted closure.'

Beth's dark head tipped back, rolling gently on her shoulders to ease the ache. His eyes followed hers upwards. It seemed bizarre to notice, through the death and the pain and the blistering cold, how pretty the night was. It truly was a beautiful Australian night. More stars than he'd ever seen in his life—that was what he'd thought when he'd first moved to the deep south of the state. The Milky Way in all its blanketing glory. It was kind of nice to see someone else appreciate it.

Beth arched her head back so far she almost stumbled. He twitched to race to her—even knowing he'd never get there—but caught himself just as she did.

'We're so small,' she murmured, regaining balance, her face still turned heavenward. 'Do you think that there's a Marc and a Beth and a whale somewhere out there fighting for life, just like we are?'

Marc followed her glance up to the sky. 'I guess… statistically. Could be.'

Her thoughts were as far away as those stars.

'It seems impossible that life could only exist on one planet out of a million twinkling lights.'

'You aren't seeing the planets. Only the suns in solar systems full of other planets.'

She turned cold-drugged eyes on him and considered what he'd said for an age. Marc frowned. Her speech was getting slurred, her lids heavy. He'd have to get her out of the icy water soon. She was turning hypothermic. And talking about space.

'We're such an insignificant part of an insignificant part of something so big,' she murmured. 'Why do we even worry about things that go wrong? Or things that go right. Our whole drama-filled lives are barely a blink of the universe's eye. We make no difference.'

Marc stopped sloshing. 'It makes a difference here and now. And life is not about how long it is. It's about how full it is.'

'Full?'

'Full of love. Joy.' He looked back at the whale. 'Compassion.'

She lowered her face to look at him. 'Even if it's only a blink?'

'I'd rather have a moment of utter beauty than a hundred years of blandness. Wouldn't you?'

Her eyes blinked heavily. 'You would have made a good astronaut,' she mumbled.

Marc frowned.

'Fourth grade. You wanted to be a space-man. You thought there was a space princess you were supposed to save.' Her teeth chattered.

A numb smile dawned. 'I haven't thought about that for years. I can't believe you remember it.'

She returned her focus to him. 'I remember everything.'

She'd driven him crazy in the playground, insisting on being the astronaut and refusing to be the princess. Was that the beginning of her tomboy ways? An insane glow birthed deep inside him that she'd held on to those memories. It suggested she hadn't stopped caring when she'd pulled the pin on their friendship. She'd just stopped being there.

His smile withered.

'So tell me about your mum,' she murmured.

His gut instantly tightened as she forced her eyes to focus on him.

'What happened between the two of you?'

His heart started to thump. Hard. 'Didn't we already cover this?'

'Nope. I asked, you hedged.'

'Doesn't that tell you anything?'

'It tells me you don't want to talk about it.'

'Bingo.' He glared at her. 'But I'm sure that's no deterrent to you.'

The more defensive he got, the more interested she got. It seemed to slap her out of her growing stupor. 'Not particularly.'

He threw his shoulders back and shot her his best glare. Subtlety was wasted on Beth. 'If you give me a few minutes I'll see if I can find a stick for you to poke around in that open wound.'

Her face was a wreck. Grey beneath the windburn, shadows beneath her eyes. But she still found energy to fight him on this. 'I'm more interested in why you have an open wound in the first place.'

Because my mother is a nightmare.

'Family stuff happens, Beth. I'm sure your relationship with your parents isn't perfect.'

She got that haunted look from earlier. 'Far from it. I've disappointed them in a hundred different ways. But I still see them. What happened with Janice?'

'You don't remember? How she could be?'

She tilted her head in that hard to resist way. He'd never felt less like indulging her. He didn't discuss his mother. Period.

So why was he?

'I always assumed it was because she lost your father,' she said. 'That it kind of…ruined her.'

He stared. 'That's actually a fairly apt description.'

Beth frowned, stopped sloshing. Her teeth chattered spasmodically between sentences. 'I remember how hard she was on you. And on me. I remember how hard you worked at school and at the café to do well for her. But she barely noticed.'

His heart beat hard enough to feel through his wet-suit. He crossed his arms to help disguise it. 'What do you remember about her personally? Physically?'

Beth's frown intensified. 'Um… She was tall, slim… Too slim, actually. Kind of…' Her eyes widened and her words dried up momentarily. When she started again she had a tremor in her voice that seemed like a whole lot more than temperature-related. 'Kind of hollow. I always felt she was a bit empty.'

Marc stared. She'd just nailed Janice. And those were still the early years.

'I'm sorry,' she whispered, as if finally realising she was stomping through his most fragile feelings.

'Don't be. That's pretty astute. After we…went our separate ways, she got worse. Harder. Angrier. The more I tried to please her, the less pleased she seemed. She'd swing between explosions of emotion and this empty nothing. A vacant stare.'

Beth swallowed hard enough to see from clear across the whale. She'd completely stopped sloshing. Her pale skin was tinged with green.

'She'd always been present-absent. Since my dad died. But it got worse. To the point she'd forget to eat, to lock the house up, to feed the cat. He moved in with the over-the-road neighbours.'

A tight shame curled itself into his throat.

'It took me another two years before I discovered she was hooked on her depression medication,' he said, swiping his towel in the ocean ferociously. 'And that she had been since my dad died.'

The earth shifted violently under Beth's feet and it had nothing to do with the lurching roll of the whale. A high-pitched whooshing sound started up in her ears.

'Your mum was addicted to painkillers?'

'*Is*. Present tense.'

Oh, God. The unveiled disgust on his face might as well have been for her. The description of Janice ten years ago might as well be her two years before. Beth's voice shook and she forced herself to resume sloshing to cover it up. 'And that's why you don't see her?'

'I have no interest in seeing her.' He dropped his stiff posture and almost sagged against the whale as he bent to soak his towel again. 'Working on the trawlers was more than a financial godsend; it gave me space to breathe. Perspective. And an education. I watched some of those blokes popping all manner of pills to stay awake. Improve the haul. I saw what it did to them over a season. When I got back and saw through educated eyes how she was, I was horrified.' Those eyes grew haunted. 'She was my mum, you know?'

Beth nodded, her fear-frozen tongue incapable of speech.

'All Dad's insurance money, all the money I'd been sending home from up north… She blew most of it on pills. She was no further ahead financially than when I left.'

Beth wanted to empathise. She wanted to comfort. But it was so hard when he might as well have been describing her. Suddenly Janice's desperate taloned grip on Beth's forearm all those years ago made a sickening sense. 'What did you do?'

His sad eyes shadowed further. 'I tried for three years. I gave her money, she swallowed it. I signed her up to support groups and she left them. I hid her Xexal and she'd tear the house up looking for it. Or magically find some more. I threatened to leave…' he shook his head '…and she threw my belongings into the street. One day I just didn't take them back inside.'

'You moved out.'

'It was all I had left to fight back with. She was hell-bent on self-destruction and I wasn't going to watch that.' He shuddered. 'I thought losing me might have been enough…'

But it wasn't.

'Do you see her at all?' Beth whispered.

'Not for four years. The one useful thing I did do was buy out her mortgage. She can't sell the house without me so I know she has somewhere to sleep, at least. And I get meals delivered to her now instead of sending her cash, so I know she has food. For the rest…' His shrug was pure agony.

Compassion and misery filled Beth at once. For Marc, who loved his mother no matter how difficult she'd been. For Janice, who lost the love of her life when Bruce Duncannon had a cardiac arrest and who had never truly coped as a single parent. And for herself, whose path wouldn't have been so very different if not for the blazing memory one Sunday morning of a young boy who'd always believed in her.

A powerful love.

'Would you ever try again?' She felt compelled to ask. Knowing if she was in Janice's shoes she'd want *someone* not to give up on her. Deep down inside. No matter how much she protested. The way her parents had hung in there for her. Despite everything.

Marc lifted his gaze. His brows folded. His eyes darkened. 'Too much would have to change. I've accepted that the only time I'll see my mother again is if she's in hospital, in a psych ward or in the ground.'

The gaping void in his heart suddenly made shattering sense. She remembered what it was like living with Damien in the early days, before she'd succumbed to the bottle. She could only imagine what it must have been like for a child living with that. Then the man, watching someone he loved self-destruct.

But she herself was that hollow. An addict. Never truly recovered, always working at it. As if Marc didn't already have enough reasons to hate her, this would be too much.

'Go ahead and say it, Beth. I can see your mind working.'

Startled, her eyes shot up. She couldn't say what she truly wanted to say. But she found something. 'What about yourself—did you ever seek help for yourself?'

The frown came back. 'I don't need help.'

'You're her son. There's—' She caught herself just before she gave away too much. 'I'm sure there's assistance out there for you, too.' She knew there was. Her parents had accessed it.

The frown grew muddled. 'To help me do what?'

Beth lifted her shoulders and let them slump. 'Understand her.'

His expression grew thunderous. 'You think I lack understanding? Having lived with this situation since I was nine years old?'

Beth wanted to beg him to reconsider. To be there for his mother, since no one else was. But she burned for the little boy he must have been too. 'If not understanding, then…objectivity? You had it briefly when you returned from up north and look how clearly it helped you to see.'

'Objectivity did nothing more than make me realise what a junkie my mother had become.'

Beth winced at the derogatory term. She'd had similar words ascribed to her over the years. Five years ago, they struck her shielded centre and were absorbed into a soggy mass of indifference. These days they cut.

Disappointment stained his eyes. 'I really thought you'd have understood, Beth. I wasn't oblivious back in school. I know you stopped coming around because of her.'

I stopped a heck of a lot more because of her. She'd started pulling back from their friendship because Janice had begged her to. And that withdrawal led to everything else that followed.

'I just… She's your mother, Marc, and all you have left. I know it's hard but I just don't want to see you throw it away—'

'Throw it away?' he thundered. 'I *bled* over that decision, Beth, even worse than when you—' He stopped short and snapped his mouth shut, glaring at her through the darkness. 'She's an addict. You have no idea what it is like to live with someone who is controlled by their compulsion. The kind of damage it does to everyone around them. How the poison spreads.'

Tears pricked dangerously in Beth's eyes, welling and meeting the salt that still clung to her lashes. It dissolved and filled her eyes with a stinging mix that she had to blink to displace. He was talking about her. He just didn't know it. She turned her face away on the pretext of re-wetting her shredded rag. Behind her, pain saturated every word.

'I have no interest in ever putting myself in that position again,' Marc vowed.

She knew plenty about being an addict but what *did* she understand about living with one? Her response to Damien's addiction had been to cave in and join him. Hardly a battle. Walking away from Janice must have been brutal for Marc—on all fronts—but it meant he kept his sanity. He survived. He controlled the spread of the poison.

Misery washed through her.

She lifted damp eyes back to his. Nodded. 'I understand, Marc. I do understand.' Only too well. Her eyelids dipped heavily. 'I'm sorry I wasn't there for you,' she risked after a long silence, forcing her lids open.

Marc was silent for the longest time but finally spoke. 'I'm sorry you weren't too. I could have used a friend.'

Did he not even have one to turn to? 'When did you walk out?'

'Christmas Eve four years ago.'

She'd spent most Christmas Eves trying to act straight while her over-protective parents threw anxious glances between her and Damien, who'd done his best to appear attentive. Meanwhile Marc had been carrying suitcases away from his mother's house. Lord, what a contrast. 'Who did you... Were you alone—at the time?'

'Are you asking whether I was single?'

She was so tired she could have been asking anything. 'I'm asking whether you were alone.' Worrying he'd had no one only made it worse.

He nodded. 'I was.'

No father. No extended family in Australia. No friends. No girlfriend. Just a long-time addict mother.

She closed her eyes for the pain she could hear in his voice all these years later. As a boy, Marc's defence of his mother was legendary. He held on to love for a long time.

'I went back out onto the trawlers for another couple of seasons. More than they recommend, but I felt I had nothing to hang around the city for. That decision turned my life around.'

'You're still such a glass half-full person, aren't you?' She'd clung to the concept when things were at their lowest ebb. 'I remember that about you.'

He paused the sloshing. 'We're responsible for our happiness just as much as our actions. No one else is going to do that for you.'

True enough. She was a walking example. If she hadn't dragged herself back from the abyss... An exhausted yawn split her thought.

'I have to move faster,' she said to herself as much as him. 'If I keep slowing down, I'll stop for good.'

'You can stop any time you need to, you know that.'

If only life were that simple. That simply wasn't true sometimes. As she and his mother knew only too well. 'I'll be here as long as you are.'

'Still competitive?'

There was no way she was going to abandon him another time he needed her. But there was no way she was going to tell him that either. She forced her body to double its pace.

'You got me.'

CHAPTER SIX

BETH had long given up trying to control the violent shaking of her frozen body, but the advancing ice-age finally showed in the loud chattering of her teeth. Not surprising, given she'd lost Marc's fleecy sweatshirt to the dark depths of the ocean during the refloating. It meant she only had her flimsy blouse to keep her top half warm. And nothing on the bottom.

Marc had eventually accepted she wasn't going to go back to the car and leave him alone with the dying whale, but he didn't like it. Exhaustion had even wiped the frown off his face. But her loudly clattering teeth seemed to break the last of his tolerance.

'Beth, you're freezing.'

Both their bodies were well into survival mode now, her own barely conscious of what was going on around it. Neither of them could do more than lean on the whale for support and drag arm-after-painful-arm from the water to slosh onto the animal to keep it wet.

'You have to get out of the water,' he said. 'You need to warm up.'

Her chill caused her voice to vibrate. It hurt even to speak, so tight was her chest. 'It's warmer in the water than out of it. And I'm not leaving you, Marc. You'd have to work twice as hard and you have nearly nothing left now.'

'I'll feel better knowing you're safe and dry.'

'I'm not leaving.'

She couldn't see his glare in the darkness but she could feel it.

'Fine,' he finally growled. 'Give me a second.'

He spread his dripping towel out on the whale's hide and splashed slowly ashore. Beth lost him in the darkness after he passed her. It seemed like a lifetime, alone in the dark with the whale, but he finally returned.

'Take this,' he said bluntly, thrusting the last muesli bar at her.

Too exhausted to eat, she tucked it into the hip of her knickers. Too exhausted to protest, he just watched her do it.

'Now this,' he said, and thrust something else at her.

Beth reeled back and almost lost her footing, catching herself at the last second against the whale's cold body. Her mind lurched out a preventative *no!* a split second before her body hummed an eager *yessss!*

'It's whisky. Dry, but it will warm you up a bit.' He raised the silver flask right in her face and it glinted in the moonlight.

Her stomach roiled. Her blood raced. Her body screamed with excitement.

'Get it away from me.' She didn't mean to shove him so roughly, didn't even know where she found the energy, but the flask fell from his hands into the salt water. He scrabbled to pick it up, frowning in the moonlight.

'Take it, Beth. You need to have something.'

'I've been drinking water.'

'That'll keep you alive but it won't stop you getting hypothermia. If you won't get out of the water, then it has to be this.'

'I don't drink.'

Her ridiculously weak protest actually made him laugh. 'Well, you're going to have to make an exception, Princess. Survival comes first.'

He shook the water off the flask and held it out to her again.

Her chest heaved and her eyes locked on it. She could just reach out and—

'I can't, Marc…' *I can't break down in front of you.*

'It won't kill you.' He unstoppered the flask and took a healthy swallow, wiping his hand across his sticky lips when he finished to make his point. Beth had never felt more like a vampire. She wanted to hurl herself at those lips and suck and suck…

Shamed tears sprang into her eyes. 'Please, Marc. I can't.'

I can't show you what I really am…

His eyes narrowed but he was relentless. 'It's this or the car, Beth. Your choice.'

What was a bit more salt on her already crusty face? She ignored the two tears that raced each other down her cheeks. 'Do you want to see me beg, Marc?'

His frown practically bisected his face. 'I want you to be warm, Beth. I want you to drink.'

She forced her back straighter. 'And I won't.'

'For crying out loud, woman! Why are you so difficult?'

Old Beth and new Beth struggled violently inside her. Old Beth just wanted to throw her alcoholism in his face to punish him for forcing her hand like this. For putting her in the position of having to defend herself. To expose herself. To *him*, of all people. The man she'd already let down in a hundred ways. The man whose good opinion seemed to matter to her more than anyone else did. *New* Beth understood that using it as a weapon would only hurt him horribly and, ultimately, disappoint him more.

She knew she couldn't say nothing, either. But saying something didn't have to mean she was beaten. She could trust him with the information. Like she'd trusted her AA sponsor with all her deepest secrets. Couldn't she? Never mind the fact that he'd just told her his mother was an addict and made it painfully clear how much that disgusted him. This was Marc... He'd see she had her addiction under control. He'd see how hard she was working. He'd understand. He always had.

She laughed, low and pained. God, now she was lying to herself! Who was she kidding? This was *Marc*. She deserved his disgust for what she'd done and how she'd been.

She stared at the determination in his face. He meant it when he said drink or car. A numb kind of fatalism came over her. Whatever he did—however he reacted—it couldn't be worse than the wondering. Than fearing what might happen if she was revealed to the world. To him.

But her heart still hammered and it pounded into the miserable ache that filled her chest. Why was it easier to trust a total stranger with the truth than the man who'd been her closest friend?

It was hard to tell where the cold-trembles stopped and the terror-trembles started, but she thrust out her violently shaking hand towards him and raised defiant eyes and said the words aloud she'd been saying twice a week for two years.

'Hi. I'm Elizabeth and I'm an alcoholic.'

* * *

Marc's stomach tightened right before it dropped into a forty-storey free fall. His breath seized up and his skin prickled cold all over. He dropped his towel on the whale and turned away from Beth without so much as looking at her trembling outstretched hand. He marched off into the darkness, ignoring the shocked mortification on her face. He couldn't trust himself not to.

I'm Elizabeth and I'm an alcoholic.

His heart hammered. People made those jokes all the time, but the degraded, pained tone in her voice and the bleached courage in her eyes told him she wasn't kidding.

Beth was an alcoholic.

His Beth.

He kept walking, ignoring the fact he couldn't see what was two feet in front of him in the sand and his feet were dangerously bare. A deep, savage ache drove him forwards. That Beth—*Beth*—could be afflicted like his mother. That it could happen to two people he loved. What was he—some kind of jinx? All the people he cared about ended up dead or...

The living dead.

He clutched the flask—a piece of his father—close to him. Beth's eyes had shifted back and forth on it as if it were made of excrement one moment and pure ambrosia the next. He knew that look only too well. It was the way his mother used to look when she hurried past a pharmacy all stiff and tall. Just before her body caved in on itself and she'd turn back for the entrance with a hard mouth and dark eyes, dragging him along into hell.

Beth wanted this whisky. Badly.

His fingers flexed more tightly around it. Growing up, she'd been his role model. Sensible. Smart. Courageous.

Everything he valued most in a friend. Everything he'd searched for in himself. Yet sensible, smart, brave Beth had ended up addicted to alcohol. If she could succumb...

But she was fighting it. Some deep, honest part of him shouted that through the darkness. She wanted it but said no. His chest ached for the pain that had contorted her face. For the extra agony that this night must be for her. As if the cold and pain weren't bad enough.

He recognised it, even if he didn't understand it.

That thought brought him up short. Maybe she could explain. Help him understand. He owed her the chance, surely? He pivoted on his bare feet and followed the silver moonlight trail back to where he could vaguely see the shadow of a whale and a slender woman silhouetted against the rising moon.

Beth lifted bleak eyes to him. It hurt that he'd put that look there. He bent to re-drench his towel and took several deep breaths before trusting himself to speak.

'How long?'

There were probably more intelligent, sensitive questions to ask right at that moment but, more than anything, he needed to know how long she'd been struggling. Half of him hated it. The other half hated that she'd gone through it without him. She glanced away at the moon and then didn't quite find his eyes again. She was terrified. But hiding it. Something deep and painful welled up inside him, cut into the already sensitive flesh around his heart. He was hurting her.

Just like she'd hurt him. Except this didn't feel like justice.

Wide, stricken eyes returned to his. 'Eight years drunk. Two years sober. I'm recovering.'

Was there even such a state? Wasn't someone

alcoholic for ever—just a sober alcoholic? Her focus kept returning to the flask. Shifty, sideways glances. He wanted to empty the contents into the sea but, the way she was looking, she might just plunge into the water and try to guzzle the salt water. A deep hunger blazed in her eyes. It elbowed its way in amongst the self-disgust. It reminded him of the look in her eyes that day behind the library.

'Did you start at school?' he asked.

She shook her dank locks. 'About a year after I got married.'

Marc winced. Did she start the moment she hit legal age? 'Why?'

Her eyes widened and tears grew in them. 'Things got…hard.'

'Life gets hard for everyone.' Not everyone turned to the bottle. Alcohol. Pills. It was all the same—a cop-out.

'I know. I'm not special. But I made that choice and now I'm living with the consequences.'

At least Beth accepted that she was at fault. He'd heard every excuse under the sun from his mother. She had headaches, she wasn't sleeping, one medication made her crave another… It was never truly *her* fault.

His mouth tightened. Beth's eyes kept flicking back to the flask he held down at his side. She lifted a hand and pressed it to her sternum as though a ball of pain resided there and crushing it helped. Something old and long-buried made him turn and hurl the flask as far out to sea as he could. Its shape and weight gave it a heap of extra flight.

'What the hell are you doing?' Beth cried out and lurched towards its airborne arc.

Christ. Did she want a drink that badly? 'I'm removing temptation.'

'That was your father's!'

Surprise socked him between the ribs. That she cared at all. To think of that. His mother never would have thought of him through her haze. She'd have been braving the sharks to retrieve her pills. Not like the old days when he was the centre of her world. The dual centre, shared with his father. His frown doubled. 'It's just a thing, Beth. It's not him.'

'You could have just put it back in your bag!'

'Would it have been safe there?'

Her back straightened up hard, even though it must have hurt her to do it. Raw hurt saturated her voice. 'It's been safe in there all day.'

What could he say to that? He should have known an addict would sniff out the nearest fix.

Beth's breathing returned in big heaves, punctuated by bursts of compulsive shaking that rattled her bones. 'Now *you'll* freeze,' she accused.

'I'll get by. I have more insulation than you.' He folded his arms, spread his legs. Classic Marc. 'But we aren't talking about me. We're talking about you.'

'Oh, I must have missed the point where your inquisition turned into a conversation.'

His mouth tightened. But her words had an effect. He forced himself to take a step back, to ease his body language. This was clearly hard enough for her. 'I'd like to hear about it, Beth. To understand it.' Though he had to force himself to say so calmly.

'So you can decide how disgusted you should be? Or how much like your mother I am?'

He stiffened. 'We're going to be out here a long time yet, Beth. Did you really expect to drop a bombshell like that and then just go back to talking about the weather?'

No, she didn't. Then again, she hadn't planned to mention it at all—not to him—and, as it turned out, her instincts were spot on. She stared at him warily where once she would have blazed unconditional trust up at him. 'It took me six months from the day I closed the door of Damien's house behind me until the day I could stand up in AA and announce I'd been sober for a month.' She sloshed his side of the whale because he'd frozen in position. 'Then two. Then five. Then ten.' She shuddered in a breath. 'Two years of my life trying to undo what I've done. I've judged myself enough for everyone in that time.'

I really don't need it from you.

He flushed, which was a miracle enough, given the temperature. Then he cleared his throat. 'Please, Beth. No judgement.'

Uh-huh, sure. She drowned in his steady, silent regard but finally sighed, 'What would you like to know?'

His pause was eternity. 'All of it.'

Fair enough. She'd opened this door with her dramatic declaration. She might as well fling it wide and see what rumbled out. It couldn't be any worse than the raw disgust he'd failed to hide. She took a moment gathering her thoughts. Her aching exterior merged with her interior perfectly. She couldn't tell him all of it but there was still plenty left.

'I hurt my family when I married Damien so young,' she began, mostly a whisper but close enough that he could hear. 'I hurt you. Turns out I hurt myself too. But at the time he was everything I thought I wanted—a holy grail, like some kind of hall pass of credibility.

People treated me differently when I was with him and I…liked it. I'd been a pariah for so long…'

'Because of me?'

The monotonous sound of the ocean began to mesmerize her. 'No. Because of me. I chose you over all of them and their money.' She pushed the words out through a critically tight chest. Between the cold and the anxiety, it was amazing she could breathe at all. 'He found out pretty quickly that he didn't like much about married life. The responsibility. The expectation. And I was so young and trying so hard to be what I thought a good wife would be. When he insisted on a drink, what else could I do?' She took a deep breath. 'I'd ask him what he wanted and bring a second.'

'Misery loves company.'

So true in Damien's case. 'But then that point passed and it got so much worse.'

Marc stopped sloshing, his whole body wired. 'Worse how? Did he hurt you?'

She straightened up, took a moment working out how to answer. 'Sometimes.' Shame washed through her. 'I just blamed the drink. The more he drank the angrier he got, but the more I drank the less I cared.'

'So your drinking was Damien's fault?'

Her clumped hair screened her face as she shook her head. She'd never blamed her problems on anyone but herself and she wasn't about to start now. No matter how tempting. 'I made my own choices. It took me a long time to realise that, though.'

'So what finally made you stop?' The deepness of his voice rumbled in the night.

'I realised I was halfway through my twenties and I'd done nothing with it. I had a job but not a career. I had a marriage but not a family. I had a husband I didn't like

and friends who only came over if I was buying. I had
no interests.' She shook her head. 'I was a drunken bore
with no achievements to my name, married to a man I
didn't love. So I packed an overnight bag and I left.'

That made her sound stronger than she'd actually
been, cowering in the shower, sobbing, but the last thing
she wanted from Marc was more pity. Or to lose any
more face.

For long minutes the only sounds were the repetitive
sloshing of water on the whale's hide and the heaving
of their lungs. And the *tick-tick* of Marc's brain as he
got his head around her speech.

'What happened with McKinley?'

'Nothing. He didn't even try to stop me leaving. I
wasn't the only one that was miserable. We both made
the mistake.'

'You've cut all ties?'

'He signed the divorce papers without even getting in
touch. I haven't seen him since.' Although she did hear
about him from time to time. Those stories were always
peppered with sadness for the man he should have been
and relief for the woman she'd so nearly become.

'How hard was it—getting through the recovery?'

Was that more than just curiosity in his voice? Beth
immediately thought of Janice. Sugar-coating wouldn't
help him. She straightened her tortured back and met
his eyes. 'You slog your guts out getting through the
physical addiction and then you're left with the emotional dependence.' As hard as that was to admit. 'But
you can get through it. I did. Until, one day, you've been
stronger than it for longer than you were addicted.'

Until curve-balls like today swing into your life.

'You did it alone?'

'My parents wanted to help, of course, but I… It was

something I'd done to myself. I felt like I needed to undo it myself. To prove I could.'

'So what got you through?'

You did. The memory of Marc. The idea of Marc. She chose her words carefully. 'A dream of what I wanted to be.' *Who I wanted to be like.* 'And a strong AA sponsor.'

Marc was silent for a long time. He shook his head. 'I feel like I should have been there for you. So you didn't have to turn to a stranger. I should have been strong for you.'

Her heart split a little more for the loyalty he *still* couldn't mask. Despite everything. 'No, I had to be strong for me. Besides, it wouldn't work if Tony was a friend. The emotional detachment is important.'

'We've been pretty detached this past decade.'

It only took a few hours in his company for that to all dissolve. She lifted her eyes back to his and held them fast. 'Do you feel detached now?'

His silence spoke volumes.

'Will you be someone's sponsor one day?'

That was a no-brainer. 'Yes. When I'm strong enough.'

'You seem pretty strong now. The way you speak of it. Like a survivor.'

Warmth spilled out from deep inside at his praise. She was still a sucker for it. 'I have survived. But every day presents new challenges and I'm only just beginning to realise how sheltered I've been.'

Confusion stained his voice. 'As a child?'

'My parents shielded me from unpleasantness for the first half of my life and my drinking numbed me to it for the second. I've never really had to make a difficult decision or face a stressful situation. They were there for me. Or you were. I've always followed instructions or someone else's lead. Or avoided painful situations completely. I still have a lot to learn about life.'

He regarded her steadily. Was he remembering all those years where she'd tagged along with him, his partner in crime? Or the way she'd cut him from her life when things got too tough behind the library? *When the going gets tough, the tough go drinking.*

'You sought me out. That can't have been easy.'

'No. It wasn't.' But she had an unspoken and barely acknowledged incentive—seeing him again. He'd come to mean as much to her as alcohol. A yin to its powerful yang. That scrap of paper in her wallet a talisman. The painful ball in her chest made its presence felt. 'But I'd chew my leg off to have a drink right now. Do you call that coping?'

He flinched at her raw honesty. Pain washed into his eyes. But hiding who she was wasn't sustainable. He might as well see her, warts and all. For richer or poorer. In sickness and in health. Presently, sickness. But one day…

'It's been a rough night…'

The understatement of the century.

'If the flask washed up at your feet right now, would you open it?'

Her chest started heaving at the image. As though his words magicked up the little vessel, filled to overflowing with the liquid escapism she'd relied on for years.

No pain. No shame. No past.

No future.

Sadness flooded through her. 'Would you believe me if I said no?'

His deep silence brought their discussion to a natural close. She'd run out of story and courage. Her attention drifted back to how cold and how wet she was and she sagged against the whale as the after-effects of her monumental confession hit her body.

Marc frowned at her. 'I'll ask you one more time. Will you go back to the car?'

It hurt her to say no, but she'd promised herself she wouldn't leave him down here alone. And if she gave in on just one thing... She shook her head. A particularly icy shock of wind chose that moment to surge across the beach. She gasped at the savage, frigid gust and her skin prickled up into sharp gooseflesh.

Marc swore and glared at her. 'Don't say I didn't give you a choice...' He grabbed up his decrepit towel and ploughed out of the water and around to her side of the whale. Then he stepped in behind her and wrapped his whole body around her like a living, breathing wind-breaker. Her body sang at the close, hard contact, the port in this storm his strong arms represented. A moment later, the slight warmth bleeding through his wetsuit also registered.

She sighed and convulsively shivered.

Marc swore and pulled away for an icy instant. She heard the zip of his wetsuit opening, the gentle brush of his fingers pulling her wet hair to the side, and then the blissful brand of his hot chest straight against her barely covered back. Skin on skin. Fire on ice. It soaked in like a top shelf brandy.

'Christ, Beth. You're glacial.'

He took her hands in his and crossed his arms around her, closing her more fully against his warmth. Her numbness leached away like ice melting and exposed a shelf of complicated emotions she'd been doing her best to muffle. She stiffened immediately.

'Don't argue, Beth. You had your chance. Let's get back to it.'

Their two bodies formed a hypnotic rhythm—bend, scoop, slosh…bend, scoop, slosh—half the speed they'd been going before the sun had set. His towel dripped on Beth's arms as she bent to refill the two-litre water bottle she was now using to wet the re-stranded whale. If not for the awful truths she'd just shared, their position would have been downright sexy. A half-naked man glued to a half-naked woman. As it was, it was just plain uncomfortable. For both of them.

And it went on for an eternity.

Despite the warmth seeping in from behind, Beth's teeth started chattering again. Marc convinced her to pull her barely dry jeans on again as some protection from the wind and she took the brief on-shore break to wolf down the muesli bar she'd had tucked away. Her body immediately started converting the grain into desperately needed energy and warmed her briefly from the inside. It wasn't a patch on the blazing warmth of Marc's skin.

She was too cold to worry about pride as she slipped back into the surf and then tucked herself shamelessly back into his body. He received her with the practice of years, not hours.

As if it was her rightful place.

Skin rubbed against skin periodically as Marc's body followed hers down and back up. His breath was warm against her bare neck. The sensations she'd been numb to for several hours came roaring back—making her tingle, making her remember. Making her—for once—ache for something more than a drink. A neglected part of her longed to peel his wetsuit right down to his waist, to see in detail and up close just how much of a man Marc Duncannon had grown into.

But she'd have to settle for feeling the topography of his body against her back instead.

'Does it feel good?' Marc said, low and almost unwilling against her ear.

She gasped and half turned in his hold. 'What?'

'Addiction.' She could feel his tension against her back, she didn't need to hear it in his voice. 'I figure it must for so many people to do it.'

Beth thought long and hard about that. About the rush, about how it felt when it was gone. Or denied. About why he wanted to know. She twisted back around in his arms and continued sloshing. 'It's not a choice you make. For me, it wasn't about how good it felt when I was drinking. It was about how bad it felt when I wasn't.'

'Describe it to me. Both feelings.'

She swallowed the lump of tears that suddenly threatened. Even though she knew this was more about his mother. *There* was the Marc she remembered. He wanted to understand.

'Were you ever infatuated with someone?' She forced the words out. Between the cold and the strong arms cocooning her, it was amazing she could speak at all.

'Like love?'

'No, not love. Obsession. Did you ever have a massive crush on someone inappropriate when you were younger—someone you could never be with?'

Marc stopped sloshing. 'Maybe.'

Tasmin? Except that he'd finally prevailed with her. They'd started dating in the final months of school.

'Do you remember how it possessed you? How it took over your days, your nights, your thoughts? You can't remember it starting but then it just…is. It's everything. It's everywhere. Like it's always existed. Like it could never not exist.' She stopped sloshing in his hold. 'Have you ever felt something like that?'

The tightness of his voice rumbled against her back and birthed goose bumps in its wake. 'Go on.'

'It's how it was with me and my addiction. I didn't recognise how it consumed me when I was deep inside it. I arranged my day around it. I made allowances for it. It became so normal. I learned to function around the compulsion. Just like the most concentrated of adolescent infatuations. And every bit as irrational.'

She felt him shake his head and she tensed. 'Is that no, you don't remember how it feels,' she asked, half turning back towards him, 'or no, you don't understand?'

His lips were enticingly close to her face. His breath was hot against her cheek. He swallowed hard. 'I remember.'

'Then you know how it can take you by stealth. The passion. The fixation. The feeling that you'll die if you don't have it in your life. And you don't even feel like it's a problem.'

Those arms tightened. 'It feels that good?'

'It feels great because you're love-sick. And all those endorphins feed your obsession. And it's hurting you but you don't notice. You don't care. Nothing matters as much as the feeling. As the subject of your passion. It's like a parasite. Built to survive. The first things it attacks are the things that threaten its survival. Judgement. Willpower. Self-awareness.'

Marc's silent breathing began to mesmerize her, his warmth sucking her in. She couldn't tell whether her words were having any impact on him. 'And being denied it physically hurts. It aches. You become irrational with the pain inside and out and you lash out at people you care about. And the more they intervene, the more you begin to imagine they're working to keep you away from the thing that sustains you. And that's when you start making choices that impact on everyone around you.'

She felt him stiffen behind her and knew he was thinking about his mother.

'But adolescents learn to deal with infatuation,' he said. 'Or they grow out of it.'

Or they give in to it. She wasn't surprised to hear condemnation in his voice, but it still saddened her. How many people saw addiction as a sign of moral weakness. A character flaw. 'Mostly because life forces them out of it. Classes. Structure. Discipline. Financial constraints. Exposure to new people. Cold reality has a way of making obsession hard to indulge.'

She turned back towards Marc again. The unexpected move brought her frigid jaw line perilously close to his lips as he leaned in for a slosh. The hairs on her neck woke and paid attention. 'But imagine that you're of legal age with ready cash, no particular structure to your day,' she whispered, 'no restraints on whether or not you indulge it. A husband who makes drinking a regular part of his day.' *And all the reason in the world to want to numb the pain.* 'No reason at all not to allow the great fascination to continue. Why wouldn't you?'

Steel band arms circled around her and held her still. Close. Her eyes fluttered shut. He spoke close to her ear. 'Because it's killing you?'

'By then, you are so hooked on the feeling you just… don't…care.'

He turned her in his hold and looked down on her, a

pained frown marring his face. 'You didn't care about dying?'

She shook her head. Hating herself. Hating the incredulous look on his face. Not that she couldn't understand why, after everything he'd been through with Janice. She could feel it in the tension in every part of his body.

'Because you truly fear you'll die without it,' she said.

His frown trebled and he pulled her towards him. Into his warmth. The kind of moment she'd lived for back in school. It was old Marc and old Beth from a time that the two of them could have conquered the world. From inside the crush of his arms, she could feel his chest rising and falling roughly. He was struggling with everything she'd just told him. And why not? It had taken her two years to finally recognise where her addiction seeded. And when.

Emotional and physical exhaustion hovered around her. She struggled to keep her eyes open, leaning her entire upper body into his. So tired, the only thought she had about the two perfect pectoral muscles facing her was what a comfortable pillow they'd make. His hand slipped around her back to better support her.

'I don't know what to say,' he said, voice rough.

'There's nothing you can say,' she murmured thickly. 'It's enough that you know.'

'Thank you for explaining.'

'I'm glad you understand now.' Her words slurred. Her eyes surrendered to the weight on them and closed. She leaned more heavily into him.

His voice was only a murmur but it echoed through the chest she pressed against. 'You want my understanding? I thought it was forgiveness you wanted?'

Nodding only rubbed her cheek against his chest. It was perfect friction. She did it twice. 'Both. I don't want you to hate me.'

Marc's thumping heart beat hard against her ear. Five times. Six times. 'I accept your apology, Beth.'

Something indefinable shifted in her world. Like the last barrel of a lock clunking into place releasing a door to fling open. And out rushed all her remaining energy like heat from a room, finally freed from her determination to win his forgiveness. Marc was the last of her list. She'd focused on those names for so long she'd never really given much thought to what lay beyond them. A dreadful unknown spread out before her. Something she had to brave without help.

Later. When she wasn't so warm and tired.

She found her voice. 'Thank you.'

He took her face in his hands and tipped it up to his. She forced her lids to lift. Hazel eyes blazed down onto her. 'I think I've been angry at you for a really long time.'

She blinked up at him, barely able to drag her lids open after each close. Knowing these words came straight from his soul. 'I know. I'm sorry.' She laid her face back against the pillow of warm muscle and sighed as the heat soaked into her cold cheeks.

'Why couldn't I let it go?' he murmured.

I don't know. The words came out as an insensible mumble as her lips moved against his skin. His arms tightened around her, held her up.

'Why couldn't I let you go?'

His voice swam in and out with the lapping tide and, ultimately, washed clear through her head and out again as she slipped into sleep, quite literally, on her feet.

CHAPTER SEVEN

A HIGH-pitched shriek dragged Beth from a deep, uncomfortable slumber. A musty smell filled her nose and she shifted around uncomfortable rocks that had somehow found their way into her bed.

Her eyes cracked open. Not a bed…the back of a car. And the shriek was a Wedge-tailed Eagle that, even now, circled the dim skies in search of breakfast. The rocks were the detritus that littered the back of Marc's four-wheel drive, cutting into her back and thighs where she lay on them. And the mustiness was a mix of the skanky old blanket that wrapped tortilla-like around her and the salty moisture of her clothes, her hair. Dry yet damp.

God damn it, Marc!

Fury forced her upright and every seized muscle in her body protested violently. She should have kept moving. She should have kept helping. Not sleeping comfortably—or even uncomfortably—while Marc froze his butt off alone with the whale.

She lurched like a caterpillar towards the rear doors of the wagon and used her bare feet to activate the internal handle. Icy-cold air streamed in as she pushed the doors with her legs and her skin prickled all over with gooseflesh.

It took longer than it should have, but she eventually scrambled out of the car and tucked the dirty blanket more securely around her against the chill wind. Up here, exposed above the dunes, it was almost worse than down on the shore. The world around her was still muted but tiny fingers of light tickled at the horizon.

'How long have I been out?' She didn't waste any time with pleasantries as she got back to the shoreline. Marc was up to his knees in the rapidly retreating ocean, practically sagging on the whale for strength. 'Why did you let me sleep?'

He turned his face her way. Haggard but still beautiful. To her. 'You passed out in my arms, Beth. You were exhausted.'

'So are you.'

'I wasn't the one asleep on my feet.' Frost rose from his lips with every word.

Beth's whole face tightened on a frown. Anxiety flowed through her. 'How are you?'

'Freezing. Thanks for asking.'

'What can I do?'

'You can not give me grief for putting an unconscious woman into my car.'

She bit back her frustration. 'I'm sorry to be ungracious. I just… You were alone.'

'I've done this before, on my own, Beth.'

'You shouldn't be alone.'

Well…! That was a mouthful and a half straight from her sleepy subconscious. The moment the words left her, she knew she meant more than just today. This man deserved the right woman by his side, for ever. A bit of happiness. He'd earned it.

Not that she was the right woman. Beth frowned at

the instant denial her mind tossed up. It was a little too fervent.

'Why are you single?'

He lifted one eyebrow. 'Why are you asking?'

'Because you'd be a catch, I would have thought. Even in the country.' Where men outnumbered women ten to one.

'Thanks for the confidence.'

All the time that had passed might not have existed. They fitted instantly back together. Back into the gentle jibes only friends could make.

'I've had girlfriends.'

Olympic Tasmin for one. 'Anything special?'

His eyes studied the lightening horizon. 'Nothing lasting, if that's what you're asking. But all nice women.'

'So what went wrong?'

He glared at her. 'I hope you're not warming up to offer relationship advice?'

Despite herself, she laughed. 'No. I may be a lot of things, but a hypocrite is not one of them.' Her eyes went to the whale. She looked ominously still. 'How is she?'

'Worse than either of us. But hanging in there.' His words were full of staged optimism. As though the giant animal could understand him.

'You're not going to give up on her, are you?'

'Nope.' He turned to the whale and spoke directly to her. Beth got the feeling there had been several man-to-whale conversations while she was out like a light. 'I'm not going to let you go.'

She frowned, those words striking a chord she couldn't name deep inside. They seemed somehow important but she couldn't place why. The eagle called again, high up in the part of the sky that was still a deep, dark disguise.

'It says a lot about you.'

His look upward was a question.

'How hard you're fighting for this whale. To give her a chance. You really haven't changed that much after all.'

Marc bit down on whatever he'd been about to say and clenched his jaw shut. Hard. She practically felt the atmosphere shift. Maybe he wasn't in the mood for conversation after her revelations in the small hours of morning. She fought the heat of shame that rose on that thought and the sinking surge of self-doubt that followed. Then she braced herself against the cold, tossed back the blanket and bundled it into her arms. Before her body could convince her not to, she plunged back up to her knees in the icy wash and sank the blanket under the water; its frigid kiss shocked her into full awakening. She dragged its weighty thickness up and over the whale, shrouding its skin in dampness. The nasty arrowhead scar on its tail was exposed again.

That couldn't be good. It meant the tide was retreating. If it went much further out it would mean the whale would be high and dry.

As soon as the blanket was secured, she moved, aching, up the beach and collected the empty two-litre container and commenced the bend-fill-slosh ritual all over again. Her body didn't even bother protesting this time. It knew when it was licked.

Marc watched every move.

'How are *you* doing?' he finally asked. Tension tinged his voice, but it was concern etched in his face. And caution.

Oh.

She stumbled slightly when she realised he was talking about drinking. Or *not drinking* in the case of this very difficult eighteen hours. And he wasn't particularly happy to be asking.

The thought of alcohol had not even crossed her mind since she'd woken. That had to be a first. Although it shot back with a vengeance now. Hunger. Thirst. Craving. Needing. They all mixed together into an uncomfortable obsession for just about everything you could put in your mouth.

She feigned misunderstanding. 'I'm ready for a big plate of bacon and eggs, a big mug of hot tea and a Bloody Mary.'

Hazel eyes snapped to her. 'You joke about it?'

She sighed. Pushed her shoulders back. 'Keeping it bound and gagged gives it too much power. Maybe it's time I started to lighten up about it all.' *Take some of the control back.* 'Get back to a normal life.'

'Fair enough. What will you do now?' he asked. 'To make a living? To have that normal life?'

It was a good question. Her dark years were behind her. Her list was done. She had the rest of her future to think about. She blew out the residual tension from their previous question. 'I have no idea... The past two years has been all about recovery. It's been a day by day kind of thing.' She stared at him, blank. 'I suppose running a bottle shop is out of the question?'

His glare was colder than the water.

'Sorry. Bad joke.' Bleakness filled her. 'I feel like all I've done is drink and then not drink.'

'You have a decade to catch up on.' He looked hard at her. 'What about uni? It's never too late.'

Beth frowned. 'I don't think so.'

'Mature aged students are perfectly common now.'

Taverns, parties, temptation. 'I don't think I'd be a good fit on campus.'

His mouth tightened as he realised. 'Online, then?'

Something she could study in the comfort of her own cavernous warehouse. In the silence of her own lonely hours. 'What would I study?'

'What do you enjoy?'

She blinked at him.

'What about your painting?'

She shook her head. 'That's something I do for therapy. It won't earn me a living.'

'Why not? Maybe you could help others like you helped yourself. Give back.'

Her head came up. Giving back rang all kinds of karmic bells. Art therapy. She hadn't known such a thing existed until she'd needed it. But it did. And it worked.

Marc shrugged. 'There'd be no shortage of people needing assistance.'

Purpose suddenly glowed, bright and promising on her horizon. She *could* give back. Lord knew she'd had her fair share of assistance from others who gave their time. She chewed her lip. 'I could. That could work. Something simple that will help people.'

His eyes narrowed. 'You don't want to rule the country any more?'

Alcoholism had taken more from her than just years. 'If I can just rule *me* I'll be happy.'

He stared at her long and hard. Compassion filled his eyes. His voice was low and sad. 'You'll get there, Beth. I believe in you.'

A deep sorrow washed through her. 'You always did.'

Silence fell. Beth shook her head to chase off the blues she could feel settling.

'What would you change?' Marc's voice came out of the dim morning light, tossing her earlier words back at her. 'If you had the opportunity to do ten years ago over again. What would you do differently?'

Ah. This one she'd pondered plenty and she'd refined it during some of their long silences in the water. She bent to re-soak the blanket and thanked God that she had no sleeve on which to be displaying her heart. 'I wouldn't have put so much importance on what others said. I definitely wouldn't have encouraged Damien's advances.'

She kept her eyes away from his as she stretched the blanket out across the whale's back. 'I wouldn't have listened to…' *Your mother.* But now, more than ever, she couldn't say that. There was already so much lost between them. Vindicating herself would condemn them. 'I wouldn't have shut you out of my life.'

'You didn't.'

She looked up. 'I did.'

He shook his head. 'I mean you didn't succeed. I kept a low profile but that didn't mean I wasn't aware of everything you did. Where you went. Right up until school ended and I lost you, I was watching.'

Watching. Beth stared. She bled for the near-man who'd been so hurt but still so very loyal. Maybe despite himself. Her voice was tiny. 'I thought you were gone.' Present-absent in the way only a teen could be.

'No. I was still there.'

Her chest tightened. 'Why?'

He considered her from under lashes crusted with salt. 'We were friends. Friends don't abandon each other.'

Beth's cheeks flamed.

'I wasn't having a dig, Beth.'

She shook her head. 'I know. But it doesn't change what happened.' She stared at him. 'You deserved better.'

You still do. Her tight heart pushed rich pulses of blood around her body and they throbbed past her ears. Her eyes stuck fast to his. She made her decision.

'I need to tell you something. About my last days drinking.' She took a second to gather courage by trailing down to the whale's exposed tail and draping the soaked blanket over it. Water cascaded over the vicious arrow-head wound.

She took a deep breath and then met his eyes again. 'I forgot you, Marc. When I was deep in the hands of my addiction, I kind of…blocked you out. For years.'

His nostrils flared. His hands stilled.

'After graduation I thought about you every day. Wondered how you were. What you were doing. Thought about what I had done. I thought about the connection we used to have, the stories we had in common. Every day I tried to recreate with my husband what I'd had with you, and it just wasn't working. As I slipped further and further into numbness I think I just…' She swallowed and took a shuddery breath. 'Remembering you hurt. So I just stopped.'

Those beautiful hands tightened on his towel. Just as they'd tightened in her hair while he'd kissed her. Last night. All those years ago.

'I can understand that.' Hurt thickened his already gravelly voice.

She shook her head. Forced herself to continue. 'One day I woke up and there you were, blazing and persistent at the front of my mind. Like a ghost with a mission. Except I was the ghost. And I realised I'd been…non-existent for so long. I remembered how you used to believe in me no matter what but, this time, instead of that making me sad, hurting, it made me determined.'

She turned her eyes back to his. 'You gave me strength, Marc. I stopped drinking because of the memory of the boy who had so much belief in me. More than I'd ever had in myself. And because of the goodness in you that I'd always wished was mine. The strength of character.'

His eyes dropped away, which meant she could breathe.

'I just wanted you to understand the part you played in pulling me out of the morass. I can't thank you because you didn't even know it was happening. But I can acknowledge it. And I think I understand it now. What it meant.'

She clamped nervous hands together. 'Drinking helped me forget how I'd treated someone I loved. How the choices I made snowballed into a lousy life with a lousy husband and a lousy future. That I'd done that to myself. But the memory of my feelings for you saved me when everything was lost. When I was.'

His frown folded his handsome face and his jaw twitched with tension.

She drew in a massive breath for strength. 'You filled my heart in high school, Marc, and I think you filled it right through my marriage, except I couldn't bear to acknowledge it. One day I just…forced you out of my heart to protect myself.' She laid a hand on the whale. 'But then I crashed into the water with you yesterday and discovered you were still the same loyal, generous, brave person who I loved back then. You haven't changed.' She dipped her eyes, then forced them back up. Took a deep, deep breath. 'My feelings haven't changed.'

His silence screamed.

Mortification waited greedily in the wings but she held it back. 'I don't expect anything in return—' *much as she wished for it* '—I just wanted you to know. That you'd changed my life. That you'd *saved* my life. That our stories are connected.'

His neoprene chest heaved up and down, his eyes blazed hot and hard into hers. The hundred variations of things he might say whispered through her head. Then he finally spoke and it was laced with agony.

'I'm not a crutch, Beth.'

Her stomach plummeted. *What?* 'No, I—'

Sudden shouting from the direction of Marc's car split the quiet of the pre-morning. A dozen figures appeared at the dune tops, silhouetted against the dawning sun. They carried coils of rope slung over their shoulders and more blankets. Beth should have cried with relief that the cavalry had finally arrived but she wanted to scream at them for *just five more minutes*. It felt vitally important that she have just a bit more time alone with Marc.

She swung her eyes back to him.

His voice was hard. Hurried. 'I can't be the thing that sustains you, Beth. You can't swap one fixation for another, put that kind of responsibility on me. I lived with that for years.'

His mother... She opened her mouth to try and explain again as people started streaming down the dunes towards them. Euphoria that assistance had finally arrived crashed headlong into the sudden shot of urgent adrenalin surging through her body. In that moment she felt the best she had all night.

And the absolute worst.

Marc lay his shredded, saturated towel along the whale's broad back for one last time. Then he pinned her with his gaze. 'Me accepting that you're sorry for what happened a lifetime ago... Are you expecting that it will change anything? Other than for you?'

'I...' *Was she?* What did it really change, other than to mark the completion of her list? One more step in her road to healing.

'Because it doesn't change anything for me, Beth.' He cast her one final tired look and then dragged his exhausted legs out of the water.

The earth shifted under her feet. In all her imaginings, it had never occurred to her that Marc would accept her apology but that he might not truly forgive her. Realise the depth of her feelings but not value it. Each was meaningless without the other.

Her heart pounded. 'I thought, maybe if you understood...'

'I understand more than you know.' His tired eyes rested on her. 'It's been ten years, Beth. Any feelings we had are nothing but a memory. We're both different people now. If I helped you to get over—'

Could he still not say the word?

'—everything, I'm glad.' His eyes lifted. 'But I'm not some kind of lucky charm to keep you sober. And telling me you were alcoholic doesn't go any way to restoring the lost trust between us. Did you honestly expect it would?'

An awful realisation dawned with the sun that suddenly peeked its warmth above the sand dunes. She *had* expected that, yes. That her cosmic reward for finding him and confessing her shame—her many shames—would be a beginning as blazing and new as the sun climbing over the horizon. That the man who had played such an important role in her recovery would be given back to her and they could have a fresh start.

Strange hands were suddenly all over her, pulling her gently back from the water as two wetsuit-clad bodies slid into her place and plunged fresh blankets into the water. Beth ignored them and reached out to urgently snare Marc's hand as he left the water, desperate not to become separated even for a moment. Something in her knew that if that happened she'd never find him again.

His eyes dropped to where her fingers twisted amongst his with white-knuckled urgency. When they lifted, they were tragic. 'I can see that you've done it really tough since we parted, Beth, and that brings me no joy at all. But drunk Beth wasn't the one who tore our friendship apart that day behind the library. Dumping me for someone better was a choice that you made stone cold sober.'

The awful, sinking reality hit her. No matter what her motivation, how honourable, she *had* ripped apart their friendship in cold blood. She'd *let* his mother drive a wedge between them, and then she'd *let* Damien exploit the gap. She'd done nothing to stop any of it. Then and now. She still couldn't bring herself to tell him why she'd really let him walk away that day.

'But you accepted my apology…'

'I believe that you're sorry.' His words grew harder. Shorter.

'But our friendship…?'

His eyes were flat and pained. And as unmovable as granite. 'I've lived without it this long…'

Pain ripped through her as the first shards of light speared across the sky. Why had she expected more? Every part of her wanted to shut up tighter than a clam. Protect herself. But that had got her nowhere so far in life.

'Wait!' Her desperate voice broke, drawing him back as he turned towards two approaching men in Department of Conservation uniforms. 'What happens now?'

Marc's face was haggard, tragic as he shrugged. She loved every line. 'I go home. You go home. I appreciate your help with the whale but, as far as I'm concerned, we're not connected any more. Our story's over.'

Not connected?

'But...you kissed me.'

His eyes were tragic. 'Yeah.' He stared long and hard at his oldest friend. 'You'd think I'd learn, huh?'

Beth stumbled backwards in the sand as he walked away.

A gentle female voice murmured near her ear—buzzing in her throbbing head—and supported her up the beach as others draped thick blankets around her shoulders. Her eyes streamed from the sudden onset of morning light after so many hours of darkness. Dawn should have brought a bright new beginning for their friendship, not this awful gaping chasm. This was like losing him all over again. The impossibility that he could literally not want her back in his life in any form. That he could forgive her past but not her present...

She sank down into the sand as someone thrust an energy bar and Thermos of tea at her. Voices throbbed in her spinning head and she let herself be tended to like a child as they tut-tutted over the open blisters on her hands and the sunburn on her tight skin. Her head cranked around to follow Marc's progress as he dragged his feet up the beach with the wildlife officials, deep in conversation.

Someone was asking her where she was staying and she felt her lips responding, identifying her motel. Then capable hands lifted her to her feet and supported her as they moved up the beach, up a different track to the one leading to Marc's car. Her head cranked around to catch sight of him as he disappeared up the far dune.

He didn't even say goodbye. To her or the whale.

A hollow, awful emptiness filled her.

That was exactly as he'd left her ten years ago.

CHAPTER EIGHT

BETH's grungy warehouse had never been so packed. Nor so popular.

She'd opened her doors four months ago to offer art classes to women in need of some beauty in their lives. An outlet. It was full six days a week with women recovering from addiction, abuse and trauma. They fiddled with pigment, they dabbed on canvases, but, more importantly, they talked about their lives. Opened up about their troubles, in person and on canvas. Sometimes they created something extraordinary.

It was the most natural kind of therapy in the safety of a group who had all experienced loss. Discovering how many kinds there were helped Beth put her own into perspective. She'd sacrificed a decade of her life to shame; she wasn't about to let that continue. She may have lost Marc again but she knew now that she was made of more than just those events that happened *to* her.

But success led to attention and, before long, the council had been on her doorstep to discuss the running of an unauthorised home business. Which was how she came to be standing here tonight, proudly wearing a dress made by one of her students from fabric screen-printed by another, a glass of sparkling water in hand, watching forty complete strangers dissect her paintings.

Running art classes from home was a no-no, according to council bylaws. Running them in an approved art space was fine. And Beth's father's rundown old warehouse was just inside the arts precinct boundary. Two weeks of hasty framing and hanging later and—*voilà*—*Our Stories* was born: an art exhibition featuring the best student work arising from four months of therapeutic art classes backed up with her own works from the past decade.

Not paintings she'd ever imagined she'd be displaying—in a million years—but necessary to pad out the collection and, in a strange kind of way, therapeutic in itself. No one assembled knew what had driven her to paint the darkest and most harrowing images—that was true of all the exhibited works—but they knew what the theme of *Our Stories* was. Their imaginations were surely filling in the blanks.

Exhibiting the works so she could keep offering classes was the goal; selling them was pure bonus. Not for great fortunes but, in the case of Kate Harrison—a mother of two who'd crawled away from a lifetime of violent abuse—selling four paintings inspired by her gorgeous, shuttered children was the first five hundred dollars she'd ever earned herself. By her own hand.

It might as well have had six more zeroes after it.

Two of her own paintings had already sold. Enough to pay for all the framing. It was surprisingly validating to have someone willing to buy her darkest moments, and deeply healing to know that the paintings would be leaving here at the end of the exhibition. Although why anyone would want to put her greatest moments of sorrow on their wall, she couldn't imagine. The enthusiastic buyers called them bold and brave. To Beth they were time capsules. Something that belonged for ever in the past.

There were more recent works of hers exhibited too. An Impressionistic acrylic number of a man's hand, slender-fingered and stroking the curve of a woman's jaw. Another one simply entitled *Duck!* was a comical close-up of a wood duck perched in a man's lap. As she watched, someone slapped a fat red 'Sold' sticker on it.

There was only one work in the whole place that had a hasty *'Not for Sale'* Post-it note affixed to it. It was where the bulk of the strangers were crowding right now—the painting that had generated some interest from the local newspaper. The enormous canvas piece she called *Holly's Bay*. Painted from under the sea, looking back to shore, where two sets of feet braced on either side of a half-submerged whale in the shallows. She'd painted it in her first fortnight after getting home from her trip to the south coast, working day and night until she'd finally exorcised the wash of pained feelings she'd brought home with her.

Better that than what she would have done two years ago to ease the pain. Which wasn't to say she didn't still feel the emotion when her guard slipped, but the worst of the feelings were forever suspended in the thick paint, like tiny creatures trapped for eternity in primordial bog.

The crowd speculated about what was above the waterline. Only Beth really knew. And Marc.

'Tell me that's our new life model.' One of her students sat up straighter next to Beth, her eyes fixed on the warehouse entrance. Their first and only life model had been a seventy-eight-year-old man with nicotine-stained fingers who was a little too eager to take off his clothing for a room full of women. Particularly since they were only drawing hands that week.

Beth twisted to see what had grabbed the student's attention. She practically tripped in her haste to get off the sofa and behind something to obscure her. The instinct to hide was immediate and all-consuming. She ignored the curious looks of her guests as she shuffled herself resolutely behind the small cluster of people, out of view of the man who had just walked in the door.

Marc.

He's here… He's here…

Between the bodies of her human shield, her eyes locked onto him and held fast. His own moved slowly over the artworks on the far side of the building. He moved quickly past her students' unlabelled work and onto her next one, accurately scenting which had come from Beth's particular soul. There he stopped. Studied. Considered.

It gave her ample time to rediscover him from the safety of her hide. He didn't seem comfortable in his suit jacket although it fitted him perfectly. He kept rolling his shoulders and tugging at his tie. Beth's heart kicked up. Why was he here? Would he recognise aspects of himself in several of the exhibited works?

He shifted sideways again as he moved on to the next work, then stopped and stared long and hard at it—a stylised acrylic of a house, not one of her own. She shifted in opposition, keeping him in view between the bodies. Keeping herself out of view. She knew her student was glancing between them with interest and she cursed herself for being a coward. This was ridiculous, hiding out behind guests.

She straightened her shoulders on a deep breath and

stepped out from behind the gaggle of art appreciators as Marc's roaming gaze brought him to the piece called *Duck!* He stepped closer, his long fingers tracing the fine acrylic ridges in the work. His eyes trailed over every element in the painting. Shielded. Protected. Then he turned unexpectedly and his gaze collided with her own unprepared one.

She tried to suppress the excited chorus of her subconscious, but he must have seen something of it in her face because his lips thinned. He stepped towards her tightly. She couldn't help mirroring him.

'Beth.'

Potentially avid ears were all around and the last thing she wanted at her students' first exhibition was any kind of scene. Beth took his arm and turned him back to the framed work, peered up at the colourful representation of a fat little duck perched happily on a pair of blue jeans and pretended to study it. Discussing the painting was a far safer option than whatever he was here for.

'Do you know where this is?' she murmured, her mind screaming all the while—*Why are you here?*

Marc dragged his eyes off her and back onto the painting. Eventually. His words were careful. 'That's our stowaway.'

They'd been on their way home from their first and only camping trip. They'd swapped seats so learner driver Beth could clock up some obligatory training hours at the wheel. It wasn't until they were underway that the duck chose to pop its sleek little head up from the back seat, where it had presumably spent the night.

'You screamed like a banshee,' Marc said on a twist of lips.

Thinking about the past was so much easier than worrying what was about to happen in the present. He'd spent the rest of the year ribbing her and she'd defended herself till the last. Like now.

'I didn't know it had chosen to make itself at home in my mother's back seat back at the campsite. I was tense enough remembering how to drive with you watching me, without the added surprise of a little blue beak and a pair of beady eyes staring at me in my rear-vision mirror.'

Beth's high-pitched holler had sent the duck into a frenzy of terrified flapping in the small cabin of the car and it had been all she could do to keep the vehicle on the road. Marc had twisted from his front seat position to try and shoo the manic duck back out through the hastily lowered window, but had only succeeded in agitating it into a flurry of wings and webbed feet.

Eventually it had plopped, half exhausted, into his lap and sat there blinking at both of them. He'd spent a minute pressed frozen into the back of the passenger seat before realising the duck was quite at home on his lap and, by the time they pulled into a national park wetland fifty kilometres off the highway, he even had a gentle hold on its rotund little body—as though it were a football he was holding on his lap and not a hitch-hiking wood duck.

That had been the beginning of the end for Beth. Seeing him holding the bird so gently, hearing him chatting to it in improvised duck language and watching its little head twisting and perking up in response. Her heart had turned in on itself right then and there. If she had to name the moment her heart shifted...

'I'm not sure who was sorrier when we released him onto that lake, you or the duck,' Marc joked now, smiling at the bird in the painting. 'You really captured the little guy.'

But, before she could answer, he shifted and his eyes fell on *Holly's Bay*, mounted high to his right. His smile froze. Blood drained from his face. Beth stared, captive, as his eyes locked on the powerful reminder of their time in the water.

'Why are you here?' she whispered. No point making any more small talk. Not when the question clamoured in her mind like pealing bells. She locked her eyes firmly onto the feet in her painting.

He faked it as well as she did, staring up at the painting as though casually discussing its composition. 'The exhibition made the *South Coast Examiner* because of the whale. Because of our story.'

Our story is over...

'I was up in Perth anyway and...' He paused, staring at the giant painted feet pressed into the ocean floor in front of him. He cleared his throat. 'That's not true. I needed to come. I needed to see you.'

'Me?' Longer words simply would not come.

He looked down at her sideways. 'Do you want me to go?'

He'd walk through fire if you asked him to.

'No. But I need a second.' She took a steadying breath, conscious of curious eyes all around them. Mostly her students. Her heart thumped like a sonic pulse. Lucky there were no whales this far inland or she'd be throwing out their guidance systems with the waves coming off her. She sheltered in something safer.

'What happened to the whale? Did she make it?'

Marc took a second to refocus. 'They got her back out to sea.'

'Did she stay there?'

'Impossible to know. The second refloating seemed to be a success.'

Beth nodded. 'Maybe she knew she had nothing to stay for.' More fitting words had never been spoken.

'Maybe.' His voice caressed her, even though his eyes stayed carefully fixed to the painting.

'She made a new beginning for herself. I hope so. She deserves her second chance.'

Beth didn't mean for it to be loaded. But too much had happened between them for it to stay an innocent comment. Marc glanced around at the milling crowd. Then back to her. 'Is there somewhere we can speak?'

Not inside. Every inch of her warehouse held either buyers, exhibits or their artists. The only off-limits place was her bedroom and he was categorically not invited there. Not outside of her turbulent dreams, anyway.

She nodded and forced her feet to cooperate as she stepped away from him and led the way to the garden door. 'Garden' was a little too generous for the tiny courtyard space she'd filled with potted green. But it offered privacy and quiet, both of which she figured they'd be needing. She closed the door behind Marc and then turned to lean on it. He roamed the tiny space and kept his back to her.

Contradictory feelings raged through her. Excitement. Dread. Curiosity. Anxiety. Lucky she had a blank canvas in her store room. She was going to need to exorcise this lot.

'Why are you here, Marc?' She faked the same bravado she'd had to employ once when an abusive ex-husband tracked down one of her students during class. It worked then, but she wasn't convinced she was pulling it off now.

He turned. 'I wanted to speak with you.'

'Go ahead.'

Marc propped himself against a concrete bird-bath and rested both hands on its ornate edge, fingers curling around it tightly. Then he lifted shuttered eyes back up to her. 'I…regret…how I left things between us back at the Bay.'

There was nothing between them. He'd made that abundantly clear. Beth stared silently.

'I've had weeks to think about everything we talked about that day in the water and how I reacted. And to track you down.'

Thump, thump, thump… 'You've been trying to find me?'

'Your parents wouldn't give me your address.'

'They knew—' *how I was after getting back from seeing you.* She swallowed. Changed tack. 'They're protective of me these days.'

He took in her pensive body language. Stiff straight limbs, hands clenched in front of her. 'Will you sit, Beth?'

'No, thank you.' Not on your life.

He just nodded. Then he met her eyes with his serious hazel ones. 'I wanted to apologise. I didn't handle myself well that morning at Holly's Bay…'

Just the morning? Letting her hurt feelings show wouldn't help anyone. She smiled tightly.

'…I felt that I owe you more of an explanation.'

'Is there more? You seemed very sure of your feelings.'

His eyes dropped away from hers. 'Those haven't changed. But there's more to it than I…' Breath hissed out of him. 'Please, will you sit?'

This was hard for him. Every protective part of her wanted to reach out. Help him. But she did the only thing her self-respect would allow. She nodded and moved to one of the outdoor chairs. He pulled one up opposite. She fought the urge to automatically fill the silence like sea water rushing into footprints on the shore.

'I'm ashamed of myself for letting you walk away from that beach doubting yourself. Your worth. You were brave and honest with me that day and I handled everything badly. You were a friend, Beth, and that should have earned you more from me.'

Were. 'You said you weren't interested in my friendship.'

'I wasn't. I'm not.' Beth sucked in a breath and he winced. 'But not for the reason you think. I owe you an explanation.'

He took her hands. 'I can see you've done it really tough over the years, Beth. I only have to look at the images hanging on your walls to realise you've been in a dark, miserable place. How hard it must have been for you to get through it alone.'

She just nodded. Months with her students had taught her to acknowledge her own strengths rather than apologising endlessly for the weaknesses. 'Pity doesn't help me.'

His brows met in a frown. 'No. I can see that. Even more now. These past few months have obviously been good for you.'

She smiled sadly. 'Someone told me that we were responsible for our own happiness. I chose to go out and find some.'

His stare was fathoms deep. His voice flat. 'You've met someone?'

What? That would require forcing Marc out of her heart and, given how long his memory had endured her horrific marriage, that wasn't likely to happen for some

time. 'I meant I've found it in me. I'm in a good place.'
His frown intensified. He looked undecided. Was he
regretting coming? Was he having second thoughts?
'Go ahead, Marc. Finish what you came to say.'

'I wanted to... When I indicated that your friendship
was not of interest to me, that might have suggested that
I thought you were not worthy...'

Her laugh was hard. 'In a manner of speaking.'

His eyes closed briefly. 'I regret my choice of words.
That you might have thought I meant... That it might
have set you back.'

Frost snapped along her veins. Would she always be
an addict first with him? 'You're worried you might
have sent me back to the bottle?' A hint of colour crept
above his collar. Her lips set hard. 'You think you have
that much power?'

His gaze was resolute. 'You told me you loved me.'

Beth's stomach dropped and her breath caught. But,
before she could speak, he continued. 'In school, you
had feelings for me. Then, later in your marriage, those
feelings...complicated things. Was that true?'

Beth stiffened in her seat. She should just say no. All
of this would go away. 'I'm not in the habit of making
things up to suit the moment.'

He glared at her.

She hissed. 'Yes, it was true.' He opened his mouth
to speak and she rushed on. 'But I've dealt with those
feelings as part of my healing process and I know they
were based on a memory. A teenage memory. Not real
life. You don't have to worry.'

He let out a stream of repressed air and stared at her,
a tight expression on his face. 'I'm not worried, Beth.
You honour me.'

The stark pain in his eyes hit her between the breasts. Stole her breath.

'Why did you tell me?' he barrelled on. 'What did you hope to achieve?'

'I... Nothing. It wasn't a planned thing. I just felt you deserved to know. I felt close enough to you to tell you.' Until you sliced my heart out with a few lazy words. 'At the time.'

'You regret it?'

The harsh laugh bubbled back up. 'Wouldn't you?'

'That's partly why I'm here. It...wasn't easy to hear, Beth.'

Compounding the awkwardness of what had been a stunningly miserable twenty-four hours? She set her shoulders back. 'I'm sure it wasn't.'

His hand went up. 'You misunderstand me. It wasn't easy to hear because there was a time I would have given anything to hear those words on your lips.'

Beth wasn't speechless often, but this was what it felt like.

'You gave me the gift of your feelings. So that I would understand you better. I'd like to repay that.'

Beth frowned. 'What don't I understand?'

'Why I can't stay friends with you.'

A sick awareness rolled over her. He wasn't here to make up.

Marc filled his not insubstantial chest. 'I worshipped you for nine years, Beth. From fourth grade through to the end of school. You were...everything to me. My partner-in-crime. My confidante. My inspiration. Those feelings grew as we did. Us being separated was never an option in my mind.'

Mine neither, she wanted to say. But words couldn't squeeze out past the growing lump in her chest. Blind panic started to take her. She gripped the edges of the chair for strength.

'I felt the very moment when you finally realised you were a female and I was a male. When you started to look at me differently. Like a man. I started planning from that moment. Studying biology was all about you, Beth. A way to stay together. Tasmin Major was all about you. I had our first kiss all planned out in my mind. Where. When. What it would mean.' Recrimination saturated his quiet voice. 'I had our whole lives planned out in my mind.'

Too late, too late, her soul whispered. That cast her betrayal of him in a very different light. She thought back to that kiss. Marc's pain. Bad enough that she'd hurt herself so much.

She forced herself to speak. 'You never said...'

Would it truly have changed anything? She couldn't imagine how two kids could be any more interconnected than she and Marc were, anyway. His mother and her parents still would have begged her to release him from her influence. Had they seen which way the wind was blowing?

'I wanted everything to be just right. I should have told you sooner.'

'Why are you telling me now?'

Marc's eyes practically bled pain. 'If I thought there was any chance that I could put you away from me, perhaps we could stay friends.' He stared down on her, words thick with sorrow. 'But I can't. You're buried too deep in me.' His fingers pressed hard to the left side of his chest. He dropped his eyes to his outstretched feet, then lifted them again. His face hardened. 'My mother's weakness controlled her and spilled over into my life until it controlled me too. I can't let that touch me again. For anyone.'

His deep voice broke on those final words and his Adam's apple lurched up and down beneath his button-up collar. He was twenty-eight and eight years old at the same time. Beth's heart broke for the young, confused boy who'd endured a life with someone struggling with compulsion. And then it wept for her; knowing she couldn't willingly put Marc through pain any more than she could simply will alcohol out of her mind for ever.

If he cared less about her, her choices wouldn't affect him and they could stay friends. And if she cared less about him, she wouldn't fear hurting him and they could stay friends.

Caring so much forced them apart.

A bone-deep ache started up at the base of her spine. 'Irony is a bitch.'

Marc stared at her sadly.

'When we were younger, I used to think that we were two halves of the same person,' she said. 'We thought so much alike, we enjoyed the same things, we practically breathed in synch. Tearing our two halves apart was the hardest thing I'd ever done in my life but I did it because I believed it was the right thing to do.' *For you.* She ignored his frown and kept on. 'And then for years I beat myself up, fearing I'd made the wrong decision.

'But here I am, a decade on, back in exactly the same position.' Her laugh was bleak. 'Boy, the universe is really trying to spell something out for me, huh?'

'Don't take this on, Beth. This is about me, not you.'

Oh, please. 'I've spent a long time re-training myself to believe I'm about more than my addiction. But apparently that's not true.'

He flinched. 'Beth, don't…'

He'd have more luck stopping a freight train. She stared up at him, angry, hurt and confused. 'You see the addiction first, Marc. And the person second.'

His eyes blazed down on her. 'That's not true.'

'Can you honestly say—hand on heart—that you wouldn't feel differently about me if I wasn't recovering from alcoholism? If I was just a normal woman who'd been away travelling for years? That you wouldn't be back to planning our lives together? That you wouldn't be thinking about kisses and long lazy days in the bedroom and how many kids you might want to fill that big, empty, south coast homestead with?' She sure had been. In those vulnerable half asleep moments between dream and reality.

'Beth…'

He didn't have a prayer of disguising the leap of wishful thinking in his expression and Beth knew that was exactly what he wanted. He wanted normal. And she wasn't.

It hurt enough that she pushed, like pressing a toothache. 'What if I'm as good as it gets, Marc? It's been years and you're still alone. What if we are meant to be together and there's no one else out there for you? And you're tossing me aside without so much as a chance to prove myself.'

She didn't believe for one second that a man like Marc wouldn't find someone to share his life with. What did it say about her that she hoped he would and wouldn't in the same breath?

His face tightened. Colour streaked along the ridge of his angular cheekbone. 'This is about me not wanting to repeat the errors of the past. I spent half a lifetime suffering life with an addict, Beth. I'm really not in a hurry to do that again.'

Her gasp was like a horrible, pained punctuation mark. *Suffering?* That was how he'd view being with her. She ignored the splitting torture of her heart as it ripped away from her chest. Her voice shook with the force of not saying what she really wanted to.

Why can't you believe in me?

He saw her face and cursed. 'Bad choice of words. I'm sorry—'

She shot up a hand. 'Don't apologise. *I'm* sorry that it's taken me this long to catch on to how people see me.' She dropped her head and took several deep breaths. The pain welling inside her *begged* to spill out as blistering sarcasm, but she forced it down. She pressed her hand to her breast and found the courage to meet his eyes. 'I'm still in here, Marc. Your Beth is still here, trying her damnedest to get back to a place that is healthy and happy. But you can't see her, can you?'

In the dreadful silence that followed, the sounds of the art exhibition washed anxiously around her, as though trying to buffer her from the pain of what had just passed between them.

She forged ahead. 'I understand about living with someone who is controlled by a substance. I remember how that felt. What that did to me. How hard it was to fight. And I was an adult by then…'

Marc looked away.

'I've spent the last two and a half years rebuilding myself. I've spent the last four months convincing twenty women that it's okay to put themselves first, to do what they need to survive. Not to accept anything less than what is healthy for them. How can I possibly wish anything less for you?'

Or for myself.

She swallowed hard past the deep abiding sadness as a sinking wave of realisation broke around her. 'You and I are bad for each other, Marc. Maybe we always were, despite all the friendship. Maybe our parents saw that and that's why they…' She took a long breath. 'I'm dry now. *I* did that. On my own.'

'I know…'

It's not enough. His lowered eyes spelled it out. Even though it had cost her so much, her best effort still wasn't enough. The tragedy of that pricked in her eyes. But letting herself cry was not an option.

'You will always fear your mother in me,' she whispered. 'And I will always fear suspicion in you. And that's not good for me. I need to surround myself with support and strength. Not doubt and judgement.'

Raw pain soaked his words. 'I'm so sorry.'

'Don't be. Imagine if we'd both just gone with our instincts and ended up hating each other.'

Imagine if we'd ended up blissfully happy, a tiny, tiny voice taunted. She ignored it.

His hand lifted towards her and then dropped. 'So what happens now?'

She shrugged. 'I don't know. I've never—' Beth stopped cold. She'd been about to say that she'd never ended a friendship before. But that wasn't true. She blinked up at him. 'I guess our story really is over.'

Marc stared at her. Long, hard. As if memorising every detail of her face. Then he cleared his throat. 'I should go.'

'Yes. I think so.'

He didn't move. He just stared. 'Is it wrong that I want to hold you so much?'

Her struggling heart gave a final, fatal lurch. Her

throat closed right over and her words struggled to get out. 'It's wrong to tell me.'

He just nodded. Then—finally—he turned for the door. When his fingers were on the handle, he turned back. 'Be happy, Beth. You deserve…everything.'

But not you, apparently.

Her essential goodness forced her to speak. Quickly, before she lost him. 'I'm sorry about what I said. You won't be alone for ever. There is someone out there for you.' *Someone better.* It was hard not to hear the demon doubts.

'I hope so.'

She saw the scepticism in his eyes and grabbed his arm. 'You have to go out and find her, Marc. She's not going to just appear at your door one morning.'

Thinking it was agony. Saying it killed her.

His smile was tragic. He nodded. 'No. That only happens once in a lifetime.'

The memory of walking up to him in his driveway suddenly filled her mind. The heat. The nerves. The secret anticipation. It seemed like lifetimes ago.

He turned and opened the door and she followed him back into the noisy hum. The lively animation of her guests seemed cartoonesque compared to the numbness of her dulled senses. Even the anxious glances of a few of her students didn't manage to penetrate the growing fog.

This feeling was frighteningly familiar. She fought it.

'You're not selling the whale?' Marc nodded his head to *Holly's Bay* as they passed. It broke her heart anew that the last words between them would be small talk. She wouldn't let that happen.

'She represents a turning point in my life. I'll never part with her.'

Not if I have to part with you. Beth walked him through the crowd to the door. Deep, thumping pain accompanied every step. Dead woman walking.

Just before the door, he turned to the painting of the house, the one he'd been drawn to when he'd arrived. His eyes were dangerously neutral. 'This one. Is it for sale?'

'They all are.' Except for one.

Marc frowned. 'It speaks to me. I can't explain it. The colours. The empty house. Like it sums up everything we've...' He paused, blew out a breath. 'Everything that's happened.'

The pain. The loss. The waste.

Beth swallowed hard. 'It's yours.' He looked at her and reached for his back pocket. She shook her head. 'Take it as a gift.'

'But the artist—'

Beth's chest tightened at everything they weren't saying. 'The artist would want you to have it.'

He stared at her long and hard and every sound in the room seemed to drop away until her throbbing heartbeat was the only sound at all. And Marc's voice. She leaned in and gently lifted the artwork off the wall and held it straight out to him.

His eyes fell on the emotional image painted in acrylics as he spoke. 'Thank you. I'll treasure it.'

Beth glanced at the two words scrawled on the back of the canvas. Pain speared through her. For everything she'd lost. He'd lost.

Even Janice Duncannon, whose name he would eventually find on the back of his painting. 'You should. It was meant to be yours.'

It seemed impossible that the two of them could be further apart now than ever. That nothing she'd done had brought any of them closer. That so much suffering would continue. She held the door for Marc as he exited and feasted greedily on the sight of his broad shoulders and back one last time.

'Goodbye, Marc,' she whispered as he stepped through.

The shoulders shifted as he started to turn and she pulled the heavy door quickly closed before she had to endure the tragedy of looking into his eyes one final time. She turned and sagged back against the door, her eyes grabbing and holding the image of *Holly's Bay* as though it were a lifeline.

Then she pushed her heavy body away and stumbled, blind and deaf, towards the only sanctuary in her world. Her bedroom.

The place she'd done all her grieving. All her hiding. All her healing.

And knew the latter would be a long time coming.

CHAPTER NINE

BETH dashed at the salty tickle of sweat suspended on her brow and stood back to examine the painting, wedging the brush between satisfied teeth. Even a spring day could reach the high thirties on this side of Australia and today was one of them. But she'd begun this particular work outdoors and—*sunstroke be damned!*—she was going to finish here.

She'd woken in the quiet hours of the morning, exploding with inspiration, and dragged her sketchpad onto her bed. She'd started blind, no concept of what might flow from her charcoal as she sketched out the initial shape of two skydivers freefalling but, as dawn broke, she'd found herself mixing up the deepest indigos, bold silvers, the rich acrylic colours and striking contrasts of a fantastical setting, not an earthly one.

She set up her easel in her cramped courtyard as soon as the sun had risen and set to work on the acrylic incarnation of her idea.

She skipped breakfast, perfectly sustained on adrenalin and creative surge, her hand flying over the canvas until her subconscious started to make its direction known. Colours merged, images resolved. The gentle morning light bathed her inner eye with a soft glow that translated beautifully on the canvas. The scene she painted bubbled up from the depths of her imagination—her soul—and for the first time in months an immense peace flowed through her.

She changed brushes and better defined a stylised spaceship in an imaginary universe far from her little courtyard. A place where a well built astronaut protected in layers of silver spacesuit floated and stretched forward to hold something. Or someone.

Lunch was a few hastily downed crackers and a cup of tea before Beth tackled the mystery of what—or who—he was reaching for. A skydiver, according to her initial sketch. But the flowing white dress and zero gravity that flowed from her brush suggested an angel.

But no, she realised as she instinctively mixed up a bronze colour and fashioned a crooked crown on her head. *Not an angel—a princess.*

Her breath caught. Marc's space princess. With long platinum hair that flowed all the way down to a green planet that glowed beyond the spaceship. Almost like a pathway home.

Warmth surged through her.

She switched brushes again and detailed the princess's hand, stretched urgently out and barely snagging the gloved index finger of the astronaut. It didn't take a genius to recognise the desperate, tenuous hold of the fallen princess with the tragically crooked crown. Beth had held on just like that to the memory of Marc throughout her marriage, no matter how deep down she shoved it. It had sustained her like that astronaut's air supply.

She returned to the canvas. In minutes she'd outlined the astronaut's other hand, the creases in his space glove showing how tightly his fingers encircled the princess's

fragile wrist. But the more Beth fiddled with her painting, the more she discovered. Like the fact that the astronaut wasn't tethered to his spaceship. But the princess's
long flowing hair anchored her to her planet.

Beth gasped. At first glance, it looked as if the astronaut's grip on the princess's wrist was the only thing
stopping her from drifting off into deepest, darkest
space. But the strong determination with which she'd
captured his finger…the way she strained against the
anchor of her hair on the green planet to reach him…

Was she saving him?

Or were they trying to save each other? Even if it
meant they might cartwheel off into airless space, somehow she knew that they would be fine just as long as
they held on to each other.

Beth swiped at her forehead and stared wide-eyed
at the image still only partly emerged from the blank
canvas even after a full day of non-stop painting. She'd
have to go back and repair parts, let it dry overnight,
prepare it for layering tomorrow. But she'd been power-
less to stop until the whole image was purged from her
mind. Sketched out on canvas. Captured for ever.

Until she knew what it meant.

A cloak of deep satisfaction settled on her. She'd
scratched and screamed against the necessity of forcing
Marc from her thoughts, and failed abysmally. She'd
cursed and professed her outrage to the universe, uselessly. But, as she stared at the painting, she realised
that the promise she'd made herself only prevented her
from acting on her feelings.

Not having them.

Marc may not choose to be her friend, but she could
still be *his*. Wasn't that what friends did? He may not
be able to love her but she could love him. She could

maintain that tenuous finger-hold on their relationship. Stop them drifting apart for ever. She'd waited this long to find her way back to him. What was a decade more?

On that thought, she slipped into a tranquil, gentle kind of acceptance. She took all those torturous feelings, all those loving feelings, all those desperate feelings and rolled them into a tight ball and bundled them away deep. Somewhere safe. Somewhere reinforced. Somewhere just for her.

The somewhere this painting had come from.

Her demons thoroughly exorcised, Beth stretched aching shoulders and flexed her cramped back and realised how hungry she was. And thirsty.

And how late it was getting. Janice would be waiting for her.

She propped her new canvas onto a shelf to dry overnight and sprinted for the shower.

Beth passed Marc's mother a steaming coffee with a reassuring smile.

Janice Duncannon looked even more nervous tonight than the last few meetings she'd been to. And they'd been to a lot together in the eight weeks since the exhibition. Accompanying Beth to AA was one step closer—one step easier—than going to Narcotics Anonymous. But the older woman knew that was where she needed to be. She was just building up the courage. With Beth's help. This woman's son was the reason Beth had been able to claw her way out of the abyss; the least she could do was return the favour.

If not to him, then to someone close to him.

Beth had seen the ravages of addiction clearly on Janice's face the first time she'd come to her warehouse classes, but she'd also seen the signs of someone struggling to overcome it. Janice had been doing it alone, too proud to call on her only son for help. She lived under his roof and ate the food he supplied but couldn't face the man she'd thrown out on the street in a chemical-induced fog.

The two of them had built up a strange kind of friendship since Beth had first invited her to art classes. They were decades apart in life experience, but dependence had a way of stripping back the years like old wallpaper. And, of course, they were sisters in heartbreak. Loving—and losing—a brilliant, complicated man. It just happened to be the same one.

Janice's hands pressed tightly to her coffee cup and she glanced around anxiously.

Beth frowned. 'You okay, Janice?'

Life-worn eyes looked at her but, as Beth watched, determination pushed the uncertainty from them. 'Yes, Beth. Thank you. I just…' Janice bit her lip. 'Perhaps I should have told you…'

A familiar voice sounded near the doorway. She'd been hearing it in her dreams so often these past weeks she'd become immune and it took a few seconds—and the lifted heads of a few of the people around her—for her to realise Marc's voice was real this time, excusing himself through the people packed into the meeting room. Heading towards them.

Her heart contracted like bellows.

She tore her eyes back to the woman at her side, who looked both guilty and eager at the same time. 'Oh, Janice, this was not a good idea.'

Did the woman not know her son at all? He hated being ambushed. As the whole room was about to find out.

'He called me when he found my name on the painting,' she whispered fiercely. 'After four years, I was *not* going to miss this chance.'

Beth couldn't blame her. Not really. Her judgement, perhaps, but not her intent. And she couldn't know the recent history between her son and Beth.

The powerful shoulders she'd never thought she'd see again pushed through the gathered throng towards his mother, setting her active imagination whirring, remembering how they'd given him the strength to hold her in his arms in the water one frigid night. But, three metres away, his focus shifted slightly to the left and his feet froze instantly. The colour leached from his eyes.

Too late for her to flee now.

He seemed to pull energy from the people pressing against him and buttress it up around him. Then he pushed himself forward again. Her heart pounded in time with his steps.

He stopped in front of her. It was a miserable replay of the day she'd walked up his driveway. Except this time they were both on the back foot. And this time his eyes barely stopped on hers as he spoke.

'Beth.'

Words simply would not come past the sudden dryness of her mouth. But she managed to squeeze out a nod and a breathy, loaded word, humiliating in its timbre. 'Marc.'

Guarded eyes darted between the two women. Beth couldn't tell which of them he was more pained to see, but being confronted by both of them in a room full of addicts had to be more than the strongest of men could take.

He turned to his mother with accusation in his eyes.

And not an insignificant amount of pain. 'Tell me you didn't plan this.'

Janice Duncannon's hands shook, but that was the case whether she was facing her son or not. The withdrawal tremors gave her a very human kind of frailty and Beth saw its effect on Marc. She ached for the confusion and vulnerability in his face. She desperately wanted to step by his side.

'Would you have come if I'd told you?' Janice asked. Immensely brave words, given they were the first she'd spoken to him in years.

Probably not, his face said. 'I thought I was here to meet with your support group. Why are you in a room full of alcoholics?' He dropped his voice as though the term would offend those around them. As though they weren't already blindingly aware of their condition. Then his voice got tighter and he zeroed in on the real problem. 'Why are you with Beth?'

He still hadn't looked at her properly and her throat ached at being dismissed so.

'Elizabeth and I are friends,' Janice said simply.

He did look at her then. Hard. Inscrutable. It told Beth exactly how much he was hurting right now. What was wrong with her that she wanted to protect him more than herself—even when he was looking at her like that?

'How nice for the two of you. Comparing habits?'

Beth sucked back a gasp.

Janice hadn't forgotten so many of her mothering skills that she was prepared to tolerate lip from her son. Even a fully grown tree-sized one. 'It turns out she and I have more in common than just love for you.'

Beth had walked these linoleum floors too long to believe they might actually open up and swallow her but she prayed for it anyway. Marc shot her another glare, this one a tiny bit uncertain. But his words were for Janice. 'I wasn't aware that anything outside of a capsule motivated you these days, Mother.'

Janice paled, her face a tragic mix of pride, hurt and hope, but she stayed upright. Beth had seen her sag at less. Her compassion for the troubled woman rose another notch. Lots of work to be done there, but she had faith in her son. And, these days, Janice believed in herself again.

'Be that as it may,' his mother said, 'it was concern for you that saw me ask you here tonight. You and Beth need to talk.'

'I'm not sure what she's told you—'

'Beth's told me nothing,' Janice chastised. 'She's very loyal to you. But the fact she never speaks about you speaks for itself.'

Beth groaned. 'Janice—'

'I should have known it wouldn't be any kind of genuine plea for my help with your sickness,' Marc said, eyes bleak. Beth threaded her fingers together to stop her from reaching out to him. *But he came tonight*, a tiny voice whispered. That wasn't the action of a man who truly could not forgive.

But to then find he'd been set up...

'My *sickness* and I are getting along just fine, thank you.' Marc hadn't heard strength in his mother's voice for a long time, judging by the way his eyes flared wide. Janice barrelled onwards. 'At the very least, you owe your oldest friend some closure.'

Oh, God... She glanced around desperately for Tony. She was going to need a sponsor pep talk tonight...

Marc glanced at her. 'We've had our closure. Two months ago.'

Janice frowned. 'Marc... You were friends for so long.'

His grin was arctic, but he faked it for the close pressed crowd. 'I think when years spent not being friends overtakes the number of years of friendship, then it rather cancels itself out.'

Ouch. All that time so easily wiped from his mind.

'Really?' Janice straightened to her full height and a decade tumbled off her. 'Is that how you feel about your father? He's been gone for many more years than you had him.'

Marc looked thunderous.

Beth took her chance. 'If you'll excuse me, I'm just going to—'

'Stay!' both Duncannons barked at once.

Marc pinned Beth with his turbulent gaze. 'I thought we'd said everything that needed to be said, Beth. What happened to your commitment to stay away, if you'd go to these lengths—to buddy up to a sick old woman?'

Beth hissed at exactly the same moment Janice roared in outrage. 'I am fifty-two, Marcus Duncannon! Hardly old.'

'You look fifteen years older,' he shot back.

'Yes, well, drug addiction will do that to a body!'

Janice's raised voice and her confident, startling admission silenced the whole room. Beth stepped forward into the awful tension to end the rapidly deteriorating scene. She turned to Janice and wrapped her cool hand around the older woman's unsteady one.

'Janice, I recognise you mean well, but please don't get involved. I've stuffed up enough relationships without adding yours and Marc's to my list. You guys have a real chance here. Do not jeopardise that for me.'

She turned next to Marc. Just smelling him weakened

her resolve and broke her heart anew. But she found his eyes. 'I am *not* trying to keep you in my life by proxy. You made yourself perfectly clear and—surprising as it might seem to you, given the past years of my life—I actually do have enough dignity not to beg for something you're not interested in giving. And I have honoured my promise to stay away.'

Even if it's killing me. Even if it was still robbing her of sleep.

'So have I,' he snarled.

Everything about him called to her. The way his hair fell across his forehead. The breadth of his shoulders. That defensive splayed-leg stance. It had been a tough few weeks, but she'd survived. She'd just have to start purging him from her mind and heart all over again.

Thanks, Janice.

Marc's permanent absence had left a huge gaping hole in her world. It hadn't been there even when they were apart for a decade because that part of her had still belonged to him. Now it was owned by no one.

She took another breath and held his focus. 'I get that there are some actions that can't be undone. That I broke something irreplaceable back when we were kids. I'll never be able to convince you of exactly how much I regret the choices I made back then but—you know what, Marc?—I was sixteen. I was virtually a child. I made mistakes and I'm sorry for them. But I've paid for them one hundred times over. I can't keep paying for ever. Not even for you.'

There was a world more she wanted to say but the thickening of her throat cut her short. There was no way she would allow herself to cry in front of Marc ever again. 'Janice, I'll see you next week. You should stay—'

'Don't leave, Beth.' The simple words caused a hard ball of pain in her chest and her pulse kicked up. She turned cautious eyes to him, her breath suspended. But then his eyes glittered. 'These are your people, after all. I should be the one to go.'

A hundred knives sliced through her. Just when she thought he didn't have the power to hurt her any more...

Her people. Addicts. Losers.

He would never, ever see past his prejudice.

He turned to go and Janice grabbed his sleeve urgently. 'Marc, don't do this. You've been in love with that girl since fifth grade. I could see it back then and I can still see it.' She appealed up to her towering son. 'Life is so brief. I know what it is to exist without joy. The gift of love is not something that you should walk away from twice.'

He looked set to do just that but Janice stopped him with a stunning proclamation. 'It's my fault she left you.'

Beth snapped her head around, not prepared to have another sacrifice be for nothing. 'Janice, no—!'

'I told Beth to cut you loose, son.' Janice's fingers bit into his arm like they'd dug into hers when she was sixteen. Deceptively strong. 'Actually, I begged her. I couldn't watch you fall more and more in love with her, making all those plans to go to university, to leave.' She took a deep breath. 'To leave me. You were all I had.'

Marc paled and stared at Janice. She went on, relentless. 'Without you, I had no one. I was terrified. That was a terrible crushing responsibility to put on a boy—' she glanced at Beth with stark regret in her eyes '—and an awful pressure to put on a young girl. But I was desperate.'

Marc's nostrils flared. He turned to Beth. 'You did it for her? Not for McKinley?'

Beth's heart pounded. 'I did what I thought was best—'

His head reared back at that. 'In what universe was tearing out my heart *best*?'

Heat rushed up her throat and collided headlong into the blood draining from her face. *I didn't know.* The words trembled on her lips, wanting so eagerly to tumble off into the fray. But, in her heart, Beth knew it wasn't quite true. On some level she'd known just how important she was to Marc.

She reached to the nearby chairs for her purse. 'I'm sorry that I wasn't stronger. I'm sorry that I'm still not strong enough for you. I made that choice, not in cold blood, as you accused, but in hot, confused desperation. But it *was* my choice and I *will* live with the repercussions.'

She pushed without grace through the meeting attendees, who were all desperately trying to pretend they weren't there. Every one of them would have had the same or worse in their own troubled lives. She'd given up worrying about her dignity when she first stood up in front of this group and introduced herself as someone controlled by alcohol. AA wasn't the place or the time for blushes.

When she hit the stairs, she made her choice in a split second. Anyone else would bolt for the street but she wanted to hide, not run. So her choice was easy. She took the roof stairs two at a time for four floors and burst out into the cold night air, her lungs aching. Downtown unfolded in front of her in a glittery, anonymous mass of lights. A half-hearted rain shower misted down on her. She tucked herself into the lee of a ventilation duct.

When the door opened quietly behind her a few minutes later, she cursed her choice. Marc knew her too well. He stepped out onto the rooftop and scanned the dark corners.

'How did you know where to find me?' she murmured.

He turned towards her voice but didn't step closer. 'I just thought about where I'd go in the same situation. I knew you wouldn't want to drive while you were upset.'

They stood silently, together in the half dark, a light sheen of moisture forming on their hair. Beth didn't care and Marc didn't notice.

'I'm sorry for exploding in there.' He genuinely seemed at a loss to explain himself.

'You never did like surprises.'

His laugh wasn't amused. Words dried up between them again. 'I just wasn't prepared. Both of you at the same time. It was…' He looked around at her rooftop hideout. 'Are you okay?'

Part of her burned to stay angry with him. But another part vibrated at an inaudible frequency just to be standing this close to him again. 'I just wanted some privacy.'

'You got it. It's nice up here.'

'I come a lot.' After most AA sessions, at least. 'Where I can think.'

'You can see most of the city.'

'More on a clear night.'

That finally drew his attention to the fine wet mist drifting down on them. And Beth's lack of a coat. 'You're getting wet.'

She laughed. 'I think I'll survive.'

'Here…' Anyone else would have stripped off their

jacket and given it to her. Not Marc. He stepped closer, almost looming over her, shrugged his jacket up and half off and held it over them both like an odd-shaped umbrella. It was surprisingly effective against the very light rain. But it brought them into dangerously close contact and forced their respective scents to swirl under the impromptu canopy. Coconut mingled with something indefinably spicy in a heady, seductive alchemy.

Oh, dear... Beth could practically feel all her good intentions dissolving as his scent chased around her. She blurted the first words that came to her by way of restoring her equilibrium.

'I didn't know, I swear. I wouldn't have come.'

Marc stared down at her in the inky darkness of their homemade shelter and flicked wry eyebrows. 'I know. I can see my mother's fingerprints all over this.'

'She meant well.'

'Strangely enough, I actually believe that's true.' He sighed, stiff and unsure in the dim light. 'Look, Beth—'

She wasn't up to another confession. Or a rehashing of all the reasons he couldn't be her friend. Or a declaration of ancient feelings hastily followed up with a *but...* She struck pre-emptively.

'I can't do the once-every-couple-of-months thing, Marc.'

His answer was too fast. Too defensive. 'I didn't expect to see you here—'

She could be flippant. She could be hostile. Either one would keep her safe. But both were a cop out. 'But you've been checking up on me. Staying just in the periphery of my awareness. Making it impossible to put you out of my thoughts.'

He seemed lost for words for once. Caught out. Beth

barreled on before she lost the nerve. 'It was what *you* wanted, Marc. For us to have nothing more to do with each other. And I understand why now. It hurts too much.' Her voice cracked on the last word.

His eyes fell shut 'I didn't want to hurt you.'

The urgent need to protect him washed through her. *Ugh—still?* When would her heart get back to prioritising itself? 'But you keep reopening that door. Every time you check up on my classes. Or talk to my parents. Or buy my paintings through an agent. You're hovering just out of sight. I can't do it any more.'

It was exactly what he'd just accused her and Janice of. Finding ways of staying connected. No wonder he'd been so angry about it.

We despise most in others what we fear in ourselves.

'You weren't supposed to know.' Heat surged off him. Enough to feel. His head dropped and, when it rose again, his gaze was intense. 'I find myself thinking of you more and more, until the only way I can shift it is to see you or see someone who has some connection to you. I know it's ridiculous but my mind doesn't seem to care about that.'

A deep pain screwed tighter in her gut. 'Fight it harder.'

His laugh was dark. 'You're underestimating its strength.' He touched his forehead. 'In here I know it's wrong, but I find myself picking up the phone anyway. It's a miracle I can hang it up before you answer. It's like I'm compelled...'

Her heart flip-flopped. To hear these words... But they didn't undo the reality. She stared at him intently. 'Welcome to my world.'

He snapped his mouth shut with jaw-jarring force as

the penny dropped. His blush speared higher, angrier. 'This is not the same.'

'Your mind tells you one thing but your body wants another. You know you should stay away but you can't. How is that different?'

'It's totally different. What I'm doing can't…' Marc's nostrils flared and he frowned deeply.

'Can't hurt anyone? Is that what you were going to say?' Her tight voice softened with compassion. 'I think we both know that's not true.'

Confusion chased across his features. And not a small amount of anxiety. Was this the first time he'd ever seen the potential in himself?

'But you're right. There is one difference.' She gently peeled his fingers from around hers. 'I'm not judging you for it. I'm just asking you to honour the promise you asked me to make. I understand why you asked for it and now I want it too.' A deep, infinite sorrow filled her as she moved past him to the roof door. She paused there. 'One day I hope you'll remember the woman before the addict,' she whispered. 'Then ask yourself why you kept coming back to me.'

Be happy.

Marc wondered if she'd said the words or if he'd just imagined the pained whisper as she closed the door on their friendship.

Now I want it, too. Beth wanted him gone. And why not? He'd done a bang-up job of making sure she wouldn't want to stay. Laying out landmines between them. Flaying her with his words. She seemed strong but so had his mother, once. How long would it be before she slipped back into old habits when things got tough?

Never mind that she hadn't in all this challenging time.

As far as you're aware. He'd not known with his

mother. For years. His sickening fury on finding out about her addiction was as much about the many years he'd been oblivious as anything else. Anger at himself. How could a son not have noticed? If he'd twigged earlier, could he have done something? It would have to be easier quitting earlier in the addiction, surely? And with his support…

His eyes drifted to the stairwell.

It was why he was keeping tabs on her. To see if she was staying healthy or whether she'd weaken and—

His own thoughts brought him up short.

Beth was right. He did see her first as an addict. He had since the moment she'd told him about her dependence. He'd scratched the word 'recovering' from his vocab and just focused on the 'alcoholic' part. The part that said she was weak.

The part he feared in himself.

Who was he to judge her strength? He couldn't even be in the same room as Beth without wanting to touch her. He *was* the infatuated teenager she'd spoken of that day on the beach. Except he'd never grown out of his obsession. He'd gone years cold turkey and after only one day back in her influence she was back to haunting his nights. She wasn't the one who kept drifting back into the sphere of *his* life. She wasn't the one scratching around for plausible excuses to see him again. She'd been as good as her word and stayed away when he'd asked her to.

What kind of a hypocrite did it make him?

He'd judged Beth for being human. For not being able to deny herself something she craved on a cellular level. But she was fighting it. She'd gone through so much these past months and hadn't had a drink. The clarity of her skin, her eyes, the softness of her hair told him that. Her body was rebounding from the abuses of its past. Ripening.

And his was responding accordingly.

All these years later, even after a decade of alcohol abuse, she was still the better human being. Nothing had changed. She was demonstrating every day the kind of strength he'd lacked all his life. He couldn't even do something as simple as stay the hell away from her.

Addict is as addict does.

That made his decision clearer but not easier. He would make himself keep completely away. Not just because she'd asked him to and because he knew it was the moral thing to do. But because he needed to see if he could. He needed to prove that he was stronger than it was.

Dependence. Compulsion.

He was not his mother.

He would deny himself his Beth fix, next time it burned its way into his psyche and refused to be ignored. The next time it set up an infuriating clanging in his head and filled his thoughts with memories of her. He'd dig around in his soul and see if he could find the strength to do what was right for *her*, not for him.

If he couldn't beat it, how could he ever judge anyone else for failing?

The difficulty he had staying away from her was directly proportional to the importance of managing it. If it was easier it wouldn't matter.

And Beth mattered.

CHAPTER TEN

STAYING away lasted all of four weeks. But Beth could hardly blame Marc when she'd all too readily replied to his email inviting her out on this charter today, convincing herself it was important to get closure.

Again.

A third set.

Masochist.

'I don't know how you do this, day in, day out.' The shade of her skin had to be reflected in the sickly tone of her voice as the *Libertine* pitched and rolled on the southern swell. She kept her eyes firmly on the golden contours of the distant shore as a way of holding off the seasickness.

Breathe in, breathe out…

'You get used to it,' Marc said from his spot at the vessel's wheel.

'Can't imagine how,' a portly red-headed American man clutching a seasickness bag said tightly from right next to her. He and Beth had both climbed up to the bridge to escape the nauseating blowback as the diesel fuel motored them slowly through the outer reaches of Holly's Bay. Nothing short of the threat of vomit would have got her this close to Marc Duncannon. Just hearing his voice still hurt.

So why in heaven was she here?

The American picked his way to the far side of the fly bridge to peer down on his wife and the nine other passengers on the lower deck, their eyes peeled to the brightly reflecting water in search of their prey.

'Thank you for coming,' Marc said quietly, still looking out to the horizon. Dark sunglasses hid his soul from her.

Gulls squawked overhead as they followed the boat in anticipation of a snack. One of the tourists below obliged with a piece of something that sent the birds into a squabbling, diving frenzy. The ugly sound grated on Beth's already tortured nerves.

'I almost didn't. I thought we'd said everything there was to say a month ago.'

'We did.' His reply was almost lost on the breeze. Beth stepped closer to hear. 'But it wasn't quite complete. There's one more loose end to tie up.'

Ouch. 'Now we're a loose end?'

The breeze cut into her skinny frame. No sleep and no appetite would do that. She could hold it together during daylight hours but there was no one to fake it for at night alone in her studio. She wrapped her arms around her diminishing torso.

Marc frowned. 'Are you doing okay, Beth?'

'You shouldn't care.' Frustration and pain lifted her voice. 'How I am or whether we have unfinished business shouldn't be on your radar. We're not a part of each other's lives any more.' Beth pointed to shore. 'You made the call not to be friends that day on the beach last year. Then you drove all the way to Perth to tell me again a few months later. Then you followed me onto a rooftop to remind me. Now…what? We're about to cover it a fourth time?' She glared at him. 'For a man who isn't interested in friendship, you sure do a good job of keeping in touch.'

He swept the horizon in a broad arc, then those sexy sunglasses fixed right back on her. 'Yet here you are.'

She stared at him. Knew he was absolutely right. Her interest in him—her desire to see him—hadn't waned one little bit. When he wrote and asked to see her, it was a short internal battle. 'More fool me. Are you going to tell me why I'm here?'

'When I took this charter I knew I'd be calling you.'

'Why?'

His twisted smile wouldn't reach his eyes. She didn't need to see them to know that. Marc killed the motor and turned to watch her. 'Wait for it…'

Over his shoulder, a sudden jet spray of water made her leap. The tourists on the lower deck screamed with delight and tilted the boat as they shifted as one body to the starboard side. Their cameras started chattering like the seagulls overhead. Not far out, a whale breached long enough to evacuate its blowhole and suck in a giant lungful of air. Then it sank out of view again and it was as though it had never existed.

Beth forgot her anxiety instantly. Whales still got her blood racing, even smaller ones. She brushed Marc's arm with her shoulder as she crossed to the side. He seemed to lean into her touch but it had to be the lurching of the boat on the swell. Out of the corner of her eye, she saw him move to the ladder leading down to the deck and snap a barrier rope across behind the leaving American, effectively making the bridge off-limits to everyone else.

Over to the right, another whale breached, and then another, and another and Beth realised Marc had stopped

the boat in the middle of a pod of the enormous dark
mammals. False killer whales. Her thoughts immediately turned to *their* whale and how she had gone after
the rescuers finally got her back out to sea. She'd been
so tired, so dehydrated, and with that nasty arrow-head
gash on her tail. Beth had convinced herself their whale
would be fine but there was no way they'd ever really
know.

'How did you know where to find the pod?'

Marc stepped up close behind her and draped a
jacket around her angular, chilled shoulders. Her mind
instantly went back to that night on the beach. Today's
cold breeze was nothing compared to that night. She'd
never been so critically numb again.

Not on the outside, at least.

'I came across the pod two weeks ago. They've been
coming here daily. Enjoying the calm shallows of the
bay.'

She twisted around and up to look at him with one
brow arched. 'Shallows being relative, of course.'

And *calm*, as her stomach lurched on a particularly large pitch of the boat. She lost count of who was
who. There had to be a dozen whales down there. They
breached the surface in pairs, solo, spread out and close.
The occasional one leaped clear of the surface with such
power and gusto it made Beth wonder just how deep the
whales' underwater domain really was.

'The hull of your boat must look like a small solitary
cloud in a massive dark blue sky to them.' Like that night
on the beach when she'd looked up into the limitless sky,
again now she felt small and irrelevant.

Marc braced himself with an arm immediately next
to hers, his hard body leaning into her from behind.
More reminders of that night. Beth didn't care that it

was inappropriate for both of them. She let his strength leach into her. Just one more time.

'Their curiosity draws them to the boat. All I had to do was get us in roughly the right part of the bay and they did the rest.'

The water show went on and Beth's breath caught and tumbled across the laughter that she couldn't hold back. This was such a gift. Finally, one whale rolled, belly up, close to their boat and its giant eye breached the water for seconds. It seemed to look right at the two humans standing together on the top deck in a way that was inexplicably moving. Then it completed the slow roll and disappeared under the surface.

Or back above it, from the whales' perspective.

Beth turned to Marc on an exclamation but he gently guided her chin back to the waves. 'Wait…'

And then it happened. The giant spinal arch of the same whale as it curled up out of the water propelled by its mammoth tail, and then the stunning salute of the tail fins standing up tall in the water. Elegant, barnacle crusted and with only a triangular scar to mar it—

Beth's breath froze in her throat. Not a triangle… an arrow-head. She half twisted in the circle of Marc's arms, unable to tear her gaze away. 'It's our whale.'

He pressed his chin to the top of her head and let his other arm reach around her to grip the gunnel. His silence said he was just as moved as she was. They watched the beautiful, strong tail sink silently down into the dark depths with the kind of splashless entry Tasmin Major would have killed for.

Beth's voice trembled. 'Oh, my God…'

'One more surprise. Wait…'

She followed his pointed finger and stared, unblinking, at the glistening ocean. Nothing...nothing... And then—

'Marc!' she practically squealed, before clamping her lips shut.

A whale calf, no bigger than Mum's tail, breached the surface in a playful splash. Its body followed the exact arc and trajectory as its mother.

'I figure she must have been pregnant when we rescued her.' His voice was breathlessly close to her ear. Somewhere deep down that bothered her. But her eyes were glued to the calf. 'It's not uncommon for whales to have an older calf with them while gestating a new one.'

Her voice thickened dangerously. 'This is a creche?' She'd heard that whales liked to spend their calf's first months in a sheltered, food-rich bay.

'I think so.'

Marc kept her safe in the circle of his arms while she cried. Too much had happened between them to make her ashamed of the tears that streamed down her face. Joy. Relief. And sadness for the final farewell that she knew this was.

Maybe it really was closure she'd been waiting for.

After all, they didn't hate each other. They just couldn't be together. They were like humans and whales—drawn to each other by instinct but, ultimately, too dangerous for each other.

The sun had its toes well and truly in the water on the horizon by the time Marc finally pulled the pin on their private whale watch. The downstairs tourists were too worn out to keep up more than the occasional quiet conversation and one by one they moved inside the comfortable cabin.

'You should get below deck,' Marc hinted reluctantly, stroking her wind-blown hair back into some order and then stepping back, as though—finally—realising the impropriety of his earlier proximity. 'It's going to get real cold real fast.'

Beth dragged her eyes off the still frolicking beasts and turned towards the ladder, knowing this was it. Before her common sense could stop her, she curled an arm up around his neck and pulled Marc's head down to hers. Her lips pressed for an eternity against the corner of his.

'Thank you,' she whispered against his mouth. Against the pounding of her own pulse. *I love you.* 'I'll miss you.'

His hand snaked out and arched around her wrist, gently preventing her from leaving. His thumb circled her skin. He didn't bother hiding the pain on his face. 'This goodbye feels final.'

No more games. She nodded out to the frolicking whales. 'Maybe we just needed to see her for it to truly be over?'

Some distant, optimistic part of her thought maybe a bit of healing time might have worked miracles. Might have changed his heart. *Might have made her more acceptable.* Marc was so damaged by his mother's addiction that he couldn't see his way to caring for someone living with one. End of story.

'Is that still what you want?' he whispered. 'For it to be truly over?'

Her head came up. 'Marc, don't do this. Nothing's changed…'

'I've changed, Beth. I stood in a room with two dozen alcoholics a month ago and listened to their stories, imagined they were you. After you left me on that miserable rooftop, I spoke to some of them about their battles. The triumphs and the impact of the defeats. How they felt about the people they'd lost in life.'

Her heart hammered.

He shook his head. 'I spoke to my mother, which was the greatest miracle. We're now having a weekly lunch. That has all changed me, Beth.' He took a deep breath. 'I thought addiction was something that happened to weak people.'

Her eyes flared wide and he rushed on. 'I wasn't particularly disposed to view it logically and fairly because I've been on the receiving end of the effects of addiction for half my life. What are the odds that both of the significant women in my world would be fighting addiction?'

'Actually, pretty high—' she started.

He raised a hand. *Okay. Rhetorical question...*

'Beth, you showed me that addiction is every bit as illogical and damaging as the most fanatical of teenage love affairs. And, having been a teenager who loved passionately, if secretly—' those hazel eyes blazed '—I now have a bit more understanding of what it means to be addicted. How it consumes everything in its path. Warps everything. And how much courage it takes to fight that kind of compulsion, every single day.'

A whale crashed into the sea behind them but Beth couldn't drag her eyes off Marc for a moment.

His eyes dropped to the deck and then dragged back to hers. 'Turns out I don't have that courage. I don't have the strength of character I used to think I do. It took six months of desperately trying to stay away from something I craved down to my very cells. Trying and failing. Wanting it every...single...day.'

Her mouth dried up completely.

'Beth, you have demonstrated more courage in climbing out of addiction than I ever have in my entire life. I worshipped you for your fearlessness back when we were kids and, later, when we were teens and you gave the social expectations of the whole school the finger.' The small smile he conjured carried genuine warmth. 'I realised halfway through our icy adventure with the whale that nothing about your courage has changed. You just lost your way for a bit.'

He stepped closer. 'Ten years ago when you walked away from me—from us—I considered that a weakness. Something lacking in you. I closed my mind to you and to my heart. It suited me to blame someone for the pain I suffered. But I was blaming the wrong person.'

He took a deep breath. 'It killed me how cleanly you were able to excise me from your life. I thought it meant you didn't care, but I was wrong. For better or for worse, you did that for me. And at considerable cost to yourself. I can see that now. It takes infinitely more strength to walk away from something like that than to endure being walked away from.'

Heated shivers prickled through her whole body.

'Even these past months, while I've been torturing myself with the intensity of wanting to see you more and more every day, you cut the ties and left them where they lay. It burned me that you could walk away from me apparently so easily while I couldn't even honour my own promise to stay away. That I had so little strength.

'I chose to interpret weakness in you because it's easier than admitting the weakness is really in myself. Up on that rooftop you told me to fight harder, and I realised that I've fought *alongside* you saving whales, I've fought *with* you against the establishment more times than I can remember. But I have never once fought *for* you, Beth.' His eyes blazed. 'If I had, you might have stayed all those years ago. Or that day at Holly's Bay or on that rooftop.'

His voice cracked on that last word and Beth found her hands tangling in his. She felt his pain in her own body, sharp and aching. And so familiar.

'When you left with McKinley I rebuilt my life. When I walked away from Mum, I rebuilt again. I've been patting myself on the back for having the strength and courage to start over repeatedly. But it dawned on me after that meeting that I let you walk away rather than fight for what I wanted. I walked away from my only remaining family when things got too hard. I let you drive away from that beach doubting yourself because it was easier than admitting that *I'm* the one who lacks strength. In the way it counts most.'

Her eyes blurred over and she had to swipe away at both of them with their linked hands to keep him in focus. 'Marc, don't...'

'Beth, my running from you, from how I feel when I'm with you, was not just about me not wanting to repeat the errors of the past. It was about me protecting myself when I should have been protecting you. And that shames me.'

Pain lanced from him to her and his eyes darkened. 'I have my priorities straightened out now. If staying away from you is the thing I can do to help you stay strong, then I give you my solemn oath I will do it, if it's what you want.' His face and his words spoke of resilience and determination. 'But know that you are now officially on the top of *my* make-good list, and I'm a patient man. I hope that one day I have the opportunity to mark you off it.'

She shuddered. 'It hasn't been easy for me to walk

away from you. I've bled as much as you have. But I guess I've just had more practice.'

Hazel eyes blazed at her, filled almost to overflowing with blind faith. Only this time she felt as if she'd earned it. 'You do not lack strength, Beth Hughes.'

She stared at him steadily. Amazing, considering her galloping heart. 'And you are not a crutch...'

'I know.'

'...I just love you.'

His eyes glittered. His chest heaved. 'I know.'

She took a steadying breath and held his eyes. 'But I'm still an addict. That's for ever. Can you forget that?'

'Would you want me to?'

Ten years of her life. Her hardest battle fought and won. A huge part of the woman she'd become. 'No.'

'But I can understand it. If you'll let me.'

What was he offering? For all his fine speech-making, he hadn't made any promises. He was just offering understanding. Or to leave her life if that was what she wanted.

Pfff... As if that was an option now...

'What do you see first when you look at me?' she risked. But it was important that she knew where she stood. 'Addict, friend or...woman?'

She felt the impact of the intensity she'd decided she'd never see again. It washed over her like waves hitting the shore. His chest rose and fell in choppy lurches.

'Honestly?' Marc shook his head. 'All of those things. Plus I see the mother of my children.'

Beth's breath faltered completely. *Children...?*

Moments after he'd lauded her courage was not the time to have it dissolve. In the silence that followed she became aware of the tightness of every part of her, the avid fixation of hazel eyes in front of her. The time it had been since she last took a breath.

'I'd like to stay on your list,' she croaked, stepping forward into the possible abyss. 'Maybe we can start with friends…'

'I can't promise you how long that will last. I'm not feeling very friendly.'

The barely repressed hunger in his eyes told its own story. She drew herself close, smiling. Not afraid with a woman's eyes. 'For as long as it lasts, then.'

Then, as she went to circle her arms around him in a hug, he pulled her to her toes and pressed his mouth to her hungry, thirsty lips.

'Do friends do that with each other?' She wobbled as he released her for air a moment later.

He tipped his face towards her again and said, 'Okay, so we're good friends.' Then he took her chin in his hand and met her lips more fully with his hot, blistering ones. The kiss went on for eternity, deep and blazing and as comfortable as a roaring fire on a cold coastal night. He folded her into the protection of his arms and kissed her back. Hot, hard and so…*so*…much better than a decade before.

'Shortest friendship in history,' he mumbled as he finally lifted his head. Love and admiration and desire and wonder all shone from his hazel eyes.

'That's fine with me,' Beth murmured against his jaw. 'I never really wanted to be your friend, anyway.'

'Brat…' Marc swatted her behind.

Beth pulled herself free. 'Wait…' Marc stroked her hair away from her flushed face and waited. 'What took you so long? It's been a month.'

'I've spent the past four weeks trying to prove I was stronger than my feelings.'

'And did you?'

He shrugged. 'I've proven it's taxing and exhausting and exasperating to deny yourself something you want so badly. But I did it.'

She laughed. 'Not for very long.'

He kissed her again. Then slid his lips around to the side of her throat. 'Long enough to know,' he murmured against her ear.

Her head tipped back as her knees sagged in response to his marauding lips. *Oh, God...* But she managed to murmur, 'Know what?'

'That I love you because of you. Not because of me.'

Her legs buckled and Marc caught her weight against his body. She swallowed back a choke of tears. 'You've only seen me four times in seven months.'

'And that's about to change.' But he must have felt her tension because he lifted his lips and looked at her, intense and loving. 'There's never been anyone in my heart but you, Beth. Even when you weren't in my life. You said at your exhibition that I'd be alone without you and you were spot on. No one could compete with what you'd become in my heart, even while I was in denial about the place you held.'

His pedestal.

'I'm just human, Marc. The higher you place me, the further I'll fall.'

Determination and caring glowed on his face. 'No more falling. Not while I'm there with you.'

He pulled her close into a strong, protective hug. Beth's eyes washed with tears. When had anyone in her entire life made her feel so safe?

'So, what now?' she murmured against his cheek. 'Where do we go from here?'

'I'd like to take you to dinner. We've never been on a date.'

A date—when he was standing here with her body pressed so intimately into his? Beth laughed. 'I think we've skipped the dating stage, don't you?'

Marc chuckled against her ear, warm and intoxicating. 'After that, I need to get you some sea legs. You're going to spend a lot of time on my boats. You'll be my first mate.'

She pushed back to look at him. 'Oh, will I? All the way from the city? What about my students?'

His smile was as seductive as it was bashful. 'They can come down on retreat. You know…when you move into the homestead with me.'

She pushed back to look at him. 'Wow, we're moving quickly. Is that where this is leading?'

'Ultimately. Raising kids isn't going to work if we're two hundred clicks apart.' Serious, unashamed eyes held hers. 'But dinner first. You look like you haven't eaten in weeks.'

She wrapped her arms more tightly around him. 'I feel like I haven't eaten in years.'

He tipped his head down to hers and murmured against her lips, 'Then let me feed you. It would give me the greatest of pleasure to watch you eat. The rest can wait.'

Her mouth found his again in a perfect fit and her blood thrilled at the taste. But a thought pulled her back again. 'Wait…your *first* mate? I was hoping to be your only mate.'

The sexy smile he gave her then made up for half a lifetime of loss. He slid his hands down her arms until their fingers entwined and he pinned them gently behind Beth's back, pressing her more firmly against him.

His lids dropped as his lips did.

'Deal.'

Turn the page for a sneak peek at
The Nanny and the CEO, *the heartwarming*
new novel from favourite author Rebecca Winters,
available this month from all-new
Mills & Boon® Cherish™.

CHAPTER ONE

"Ms. CHAMBERLAIN? You're next. Second door on the left."

"Thank you."

Reese got up from the chair and walked past the woman at the front desk to reach the hall. At ten o'clock in the morning, the East 59th Street Employment Agency in New York's east side was already packed with people needing a job. She'd asked around and had learned it was one of the most reputable agencies in the city. The place reminded her of her dentist's office filled with patients back home in Nebraska.

She had no idea what one wore for an interview to be a nanny. After changing outfits several times she'd opted for a yellow tailored, short-sleeved blouse and skirt, the kind she'd worn to the initial interview on Wednesday. This was her only callback in three days. If she didn't get hired today, she would have to fly home tomorrow, the last thing she wanted to do.

Her father owned a lumberyard and could always give her a job if she couldn't find anything that suited her, but it wouldn't pay her the kind of money she needed. Worse, she didn't relish the idea of seeing Jeremy again, but it would be inevitable because her ex-fiancé happened to work as a loan officer at the bank where her dad did business. Word would get around she was back.

"Come in, Ms. Chamberlain."

"Hello, again, Mr. Lloyd." He was the man who'd taken her initial application.

"Let me introduce you to Mrs. Tribe. She's the private secretary to a Mr. Nicholas Wainwright here in New York and has been looking for the right nanny for her employer. I'll leave you two alone for a few minutes."

The smart-looking brunette woman wearing a professional business suit was probably in her early fifties. "Please sit down. Reese, is it?"

"Yes."

The other woman cocked her head. "You have excellent references. From your application it's apparent you're a student and a scholar. Since you're single and have no experience taking care of other people's children, why did you apply to be a nanny?"

Reese could lie, but she had a feeling this woman would see right through her. "I need to earn as much money as possible this summer so I can stay in school until graduation. My academic scholarship doesn't cover housing and food. Even those of us born in fly-over-country have heard a nanny's job in New York can pay very well, so I thought I'd try for a position." Hopefully that explanation was frank enough for her.

"Taking care of children is exceptionally hard work. I know because I raised two of my own."

Reese smiled. "I've never been married, but I'm the oldest in the family of six children and did a lot of babysitting over the years. I was fourteen when my youngest sister was born. My mother had to stay in bed, so I helped with the baby. It was like playing house. My sister was adorable and I loved it. But," she said as she sighed, "that was twelve years ago. Still, taking care of children is like learning to tie your shoes, don't you think? Once you've figured it out, you never forget."

The other woman eyed her shrewdly while she nodded. "I agree."

"How many children do they have?" *Please don't let the number be more than three.* Although Reese wouldn't turn it down if the money was good enough.

"Mr. Wainwright is a widower with a ten-week-old baby boy named Jamie."

The news concerning the circumstances came as a sobering revelation to Reese. She'd assumed she might end up working for a couple with several children, that is if she were ever offered a job. "Then he's still grieving for his wife." She shook her head. "How sad for him and his little boy, who'll never know his mother."

Reese got a swelling in her throat just thinking of her own wonderful mom still remarkably young and vital, probably the same age as Mrs. Tribe.

"It's a tragic loss for both of them. Mr. Wainwright has arranged for a nanny who's been with another family to start working for him, but she can't come until September. Because you only wanted summer work, that's one of the reasons I was interested in your application."

One of the reasons? She'd aroused Reese's curiosity. "What were the others?"

"You didn't name an unrealistic salary. Finally, one of your professors at Wharton told me you've been on full academic scholarship there. Good for you. An opportunity like that only comes to a very elite group of graduate students. It means you're going to have a brilliant career in business one day."

To run her own brokerage firm was Reese's goal for the future. "That's my dream."

The dream that had torn her and Jeremy apart.

Jeremy had been fine about her finishing up her undergraduate work at the University of Nebraska, but the scholarship to Wharton had meant a big move to Pennsylvania. The insinuation that she was too ambitious led to the core of the problem eating at him. Jeremy hadn't wanted a future-executive for a wife. In return Reese realized she'd had a lucky escape from a future-controlling-husband. Their breakup had been painful at the time, but the hurt was going away. She didn't want him back. Therein lay the proof.

Mrs. Tribe sat back in her chair and studied Reese. "It was my dream, too, but I didn't get the kind of grades I saw on your transcripts. Another of your professors told me he sees a touch of genius in you. I liked hearing that about you."

Reese couldn't imagine which professor that was. "You've made my day."

"Likewise," she murmured, sounding surprised by her own thoughts. "Provided you feel good about the situation after seeing the baby and discussing Mr. Wainwright's expectations of you in that regard, I think you'll do fine for the position. Of course the final decision will be up to him."

Reese could hardly believe she'd gotten this far in the interview. "I don't know how to thank you, Mrs. Tribe. I promise I won't let him, or you, down. Do you have a picture of the baby?"

A frown marred her brow. "I don't, but you'll be

meeting him and his father this afternoon. Where have you been staying since you left Philadelphia?"

"At the Chelsea Star Hotel on West 30th."

"You did say you were available immediately?"

"Yes!" The dormitory bed cost her fifty dollars a night. She couldn't afford to stay in New York after today.

"That's good. If he decides to go with my recommendation and names a fee that's satisfactory to you, then he'll want you to start today."

"What should I wear to the interview? Do I need some kind of uniform? This is completely new to me."

"To both of us," came her honest response. "Wear what you have on. If he has other suggestions, he'll tell you."

"Does he have a pet?"

"As far as I know he's never mentioned one. Are you allergic?"

"No. I just thought if he did, I could pick up some cat or doggie treats at the store. You know. To make friends right off?"

The woman smiled. "I like the way you think, Ms. Chamberlain."

"Of course the baby's going to be another story," Reese murmured. "After having his daddy's exclusive attention, it will take time to win him around."

Mrs. Tribe paused before speaking. "Actually, since his birth, he's been looked after by his maternal grandparents."

"Are they still living with Mr. Wainwright?"

"No. The Hirsts live in White Plains. An hour away in heavy traffic."

So did that mean he hadn't been with his son for the

last couple of months? No…that couldn't be right. Now that he was getting a nanny, they'd probably just left to go back home.

"I see. Does Jamie have paternal grandparents, too?"

"Yes. At the moment they're away on a trip," came the vague response.

Reese came from a large family. Both sets of grandparents were still alive and always around. She had seven aunts and uncles. Last count there were twenty-eight cousins. With her siblings, including the next oldest, Carrie, who was married and had two children under three, that brought the number to thirty-four. She wondered if her employer had any brothers and sisters or other family.

"You've been with Mr. Wainwright a long time. Is there anything of importance I should know ahead of time?"

"He's punctual."

"I'll remember that." Reese got to her feet. "I won't take any more of your time. Thank you for this opportunity, Mrs. Tribe."

"It's been my pleasure. A limo will be sent for you at one o'clock."

"I'll be waiting outside in front. Oh—one more question. What does Mr. Wainwright do for a living?"

The other woman's eyebrows lifted. "Since you're at Wharton, I thought you might have already made the connection or I would have told you. He's the CEO at Sherborne-Wainwright & Co. on Broadway. Good luck."

"Thank you," Reese murmured in shock.

He was *that* Wainwright?

It was one of the most prestigious brokerage firms in

New York, if not *the* top one with roots that went back a couple of hundred years. The revelation stunned her on many levels. Somehow she'd imagined the man who ran the whole thing to be in his late forties or early fifties. It usually took that long to rise to those heights.

Of course it wasn't impossible for him to have a new baby, but she was still surprised. Maybe it had been his second wife he'd lost and she'd been a young mother. No one was exempt from pain in this life.

EXPECTING ROYAL TWINS! *by Melissa McClone*

Mechanic Izzy was shocked when a tall handsome prince strode into her workshop and declared he was her husband! Now she's about to face an even bigger surprise...

TO DANCE WITH A PRINCE *by Cara Colter*

Royal playboy Kiernan's been nicknamed Prince Heartbreaker. Meredith knows, in her head, that he's the last man she needs, yet her heart thinks otherwise!

HONEYMOON WITH THE RANCHER *by Donna Alward*

After Tomas' fiancée's death, he sought peace on his Argentine ranch. Until socialite Sophia arrived for her honeymoon...*alone*. Can they heal each other's hearts?

NANNY NEXT DOOR *by Michelle Celmer*

Sydney's ex left her with nothing, but she needs to provide for her daughter. Sheriff Daniel's her new neighbour who could give Sydney the perfect opportunity.

A BRIDE FOR JERICHO BRAVO *by Christine Rimmer*

After being jilted by her long-time boyfriend, Marnie's given up on love. Until meeting sexy rebel Jericho has her believing in second chances...

Cherish

0211/023a

THE DOCTOR'S PREGNANT BRIDE?
by Susan Crosby

From the moment Ted asked Sara to be his date for a Valentine's Day
dinner, the head-in-the-clouds scientist was hooked; even if she seemed
to be hiding something.

BABY BY SURPRISE
by Karen Rose Smith

Francesca relied on no one but herself. Until an accident meant the
mother-to-be was forced to turn to fiercely protective rancher Grady,
her baby's secret father.

THE BABY SWAP MIRACLE
by Caroline Anderson

Sam only intended to help his brother fulfil his dream of having children,
but now, through an IVF mix-up, enchanting stranger Emelia's pregnant
with his child!

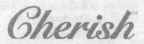

Her Not-So-Secret Diary
by Anne Oliver

Sophie's fantasies stayed secret—until her saucy dream was accidentally e-mailed to her sexy boss! But as their steamy nights reach boiling point, Sophie knows she's in a whole heap of trouble...

The Wedding Date
by Ally Blake

Under no circumstances should Hannah's gorgeous boss, Bradley, be considered her wedding date! Now, if only her disobedient legs would do the *sensible* thing and walk away...

Molly Cooper's Dream Date
by Barbara Hannay

House-swapping with London-based Patrick has given Molly the chance to find a perfect English gentleman! Yet she's increasingly curious about Patrick himself—is the Englishman she wants on the other side of the world?

If the Red Slipper Fits...
by Shirley Jump

It's not *unknown* for Caleb Lewis to find a sexy stiletto in his convertible, but Caleb usually has some recollection of how it got there! He's intrigued to meet the woman it belongs to...

On sale from 4th March 2011
Don't miss out!

Available at WHSmith, Tesco, ASDA, Eason and all good bookshops

www.millsandboon.co.uk

2 FREE BOOKS
AND A SURPRISE GIFT

We would like to take this opportunity to thank you for reading this Mills & Boon® book by offering you the chance to take TWO more specially selected books from the Cherish™ series absolutely FREE! We're also making this offer to introduce you to the benefits of the Mills & Boon® Book Club™—

- **FREE home delivery**
- **FREE gifts and competitions**
- **FREE monthly Newsletter**
- **Exclusive Mills & Boon Book Club offers**
- **Books available before they're in the shops**

Accepting these FREE books and gift places you under no obligation to buy, you may cancel at any time, even after receiving your free books. Simply complete your details below and return the entire page to the address below. You don't even need a stamp!

YES Please send me 2 free Cherish books and a surprise gift. I understand that unless you hear from me, I will receive 5 superb new stories every month, including two 2-in-1 books priced at £5.30 each, and a single book priced at £3.30, postage and packing free. I am under no obligation to purchase any books and may cancel my subscription at any time. The free books and gift will be mine to keep in any case.

Ms/Mrs/Miss/Mr _____ Initials _____

_____

Surname _____

Address _____

_____

_____ Postcode _____

E-mail _____

Send this whole page to: Mills & Boon Book Club, Free Book Offer, FREEPOST NAT 10298, Richmond, TW9 1BR